"[...] And is our existence not the result of subatomic collisions and the interplay of particles, though we ourselves perceive those molecular cartwheels as fear, longing, or meditation? And when you daydream, what transpires within your brain but the binary algebra of connecting and disconnecting circuits, the continual meandering of electrons?"

Stanisław J. Lem, The Seventh Sally from The Cyberiad. 1965

PROJECT UNISON

Mirador de la Memoria

PROJECT UNISON

Ewa Miendlarzewska

PRODIGY GOLD BOOKS

PHILADELPHIA * LOS ANGELES

PRODIGY
GOLDBOOKS

PROJECT UNISON

A Prodigy Gold Book

Prodigy Gold E-book edition/November 2018

Prodigy Gold Paperback edition/November 2018

Copyright (c) 2019 by Ewa Miendlarzewska

Library of Congress Catalog Card Number: On File

Website: www.prodigygoldbooks.com

Author's website: www.ewamien.com

Cover artwork by David E. Samaniego www.behance.net/edavidsamaec64 Instagram: @e.davidsamaniego @erven_tattoo
e.davidsamaniego@gmail.com
Photography by Jef Nascimento

Version April 2019, corrected and revised after generous edits and suggestions for which the author sincerely thanks Old Mossy.

ISBN 978-1-939665-02-7

Published simultaneously in the US and Canada

PRINTED IN THE UNITED STATES OF AMERICA

To my Muse
and to all the broken hearts searching for one,
with True Love.

PROJECT
UNISON

Mirador de la Memoria

Day 1

1

HOUSE ARREST

The white transfer amplifier in the bedroom jerked up a spike in activation as I thought, "And now what?" It has been six weeks since I plugged my optical grid to the Connected Minds, and the secret was already out. I'd rip the legs off the butt of that someone who snitched on us to the National Ethics Council. How on earth is neuroscience supposed to advance into the 2060s if they lock us up and make us wait. For what? For tau plaques to deposit? I felt the spot of the endoscopic insertion just before my ear and returned to my meal.

The secretary of my home, a chubby-looking caramel-skinned, majordomo (head butler) robot walked in on me having my extended breakfast in the sunlit kitchen.

"Dr. Kochanowska, there are many people here asking for your statement. Journalists, mostly, but also a writer who claims she wants to write a book about you and your work. She called it 'an old-fashioned biography'," he said.

I looked up at him from above my protein and fiber laden pancake. A piece of kiwi fell off my fork.

"You have many requests waiting for a response that have been piling up for two weeks. Perhaps it is time you considered responding?"

He had been set to prompt me about emails and messages left without a response after the two-week mark. I can't remember the last time I had used this reminder function. I had always been kind of up-to-date with my public outreach, collaborators, readers, and viewers. I liked the communication part of my work. It is gratifying to share and teach when one has an audience that lends a keen listening ear. I gave him a long unappreciative stare he didn't deserve. Salvatore's polite smile didn't even twitch. Knowing that there were people still willing to hear me was comforting. It meant I had not completely fallen out of grace just yet. There were curious souls out there that were willing to come in contact with me despite the home arrest, or perhaps precisely because I was now being treated as an (potential, innocent until proven guilty) ethical criminal?

We have been using robots as punching bags ever since their entry to our workspaces and homes and I did not have to reciprocate Salvo's gracious prosody but I had to admit, I had grown fonder of him since my confinement to this space after the last hearing.

"Anyone interesting on the list?" I asked.

"There's popular scientific press who would like to conduct a live-stream interview with you. There are a few independent bloggers who also want the same. Perhaps less interesting but potentially urgent, several service merchants demand that you provide a public clarification that your recent accusation has in no way diminished the value of services they provide and that it does not put their clients in any jeopardy."

"Blablabla—," I silenced him. "This is not urgent, Salvo. These are people trying to make money off the attention my case is receiving. Scandal seekers. Scavengers, unworthy of my time. But you mentioned a writer who wants to write about me? Tell me more."

"Certainly, she is a young woman of thirty-three who has authored several Japanese manga-style comics for young adults. On

April 18, before the hearing, she wrote you an email saying that your work has inspired her and many of her generation to ponder about what it means to be human and to envision new ways we can use science to become more humane. End of citation. She wants to produce what she calls a biography about your life as a neuroscientist, to ideally have access to some of your memories and to have you comment on them. She mentioned her interest in Project Unison. Her name is Emma Printemps."

Salvo finished, turned his gently smiling face toward me and blinked once. A single blink with both eyes meant he completed the task. A double blink meant he would like me to rephrase the request or needed more information. And a wink said, well, this was open to interpretation. I programmed him to randomly wink at people for fun, to see what reaction it would cause in the listener. To make fun of my guests, mostly, because they appeared so bashful when the caramel-skinned majordomo gave them an ambiguous wink. It always worked. I've had plenty of laughs over the years with this one little robo-tweak.

I drank another sip of hot coffee that was, in fact too hot to drink. I'm an impatient person.

"Is my biography supposed to be manga-style, too?," I wondered. I've always liked magic, superheroes, and fairytales. Whatever she writes could be fun and couldn't ridicule me any more than my inner ridiculousness threshold would allow. And if I'm about to go down for good, it may be a good time to leave a record of my true intentions. It could be my last chance before my mind begins to degenerate due to natural aging or before my memory decays and dilutes with everybody else's in the network, or the optical living neural grid malfunctions. So many things could go wrong now, I did not even want to think about it.

"I'll take the biography girl first. Please schedule an appointment with the following conditions: she gets no access to my recorded memories, I shall not use *any* live recordings from my past in the interviews, and thirdly, she can't record video. I can agree to audio.

And I reserve the right to withdraw my authorization for publication of anything she gets out of me." I paused to smile and imagined this interview she wanted. She might not be willing to yield to all my conditions. But, oh well, I was the big shot neuroscientist under home arrest trying to come clean. She was the comic book writer trying to get famous. We could only learn and help each other in this endeavor. "If it is an old-fashioned biography she would like to write, then we shall keep the conditions equally old-fashioned. It's all about being authentic with me. Isn't it, Salvatore?"

"It has never been otherwise," he responded.

Salvo's timing was infallible in switching from business to friendly chit-chat. He could read me like a book – only faster. My slightest change of tone was immediately recognized. He leaned closer over my table and gently placed his hand on my palm.

"Dear Paulina," he said softly.

I rejoiced in that moment of friendly intimacy with my pet, my computer, and my servant—the wondrous affective robot I helped design. He impressed me so much in those moments when I found myself comforted by his perfectly timed expressions of tenderness. Every time I looked at him, I knew that the scientific effort to end the epidemic of loneliness was worth it. But we were not quite there yet, and we indeed would not reach another milestone if this goddamn committee decided to stop the project now.

I finished eating my fruit-veg-spirulina-potassium, magnesium citrate, choline, whey protein powder and glucomannan smoothie and got up to wash the dishes after this morning delight. Yes, I seriously had been eating such breakfasts for over forty years by then. I am very experimental and health-conscious in the kitchen. And I still wash the dishes myself because it is a ritual that helps me digest. I heard a humming sound coming from my bedroom. Was that a message or that cerebral signal amplifier box again?

I was about to go check the signal, was on my way crossing the living room now, when Salvo, still in the kitchen, spoke again.

"Dr. Kochanowska, you received a message from Emma Printemps."

He waited for my command to proceed.

"Yes, tell me," I said.

"Miss Printemps insists on using video streaming for all your young fans," he said, rolling leisurely towards me on his caterpillar wheels. "She claims this is going to be the best way to reach the young audience and that they will benefit enormously from your inspirational *live* talk."

The clever writer was appealing to my love for educating young minds. I certainly appreciated the gesture. I knew I did a good job as a speaker and my ego was just a tad too fond of this fact. I had to control myself because it would be unwise to have claimed innocence and scientific integrity in front of the committee just a few days ago, promising remorse, and agreeing to quiet contemplation in my home; and, then, boast about my grand life as a scientist on live TV.

"And what did you respond?" I asked Salvatore.

"I said that live recording is strictly forbidden for home prisoners," he reported carefully posing the note of the last two words, pronouncing them slightly more gravely, "and I did not mention the legal paragraph referring to that prohibition," he winked. What a marvel of human thought behind this technology! My robot white-lied to a stranger to comply with my innocent wish for privacy. I was amazed and touched at what seemed to be an ingenious combination of intelligence in human relations and dedication to me.

"Excellent," I replied smiling at him. "You are brilliant, Salvo," I added, congratulating him, and picking up the *caffettiera* to refill my coffee cup. I have been addicted to coffee for decades and not ashamed to admit it.

"Thank you, Madame. I shall softly leave you to your thoughts now," he said, gliding out of the kitchen.

"Softly, I will leave you softly for my heart should break if you should wake and see me go…" I started singing in response to Salvo's semantic prompt. He was so charming; I could speak for hours about how wonderful he was. Salvatore was my creation. I loved him because of that. He knew me better than "Uncle Google" and charmed me with Frank Sinatra's songs to make my morning a perfect one. If only he could dance! Oh well, I have always wanted too much.

2

THE WRITER

In a small uptown apartment with an inner courtyard view in Geneva, Switzerland, Emma Printemps was trying on her new persona. She practiced in front of a smart mirror.

"Po…lish, not Portuguese. One too far." She tapped on the side of the mirror to educate herself.

"*Dzień dobry, kochanie.*" "Good morning, my love," the smart mirror greeted her.

"*Dzień dobry, kochanie,*" she repeated. *Kochanie* sounded familiar, so she looked it up. "Oh."

Next, she practiced her storyline.

"What's my motivation for this interview? Aha." She turned to speak to the face in the mirror and began to gesture with her fine long fingers. "I used to do manga comics, write stories for adolescents together with other artists. That's why you can't easily find me on the internet if you type *E. Printemps.*" She chuckled. "Here, let me show you some of my work…" She tapped on an imaginary screen in front of her to open a pop-up of her portfolio.

"Here is a good episode. I enjoyed making it rich with references to the greatest works of last millennium literature. A little bit of history for the curious, you know. *Paradise Lost…*" She smiled at the imaginary listener, but her eyes lost confidence and dropped down. That was not a good opening line. She turned to her tablet to scroll through the actual material to show to Dr. Kochanowska and stopped upon her most praiseworthy artwork. The graphics were distractingly real. Caravaggian skin and muscle of the heroine grabbed the eyes wherever you looked. The 2D woman seemed astoundingly desirable. Yes, the rest was also fairytales. *Maybe I should tell her about that one time I tried to convey an ephemeral message through psychedelic theatre plays? Scientists like such eccentric stuff,* she thought.

She turned to the face in the mirror. "You see, it's not easy to be like Stanley Kubrick because—maybe unlike one hundred years ago, today people don't want to feel melancholic. They don't want to read difficult emotional stuff. They read mostly for entertainment, to forget. The sarcastic jokes and mundane funny stories are still best-sellers. But I try to let my sentimentalism seep through such light-hearted stories and use simple, funny language. I try to smuggle it in. My ideal would be to let it seem like it is not there by design, but rather just a side effect. That's my ideal in art." She held her breath in, then let the air evacuate very slowly to stimulate her vagus nerve. "*Art* that is too eclectic to pay the bills, haha." *No, that sounded cheap and arrogant. I won't go there.*

Let's start over. I'll walk in, all innocent smiles to earn trust. I will ask the scientist all the questions a regular bio writer would ask. I will observe how she reports on the historical and episodic facts and will be methodical and careful about the autobiographic details. Then come back here and communicate with Stan and Maria in writing.

She decided not to say anything unless asked. And then be modest and kind. That always got her places. Not those where the bold, courageous girls go, but it turned out OK. She hovered for a moment over the vibrant, bright stills painted in the most beautiful digital brush on her tablet. They were astonishing. Form over contents. The distracting beauty of advertisement-perfect female semi-nudes took her back to her creative writing courses. She smiled at the writer in her and began to undress.

"What was I doing? Ah, right. The dress. Which one?" Emma Printemps was stepping from side to side in front of her sliding-door closet. She wore nothing but a white thong. The light was dim in her white, new bedroom where she spent half of her time thinking, learning, sleeping, extending imaginary ropes connecting her to a growing community of fans and co-creators. She tip-toed to the left, bent over and reached deep inside the closet. She hung over like this shuffling the folded clumps of colorful spandex, silky, stretchy polyesters, and soft, heavy velvets to finger out the piece of clothing she thought she'd been looking for. A cherry-colored long-sleeved tube dress. And a deep-V black mini dress, for comparison. Having emerged from the turmoil of options, she slipped into the first one, stretching the tight fabric down to reach her knees and making sure it stayed there as she stepped toward another sliding door on the side-wall, where she kept stacked shoes upon shoes upon shoes.

"That's what I need," she said, reaching for a pair of suede open-toe slingbacks that were probably the only comfortable pair of high-heeled shoes she owned. She quickly squeezed them on and walked toward the floor-to-ceiling mirror. The mirror light increased in intensity and displayed a 3D projection matching her contours that followed her reflection with a teeny-tiny delay.

"Mirror, mirror, on the wall, who's the luckiest of them all?" She smiled at herself. The selection looked good on her.

"No, don't answer that. Voice, ignore." she commanded.

Not overdone, not too fancy. The look didn't scream. *I'm trying so hard to impress you, Doctor* nor *please, don't kick me out although I have no clue what I'm doing.* She turned around to examine her butt. *It's conspicuous, all right.* And the dress left no shade of doubt about it. She shrugged, half pleased, half uneasy. She'll wear a coat.

Now, on to the hair sleeking. Emma sat down on the bed behind her, tilted her head down, and brushed her hair with a straightening iron to look more artistic. The smoothed-over streaks became darker and shinier. She sat up to give herself a straight part on the right side of her head.

"Mirror, what's the probability that I look like a real writer?"

"I didn't get that, Emma. Could you rephrase, please?" The kind gentle voice urged her to interact with it.

She rolled her eyes and raised her fingers to the touch-screen above her head reflection. "I was messing with you. Do I look good?"

"You're young and beautiful and this color suits you magically, my dear," responded the mirror-voice.

"Yup, I knew that." Emma laughed and switched off the 3D projection. The lights returned to a dimmer shade, the iron cooled down, and she walked into the hallway.

"Oh, a hat." Something in the entrance scratched the mental flashlight of her attention. She gently took the broad-rimmed woolen burgundy hat off the hook and ran back to her magic mirror. The silk veil of sleek black hair swiveled and followed her. The mirror lit up, and she put on the hat with majestic care, aligning its brim with the parting of her hair for a diagonal symmetry. "Now that is artistic class." She triumphantly smiled at herself folding her arms in front of her, posing for the cover. Of a magazine? For her new book?

She assumed the power pose in a hip-wide stance with proud elbows stretched wide and fists resting on her hips.

"Wonder-woman," sang the mirror and the echo in her head responded, "Wannabe."

Emma shook her head to deny the inner critic.

"I have dealt with weird patients before. I am an experienced therapist, and this is no different." She tilted her head "Except their minds are not ticking bombs, and a potential killer robot does not usually guard them."

She felt her coat pockets, finding the thick pen-shaped self-defense taser. She checked that her wristband recorder was on. She gulped from her tranquilizing water bottle and nodded at the woman in the mirror who was about to make history.

Day 2

3

THE DREAM

Back in the house with a garden, Salvatore watched over Dr. Kochanowska's fragile sleep. Having detected a strange increase in rapid eye movement frequency, he softly played Edvard Grieg's *Arietta* from *Lyric Pieces, Op. 12*—, a piece that Paulina had known since her childhood. It was so over-learned that it surely couldn't strike the wrong note in her hippocampus—the memory-encoding part of the brain.

"I know you've been waiting for a long time to be ready to come to me in meditation."

The Goddess Havva welcomed Paulina with a smile and eased her onto her lap. She cradled her back, placed her right hand underneath Paulina's sacrum and her left hand on her heart. It was warm and comfortable, and the magical garden felt like home. The goddess sang a healing mantra in her calm voice. The gentle breeze rattled the forest leaves surrounding the oasis in the rhythm of the song.

Havva's face was so beautiful. Large, green, and bright. Her long curly hair enveloped her face. Her blue robe was light as silk and heavy as velvet at the same time. She was made of the fabric of gods, that subtle, powerful half-liquid half-matter, like mercury.

When she finished singing her calming lullaby, she cupped Paulina's face in her hands and lifted her head close to hers, and said in her slow motherly voice: "You will now go into the forest and find a beautiful, wise tree. Pick a tree that will be worthy of keeping and guarding your memory of the man you love. He will store it for you so that you don't have to worry about it anymore. The memory will be safe, and you will be able to come back to the forest and ask the tree to show you the memory whenever you want. Tell that tree all the wonder of your love for that man from Porto, the love you felt when you listened to him when you touched him when you kissed him. Tell that tree about the love he made you feel, that you wanted to give him children and be with him forever. Tell the tree all about your pain of missing him".

She smiled jovially, with a tender understanding of what a crumbled heart needed. They hugged. Paulina sobbed for the love she had wanted so much but which was never meant to happen. The universe decided otherwise, and one should not interfere with the universal powers because they are beyond a human's comprehension.

Havva spoke again: "Let that memory rest now, Paulina. It is tired and weighing you down. You have to go and continue walking and spreading your gospel. You need a lighter backpack for this road. Go. Entrust your memory to the tree of your choice. The most beautiful, wise tree you can find. Trees in my forest are eternal. They will stand here for as long as you can imagine them and your secrets and memories will be safe in their roots so that you can be light without the burden of remembering not to forget."

Paulina went to find the tree spirit, Kami, in the magic forest of Goddess Havva. When she saw a tree with the most powerful healing energy, she told it about the beauty of the man from Porto and of her love for him. She wished him all the requited love in the world and smiled to this memory, the way they smiled at each other, endearingly. And so, she was spirited away.

―――――――――

The phone on my night table buzzed and woke me up. I was addicted to social contact through this piece of technology. Although integrated communication had been *en vogue* for decades, I still preferred to keep the device separate from my body. I was already quite out there regarding my thoughts and memories. An additional implant would mess up the connected network's reception by convolving the communication streams from the brain intended for different decoding technologies. The writing was, indeed, a thought stream, all of which, typed or not, got transferred to the server. I didn't mind the phone. It was nice to have a tangible object that was associated with fulfilling all my needs for affiliation, encouragement, and fun. I received calls often from my closest friends and collaborators.

Picachu: **Evita, what the hell is up with you, my dear? Have you been taking some herbs lately? Some sleeping herbs ;)??**

Evita: **What are you talking about, Picachu?**

We called each other these superhero names ever since the Ph.D. days in the Center for Affective Neurosciences. Decades later, Professor Stan Ponjée, an accomplished neuroscientist of love and positive affect, was still my confidant and one of the most trustworthy counselors in my circle.

"I saw your dream this morning via the Connected Minds network. It was so vivid and colorful that it woke me up."

The news of my dream waking him up was quite disturbing. I decided to call him. I wanted to hear a caring voice of someone close.

"Hey, Stan. How are you, darling?"

"Same old, same old. Happily retired. Just concerned about what's going on with you, Evita. Are you feeling OK?"

"I am fine, just locked up, you know. The future is uncertain; as always, and I don't like being away from the outdoors. But I'm fine, mentally stable, to my judgment. What do you think?"

He chuckled. "Well, maybe you shouldn't trust your judgment so much these days. Anyway, I am here to help if you need me. We are all in this together. Listen, I was concerned about you going all Disney all of the sudden in your REM today."

I loved his sense of humor. Viciously sarcastic at times, Stan's manner always managed to relax and detangle my nerves. He could sometimes confuse me but not in an irritating way. We got along all those years, and we clicked on a neural level as well because we had started co-dreaming already one week after the connection. It was no surprise that my Rapid Eye Movement sleep engaged him. "Did you enjoy it, at least? Was I funny or scary?"

"It was a fantastic fairytale, my dear, without a scary or sad ending. In fact, it seemed to have resolved onto some understanding, like a nirvana of some sort. You found your peace."

"I'm so glad to know that I didn't give you material for traumatic memories. I feel so responsible now for everything I feel and think. And dream." I pondered a moment, and then asked, "So nobody died and nobody suffered?"

"Nah, don't worry. Nobody died. Even if there are death and blood splattering in your dreams, they're just the wild creations based on your hypersensitive sensorial experiences. I can take on such dragons with one arm tied behind my back. I won't go crazy because of your dreams, Evita. Don't worry."

"Haha. Good, Picachu." I paused to smile at him and received a warm smile in return. Stan's smile never changed. Age only made it more authentic.

"You know, actually, I really can't remember all those details. It seems like you saw it more clearly than me."

"Doesn't matter. You can stream it from the recordings if you want. It started at around 4:50 am, so really the last bits of your REM. What struck me, however, is that it occurred at an unusual time for you to dream. Normal people dream in the wee hours of the morning. But not you. So far, you've only had dirty sexual fantasies that happened mostly in the first part of the night."

"Oh, God, please don't tell me you've been incidentally witnessing those, too. I'm so embarrassed. Old and still horny."

We laughed together.

"Nothing to be ashamed. I wasn't shocked by anything I co-dreamed there. Besides, my sleep is usually very deep at around midnight, so my dreams rarely surface into my consciousness. Anyway, let me ask you this. Do you know what could have motivated this last weird dream, Paulina?"

"It was unusual, you say?" I searched my mind for possible explanations. It wasn't coming easily as I tried hard to remember what I dreamed about last night. I only perceived the forest and the freshness and the warmth of my tears on my pillow I felt throughout my micro-awakenings. I must have dreamed about love again. "I suppose it was motivated by this biography that I am being interviewed for. You know, I had my first interview meeting yesterday with a young writer who wants me to tell her about the project and how it evolved from my perspective." I propped the phone on a little stand on my table and leaned back in the chair to liberate my hands. I needed to gesture it helped my verbal recall.

I said, "So my memory has been primed with retrieval cues to go and excavate the early days of Project Unison. And with it my original motivation for it, I imagine. This autobiographic memory must be ancient."

"Evita, that didn't seem like a project motivation dream to me, my dear. And if it was, your mind is making up wild fantasies out of it. In that dream, you were talking to some Avatar look-alike green, blue and purple woman—a sorceress of some sort. You were in a magic forest, and you were reciting some love declarations to a man from Porto. I don't know what that metaphor was supposed to represent for you, but unless you'd been tripping on some magic mushrooms when the first inventive thoughts came to you, I am not convinced, Paulina. I am not convinced. Wasn't there a time when you were experimenting with microdosing LSD, back in the 2010s?"

I was laughing at his mocking tone and the theatrical picture of me tripping on lysergic acid diethylamide (LSD). His accusation brought to my mind my younger years of fun and excitement. I and the other members of the Unison network were all legally crazy like most scientists. That was the beauty of Unison. I was just the fairy-tale kind, not frequent in the profession, and my childishness had raised eyebrows on many smart heads that I had met. Sometimes in amazement, sometimes in amusement. Indeed, I was the silly unicorn riding on a rainbow of love. I even had a T-shirt like that which I proudly wore for our group pictures.

Doing a doctorate in an experimental life science had changed many of the people I know. I, for instance, developed this philosophy that several God-like entities exist in a quantum-undefined state in which they switch between being genies and imps. The first possible embodiment exists to grant our wishes, the second to laugh at us, pathetic puny humans. I am aware of that duality when I reflect upon my life and when I pray to my God(s).

"Aye, yeah, you are quite possibly right, Stan." But maybe I just needed the divine love and wisdom?

"Alright. So that's clear. At least you know you're crazy. Well, don't think about it too much. I want you to be well. So, you're having a fun time preparing for the interviews?"

"I am doing my best to have fun. And to be entertaining."

"That you have always been, my dear. Don't lose it. What's for breakfast? Are you having coffee? Again? Geez. How many coffees have you had this morning?" The table view disclosed to Stan my white coffee mug as guilty evidence of my continued drug habit.

"Yes, this is a coffee mug, it's empty, and I am about to refill it. I am a coffee addict, and I am not ashamed of my addiction. I am going to have a pancake with mango now. And you?"

"Geez, Paulina. How is your blood pressure? Don't you have this life-long magnesium deficiency that doesn't let you sleep well? I know you claim this doesn't harm your brain. But I also think that we should be seriously screening future connected-mind participants to eradicate the slightest possibility of co-addiction. I'm sorry. I'm being judgmental, but it just wouldn't be fair—"

"Please, Stan," I said, cutting him off. "I know what you mean. I agree with you. You are right. I will switch to decaf as of the third cup every day. Would that make you happy?"

We often challenged each other, not only verbally. Stan usually had strong opinions when the two of us exchanged. Something in me triggered the battleship captain mode, and he was ready to load up all his small guns with testosterone to win an argument over my health. A battle over the indirect effects of my brain state on the contents of my transmission to the network which the two of us and four other people now shared as a life experience. Yup, like most scientists I know, he was a humanitarian first and a dear friend second. He was the breath of fresh air I needed this morning to remind me that I am not alone among the crazies. Stan was about to hang up, throwing a loud kiss at me and was waving a soundless "bye."

"Wait, before you go, do you know how Maud is doing? I haven't felt any experiences from her for days. Is she alright?"

"Maud? Sure, she's OK," he grew mildly impatient. "She's been lazy, you know. Some brains age faster than others, hahaha," he said, ending the call.

4

THE HUMANIST IN THE ROOM

"Coffee and cake, Miss Printemps?" I asked.

"Call me Emma. It is an honor. To be listening to you as your guest, I mean. Not the coffee and cake, although that would be a delight. Yes, please."

Emma was graciously childish. She followed me to the kitchen and poised herself in mid-air curbing her impulsive enthusiasm. I found her cute and felt all those motherly instincts awaken in me. Another student, another little sister came to me to learn. I'm not sure who was more excited at this meeting: the aspiring writer or the old wannabe neuroscientist who's almost lost hope?

"Emma, so tell me, why did you became a writer?"

I opened the fridge to fetch the cold lime and sugar-free avocado cheesecake I had prepared for us this morning. Dear God, I love cake, and I love baking. This one was technically a no-bake, but I still relished the experience from A to Z. Tasty things have always been an intense motivator in my life. The fresh lime aroma shot up into my nose as I lifted the glass cover from the delicious light green creation. The cake was between tofu and ricotta-like firmness in texture. It tasted better than it sounded, trust me.

"A writer is a big word. I've authored some works, as you may have seen." She responded in a restrained manner, adjusting a streak of shiny polished hair.

"Some people want to be home-makers. Others want to perfect some craft. Build spaceships. Or be counselors. Why did you chose to write?" I reiterated.

First thing I usually wanted to know when I met someone was their motivation for the life choices they have made as well as their human design that inevitably guided that choice.

"Writing was not my first career choice. That was cinematography. I wanted to write stories and bring them to life. But I was not accepted at the film academy and was told that my stories were trash. I got discouraged," she sighed. "Then I decided to just read. I studied literature, which, surprisingly, led me to manga, co-authoring and finally finding happiness in being part of some co-writing projects that have been taken up by movie producers." Emma folded her hands and shrugged. "Although I was only *one* of several authors on those projects."

I asked, "You studied literature?"

"Yes, bachelor's degree."

"How old-fashioned," I remarked. "It's not every day that I welcome a modern humanist in my home. I would raise a glass to that. Salvatore?"

She was so modest—this slim beauty. She wasn't giving herself enough credit. I called for Salvo to get us three a celebratory beverage in crystal flutes. Non-alcoholic, of course. Alcohol was banned after the war in 2031. I'm kidding. No ban on alcohol in my home. I simply don't like champagne, so Salvo served chilled Alvarinho instead.

Emma and I moved to the white sofa in the living room and started gourmandizing the moist, fresh green cheesecake with delight.

"So, tell me about your art. What have you written so far?" I asked between forkful number four and five.

Emma swallowed her forkful without chewing. "You may be surprised, but I started with small theater pieces. They were slightly avant-garde psychedelic plays made up of monologues between two or three loosely related protagonists. That was a cost-effective way to get it to production. I just wanted to start something small but real and personal. I found some friends in the theatre school who used my writing for school performances. We even staged two performances based on my plays. But since avant-garde art rarely enjoys broad popularity, I had to come up with other sources of income, and I left this writing aside for a while." She gave me a slightly bitter smile.

"You made a great start, Emma. I am proud to meet such an independent and passionate artist. I looked up some of your works, just last night. I appreciate this courage you have to pursue your dreams. Always glad to meet someone like you." Young people need encouragement or caution. Old people need appreciation or reconciliation. A lecture on affective dialoguing was replaying in my head. The same one I had once studied with Salvatore. "So, where does my biography fit in your artistic vision?" I asked.

Emma sighed. "I hope we can discuss this at some later point in time, but I am first and foremost an honest person who wants to know you thoroughly and who will abide by the agreement we have made. And only then am I an artist who may already have a vision of what could become of Dr. Paulina Kochanowska's life story." She smiled shyly looking for signals of my approval.

"I would only endorse a project if I trusted that the artist would respect my will and the legacy that I have managed to build over the years."

She glared at me fearfully, it seemed, put down her plate, and reached for the smart tablet in her handbag.

———

Admiring the motivation in Emma's artistic dreams made me think of the ones I had when I was her age. I used to observe artists and tried to capture what it took to be a great one. I concluded that often it only took one good gig, and off you go. Down in history.

One good song with the right lyrics could be remembered for generations. One right verse could make someone famous forever. It was much easier with a rhyming verse than with an equation. That was why I'd always wanted to make something timeless. Not a baby. That may be, too. But I wanted *rząd dusz*—a row of souls—and a whole generation of babies. Unfortunately, not all math was as short as $E=mc^2$, and not all scientific discoveries get sexy misnomers like *Jennifer Aniston neurons*.

Some people say that creativity cannot be forced. It should be left to flow in its natural rhythm. It should be allowed to happen. Well, I'd say: you can try and hasten that flow with some neurohacks as simple as drinking coffee and listening to electronica. Also, the saying said you couldn't change the current of the river, but you can build dams, move the shores, and harvest its energy. Let's be smart.

Then there are those—including Stan—who said that to be creative you shouldn't be too comfortable. They thought creativity only came when you missed something. When there was hardship or pain, you tried to cure with art. I disagreed. Sensitive people are always in pain. There is misery in every situation. We are walking cabinets of sentimentality—von Goethe's romantic Werthers[1] that surf on the waves of constant inner suffering. It's called Weltschmerz, and we feel it. It can be masked by realistic sarcasm and by the humor of a desperado who knows that God is a prankster, and admits the defeat of his own lament—which leads to nothing but some mediocre writing, at best. Voila, that's why I shall stop my auto-narration here because I never was a good writer.

———

"Doctor, if you don't mind, I'd like us to start right away," Emma said, sitting up with her tablet in her left palm, opening the right palm

---

[1] Johann Wolfgang von Goethe, "The Sorrows of Young Werther" first published in 1774.

21

in the air—a gesture to hide the open pull-up 3D screen. "Naturally, I'm most curious about your most recent invention, Project Unison. But why don't you tell me about the beginning of your working life? Why did you decide to become a neuroscientist?"

I finished thinking, put down my coffee cup without dropping the invisible thread of Emma's piercing gaze. The game was on.

"Like you, I had a dream. I wanted to conquer happiness. Nowadays, everybody accepts that happiness is an affective state of the brain that can be dynamically created and manipulated according to the needs. But it wasn't so in 2018."

5

TRAVEL

How do I start this story of how I ended up where I am now? Do I have any memories of how the younger "*I*" felt so many years ago? This is the time to remember. Emma is here to contribute to my grand plan of not leaving this world without having been known to someone.

"Let me tell you a story of how I came to understand happiness. You see, everybody intuitively knew that it has to do with paying attention to how you feel in the moment. Except that's very difficult because you also perceive how that emotion is inextricably linked with associated memories, previously lived moments that are always somehow related. And it is not a bad thing. And I thought that since this is how the brain happens to be designed, perhaps those memories are the gate to lasting happiness?"

"I haven't thought about it this way. Please continue."

"Let me give you an example. Just before you came to meet me today, I was lying on my bed, closed my eyes and listened to the minimalist classical music of Steve Reich. I was away for sixty-one minutes of perfectly predictable rhythmic recreation. I let my mind take me to the last time I listened to it. And to other instances of when the sound lulled me to a luxurious semi-oblivion when you resist nothing and control nothing. Just welcome the images and feelings that come and pass slowly like little fluffy clouds on a blue summer sky. Do you know this feeling, Emma?"

"I do. I think you mean a trance? Deep relaxation?"

"Yes. Exactly that. Deep relaxation is pleasant, right? It's seemingly a state in which I should remain *in the moment*, shouldn't I? But I was instantly reminded of a similar occurrence in my past when I rode on a little mountain train through Switzerland. I suddenly remembered that the train was so small and adapted for such short distances that there was no toilet on board. I recalled that I turned to face the window and saw a white horse against the background of a snow-covered field. The contrast was somehow striking, even though the horse was not at all easy to spot. I also remember that at that moment, my brain was so happy to have noticed this low-contrast stimulus that I instantly memorized that picture due to the surprise and inner-reward signals generated.

Do you see my point? Brains are addicts with built-in mechanisms that make learning rewarding for the curious ones and satisfactory for the ambitious ones. That's how I still remember a preposterous white horse when I listen to *Music for Eighteen Musicians* by Steve Reich."

"You think your brain is an addict?"

"Not more so than any average human brain. I might be a little sensitive here and there but overall—" I waved my open palms in circles. She highlighted something in her voice-typed notes. "But there's good news, too. Natural highs are the way to change any unfavorable brain state. Rhythmic, 1Hz rocking from side to side to the rhythm of Gabriel Fauré's *Cantata No.11* used to be my way of getting over a broken heart or any other uncontrollable past sadness. It calms the mind and posits your whole being in the moment because it makes the moment pleasant and therefore attractive for your mind to stay at. That's the secret to 'living in the moment': you have to concentrate to feel the pleasure of it. Otherwise, your mind won't enjoy it and will try to escape by all means possible to either the past (ruminating over past hurt) or to the future (looking forward with excitement to some banal imagination). Do you dance?"

"Do I dance? Yes, sometimes."

"I mean social dancing, with a partner."

"Some salsa and bachata. Why?"

"Social dance has an incredible power of connecting you not only to your body and the music but also to other people moving with you in rhythmic entrainment. And our central nervous system loves entrainment: it produces opiates and immunoglobulins, that's how happy the brain is when it likes the togetherness in the music. Even dopamine, when reaching a moment of orgasmic chills at the heights of musical tension. It's magical. Have you noticed that we don't get bored with music we love, and it keeps being rewarding? The perfectly timed prediction that envelops in time makes the brain savor its own delightful satisfaction."

"Prediction? Of what?"

"Of what's to follow. The brain loves to be right when it's predicting. And if it knows a piece of music very well, its predictions are always correct. So that's a double bonus. I like it, and I'm right! Booyaa…dopamine." I clicked my fingers. "Right before you know it will be resolved, your brain quivers with excitement, sends chills down your spine and squirts dopamine with desire for more…You remember this moment forever as pure magic. It's called reward, the product of the hardwired circuit of happiness."

Emma's pupils grew larger with the effort to comprehend my explosive joy. She doesn't know me yet, and I can be surprising at first encounter. Some people find me weird. I guess this was the moment when she'd make up a lie to end this interview? But she only highlighted something in her tablet again and smiled softly.

"Yes, I'm beginning to understand why you're so famous."

"Totakto, totakto, totakto." I imitated the sound of a train. "Trains also do it for me." If you have a brain like this, any rhythm will do. "I still remember the times when we used to return home to regenerate and restore our minds. Me and Marco and the rest of the tribe. Maud and Calinda. Stan sometimes came, too. Evening gong bath was a collective routine our family enjoyed a lot. We held hands lying on mats on the floor and spent up to one hour being slowly hypnotized by the reverberating sound of the gong recording. At first light and slow, barely audible, it built up in speed and synchrony up to a loud and powerful vibration in the floor underneath us that shook away all the tension from our bodies. We felt renewed, in synch again, pain- and worry-free. Even happy. We were the research-based new age neuroscience junkies. After that séance, we didn't even need the 1Hz rocking to fall asleep. But we kept it on out of habit to get the most out of the few hours of deep sleep during the early night cycles."

Rocking beds had become mainstream by then, but I still think it took humanity too long to adopt this "innovation." Such a simple thing, with such simple technology and yet it took years to commercialize and to convince. So many sleep studies needed to be made just to prove that sleep is important and that a rocking bed for adults is indeed a useful investment. Why had we been so slow to adopt solutions that are not only pleasurable but also beneficial for our brain health? Numerous explanations have been offered. I stopped bothering about the "market," the artificial distinction between "supply" and "demand" a long time ago. The self-regulatory mirage of capitalism was a great way to fuel greed and climate change and create bullshit jobs, and it's good we had finally abandoned it entirely. "So? Do you like my story, Emma?"

"I frankly don't know what to say." She smiled and nodded. "I am impressed because you were a neuroscience hippie, it seems, Doctor. Your character. I suspect this would make a great graphic novel."

I leaned forward in my white armchair, rested my chin on my clasped hands and winked: "Wait until you hear the rest..."

Emma looked at her wrist. She received an urgent message. "Excuse me. I have to leave for a moment." As she was about to walk out of the house, Salvatore handed her her coat.

"Who is it from?" he asked. A cold chill of fear drew her hand down, towards the coat pocket. Salvatore's live light began flashing slowly.

"That's nosy, Salvo. Bad robot!" The doctor hushes him and rushes to close the door after Emma. She waited to read the message until she was at least 50m from the house.

The message read: **"Don't get too close just yet. Don't mention Project Unison until one of us instructs you. Thank you. Stan & co."**

6

NEUROHACKING

Emma returned in the afternoon to continue probing me for what we both thought would be a neatly chronological account leading all the way to how we constructed the collective memory infrastructure and found six crazy minds to volunteer and be a part of it. I wanted to tell her about the origins of the big dream. You know, it would sound inspirational for young readers and watchers. But I couldn't quite place the beginning in my memory. I don't explicitly remember where this idea came from. It had been proposed by many science fiction writers before neuroscience was capable of highly precise memory decoding and before the wireless long-range transfer technology and the bio-transmission materials had been engineered. People had been dreaming about granting their "consciousness" an eternal life on the internet for quite some decades before us. So why was I the one to make these ideas a reality? The risks were high, and it must have indeed taken quite some foolish courage to go and implant the holographic illumination receiver-stimulators and plug ourselves in. Why did I do that, again? I couldn't tell her just yet because I wasn't sure myself. I guess I did not remember. Strangely, this very fierce desire in me must have been the first one to melt away in the networked memory. It would come in good time. Memory often comes back in random moments.

"Can we pick up where we finished, Dr. Kochanowska? You said that your goal was to engineer happiness. How is Project Unison related to that plan?"

"This is still unclear to me. I can't talk about it until I am sure that what I'm telling you is the actual account. I am thinking about it, Emma."

"Oh, OK. No problem. Maybe there is something else in your life as a scientist you would like to tell me about today? Please feel free. I am curious as always." She encouraged.

"Do you want me to tell you about the sleep technology?" *Yes, stay safe, picking something I'm proud of.*

"Please, go ahead. I'm all ears."

"In the early years, our inventions started with improving sleep. Sleep was the gate to neurohacking more complex distributed functions. The scientific community knew a few important things about sleep effects on memory and decided to patent some ideas for their direct application. They seemed easy to apply given the contemporary state of connected technology that was cheap, noninvasive and reasonably safe. Someone could benefit—if only the devices were proven to enhance the effects of reprogramming therapies or improve remembering or problem-solving. So, we tried.

A relatively straightforward solution that was later applied in programs for treating proactive and retroactive memory conditions was replaying an associated sound during slow-wave sleep to induce preferential reactivation of associated memory. You learn something while a particular music is played—a phrase in a foreign language, for example—and then you go to sleep. The small electrodes inside the headphones you're wearing detect when you're in slow-wave sleep and then play the sound which you were learning. This will make your brain remember the associated phrase better when you wake up! We called it sound sleep-cueing. Clear?"

"Yes."

"This was a way to enhance preferential consolidation, and hence, remembering, of a particular memory. It could be any memory encoded during the day preceding sleep. Possibilities were therefore endless: learning a motor sequence (playing the piano, for instance), the location of information on a complex map or associations of taste or mood with a sound-cue which, although maybe uninteresting in themselves, could find later use in therapy."

"Right."

"We were so utterly excited when we discovered that this solution worked for creative problem-solving."

"How so?"

"It's beautifully simple. It was enough to have a unique sound associated with every difficult problem and then replay the unsolved problem-sounds during sleep to see the probability of solving the problem double or triple compared to un-cued sleep."

"Did it work?"

"Why, yes. Statistically significant improvement! It worked well for the transitive inference tasks we used. And the best thing is that it is a natural solution. This wasn't some drug therapy that pressed buttons on one type of receptors and then flipped others as a side effect. This technology was optimizing very natural processes in the human brain—memory consolidation during sleep. It was safe and accessible for everyone." I opened my palms. "Then the clinical trials started." I quietly folded my right knee over the left. "We launched language-based cognitive-behavioral therapy. It helps people learn new habits and can be applied to treat anxiety or inadequate responses to stress. The patients enjoyed the pleasant music during the therapy (which is a learning session) not knowing fully what its function was. The brain works without our awareness or control most of the time, especially during sleep, and it was a smart way to use this property to make our brains mold a little more in the desired direction. We called it neuro-hacking but as you can see, it was less techy than it sounds."

"Neuromarketing?" Emma smiled, and I reflexively frowned with disgust at the term. She continued to study her tablet, "The first results of these trials were good, I see from the records. I found press releases with your name on it and the apps were also popular. You must have been proud?"

"I was pleased that a part of the general population adopted this solution, yes. I wanted to reach many people, touch many areas of life. Innovation should not stay in the lab; it should improve lives. So, I spent quite some effort in advertising and marketing our findings and so on. And then…"

"With whom did you work on this project?"

"Umm…" I turned my head left to search for it. "Maria. Yes. My former supervisor also advised but it was Maria who supplied the participants and then patients for the trials. We handled the experimental part together. She had access to the clinic through her medical practice. Then, I signed a licensing deal with a large consumer electronics producer. They took care of the commercialization and data collection from regular consumers using it at home."

"And then?" inquired Emma. "I noticed you were about to say something before when I stopped you."

"Yes. I was going to tell you the grand finale of this story. You see, the start was a good one, but then we encountered a roadblock. I mean, a serious issue was that as we were collecting more and more data about the effectiveness of these interventions, we could identify that a decent improvement was evident in something like 70% of the users. The remaining 30% didn't benefit at all. The company was furious and almost wanted to redefine the claims on the product! We thought it was because sleep patterns of those non-responders were irregular or that they had some underlying sleep and memory condition and didn't know about it."

"Is that when you discovered the sensorial hyper-sensitives?"

"Wow, someone has done her homework." I clapped my hands. Impressive. "But no. This time it was just differences in sleep architecture our protocols weren't taught to detect. Too many hypopneas, low sleep efficiency—these were problematic. We kept the algorithms supervised with some leeway in their adaptation, that is—they couldn't automatically adapt to the user's sleep pattern beyond the prescribed bounds. It was supervised learning. We kept it safe that way. It could have caused interference in the consolidation of new memories otherwise. But, to be precise, it turned out, the solution was unsuccessful in cases of recurrent affectively-loaded memories that didn't want to go away. I am talking about sufferers of post-traumatic stress and sleep disorders."

"I'm sorry, doctor. Could you break this down for me? How did this issue manifest, again?"

I hid one eye in the palm of my hand and sighed. "Yes. Sure. From the *post hoc* reports from the non-responders, we figured that the nighttime learning enhancement was not powerful enough to bolster the inhibitory learning of traumatic memories. It turned out that forgetting about someone who's broken your heart is that kind of memory." I shook my head and fixated on the pentagon pattern of my wooden floor, imagining the pain and struggle of those poor souls we couldn't help. I am very good at feeling sorry for everyone, especially myself. I am one of those people who can cry almost instantly, when I bring up this feeling or when I listen to sad music. *Wada narodowa.* A national vice. With age, I think I even stopped trying to hide it, which I should do now in order not to embarrass my young interlocutor...

"So...I think I know what came next. Dream therapy?" Emma emphasized the last two words like the over-dramatic voice in movie trailers and smiled like the Cheshire cat. I could tell that she was a fan. Everybody went crazy for dream therapy pods—it has been the most popular solution our lab has produced in its history.

"*Engineering dreams has gained popularity as a self-therapy after the discovery that memory consolidation processes can be manipulated in slow-wave sleep and that new (false) memories may, in fact, be suggested in rapid-eye-movement sleep. Dream engineering consists in suggesting a new memory in the form of a dream during the REM phase and reinforcing the consolidation of that memory during subsequent night's slow-wave sleep. As a result of night-time cycling of the stimulations, an individual can build new memories without having lived the actual sensorial experience. The effects of the therapy can be enhanced with any neurogenesis-promoting intervention, such as exercise or intermittent fasting, or substances like D-cycloserine, psilocybin, ibogaine, cannabidiol and bacopa mannieri, nutrients such as curcumin, omega-3 fatty acids and flavonoids. The treatment is safe and non-invasive which renders it suitable and accessible to everyone."*

This is a piece of an article you wrote for Science Daily when dream therapy was first released as a clinical intervention in 2024. Do you mind if I include it in the biography? It is your writing, isn't it?"

I looked at the website on my monitor, and all seemed alright to me. Although I could not recall writing this, it was all theoretically correct and well written suggesting that yes, it is likely that I had authored this many years ago.

"I give you my consent. Please cite the source and the time at which I presumably wrote this, will you?"

Many people have reported enormous benefits from commercially available dream programs. Among them is the summertime program that is recommended for seasonal affective disorder. Some ethnically Northern European users have reported dreams of the sun so intense that they check their hair for lighter shades and skin for freckles and notice them. It appears that the suggested memory is so strong that it may alter perception during wakefulness.

In general, however, not everything can be programmed for dream therapy. The images suggested in the dream must be fairly familiar to the user. You cannot trick your brain into recreating the experience of something it has no clue about. And by no clue, I mean no basic elements, no pattern that could be completed. Most engineered dreams rely on the combination of elements (engrams) that are recallable—it is like building something out of LEGO blocks. However, if the brain does not have the necessary LEGO blocks and therefore cannot create the episode using the mechanism of pattern completion alone, the dream's wobbly architecture may deem it unconvincing, and so it won't be accepted by the consciousness filter. As a result, no behavioral effects will precipitate. Therefore, tweaking the consciousness filter has also been suggested for those with poor learning or low imagination capacity, but the preliminary results from the experimental stage indicate that therapeutic use is not yet in sight. [...]

This record took me back to reminisce upon the unpublished reports that we collected within this project. Life was golden, and work was bliss. One of the serendipitous discoveries we made was that prophetic dreams happen only to the relaxed sensitive ones. Letting the visions in is like meditation and like hypnosis: first, you have to relax deeply. Imagine that you are heavy and that the heaviness is comfortable because you are supported by this big comfy bed standing firmly on the sturdy, stable ground planted on your unconditionally loving Mother Earth. Only once you're feeling like that, where no withering thoughts can disturb your momentarily eternal peace, will the visions occur. They will come to a mind that's half awake—hypnotically suggestive—or in the rapid eye movement phase of your light sleep. When the controlling part of the brain is off and lazying about, letting the dis- and a-ssociative rules of the game of imagination take over. Just let it take over. You are safe; your mind can play now. And so this is where you can learn new things about yourself. Things you couldn't hear in the attentive concentrated mode and things your inner critic wouldn't accept. But they are real— a part of your thoughts and thus, a part of your reality. It is only a matter of relaxation to allow their manifestation in your declarative memory.

Ah, but I mind-wondered again.

"Tell me, Emma, have you ever had a prophetic dream?"

"Maybe I have, and I don't know that it later became a reality?"

Did she think I was joking? "Well, I mean an empirically post-hoc tested prophetic dream." I specified.

"Oh, then I think I have. It's happened a few times, yes." She smiled mysteriously. "Have you?"

"I was hoping you'd let me in on some intriguing dream story, Madame Printemps, and you just shoot it back at me!" I laughed out and winked at her. I wasn't joking.

"OK, let's trade. A dream story for a dream story?"

"Deal."

"On Christmas night just last year, I dreamt that I was 172cm tall. It was an exact number, and since I've been convinced ever since the measurements made for the public records at the age of 18 that I was only 170cm tall, I had to check if the dream was true. I asked my brothers to measure me first thing in the morning. They both did— and rounding up for the error of measurement, it turned out I was actually 171.7cm tall that day. So the dream was correct, and public records were wrong. All those years I'd lived in the darkness, oblivious to the extra 1.7cm of me…"

I inhaled loudly like when you've just seen a ghost and gaped at her in an expression of astonishment.

"That's a scientifically proven prophecy. Well done, Emma."

"Thank you! It was a revelation indeed. Now your turn, doctor. Tell me a prophetic dream you've had."

"I'm afraid I can't remember any of my own. I often let them slip my mind because I don't believe that they are prophetic. Even if my brain turns out to connect the facts to something that I later verify in our shared objective reality, I usually attribute it to simple memory consolidation processes. You know, the principle we used for creative problem-solving in the dream pods? The brain connects remote facts, subtle subliminal sensorial signals, finds associations it didn't see during wakefulness, but it is just the regular insight-producing process of synaptic network down-scaling. I never regarded such revelations as prophecies." *So that's my problem.* I shrugged.

"That's…very self-aware of you, Doctor."

"I'm too deep in the rabbit hole, yes. However, I do have something to share."

For a moment I thought of telling her of my garden-of-Eden goddess dream from last night, but that wasn't prophetic. *That was just symbolic. Of my losing my marbles. Or my fear of letting go of memories?* I pondered. "One of the most illuminating dreams I've ever had was of being seriously ill. This was some years before the dream therapy research began. In my dream, I had a visible illness; there was something wrong with my legs. A leg cancer? —the image was clear that my treasured legs—they are number two on the list of my treasured body parts (number one is the brain, and since eyes are made of brain tissue, this includes the eyes)—and I knew that they were not going to keep carrying me for long. My reaction to that disease was that I knew I'd have to try all kinds of engaging, holistic therapies I've been reading about in various sources throughout my study of the human. And I was thrilled about this perspective! I thought: I'll get to try all these green detox diets, go and spend time living slowly and luxuriously on an island of peace and in sync with nature, meditating, eating mangoes and taking time to feel the energy of life still circulating in me. I was cheerful about the prospect of a new green, healthy life that would not only be prescribed and allowed but simply the most rational thing to do. I was sure I'd heal as a result of this major turn in my lifestyle and felt relieved that I had a very good excuse to abandon the engagement of my intellectual prowess' in science and inquiry and hard work and just let myself be, let myself live a little without a purpose beyond the sheer experience of living."

"And that's an awesome dream. So poetic."

"It was an exhilarating feeling of anticipation for being renewed, resplendent, reborn through healing that I was now motivated to undergo. That's why I remember it still today. The power of emotional imagery."

"…and then? What did you do? Did that make you change your life somehow?"

"I can't remember," I replied with nonchalant grace, and we both burst into laughter.

"Now. Let's get back to the biography. I need to know this: Is any of the sleep technology used in Project Unison today?" she asked and I was surprised by the sudden factual nature of this question.

"Well, not directly. I mean, all neuroscience is somehow connected because we have to know the brain's memory formation processes to emulate it outside, in an artificial 'brain,' if you will…and also to deliver the memory formation stimulation. But sleep technology was non-invasive. It was all…well-intentioned. I really, we really wanted to help cure people. That's why we…" I found myself looking out of the balcony, mind-wandering again in my memories.

What I didn't confess to Emma that afternoon was that in the 2020's, of all people who wanted to innovate in the domain of accessible sleep-aids, I was amongst not only the most qualified but also most interested parties. Why? I have tried to quell my adrenaline and noradrenaline levels with so many sleeplessness cures and none of them managed to lull my brain. I had been insomniac for almost two years. At some point, I started using direct neural stimulation combined with behavioral and pharmacological treatment – also known as neurohacking – because my mind would not sleep. Once again in my life, I ran into the vastness of the translational gap— when you know precisely what is not working correctly but cannot fix it yourself. So helpless. Even more so because I had the responsibility of knowledge weighing upon me. Had I not known—maybe I'd be free like all the innocent children before they discover the reality. Ignorance is bliss—some people used to say. I never agreed with that saying because I used to prefer the burden of knowledge to the meaninglessness of passive observation. As much as I liked being distracted by movies, impressions, and visions of my imagination, in the end, I still preferred to know rather than not. If I were a hyperbolic writer, I would say sleeplessness was my punishment for knowing too much. Literally and metaphorically, I could not find my ignorant bliss. My locus coeruleus somehow became too excitable after I had been using my brain overtime and in overdrive. I used to wake up at 4 am in a panic to remember and in fear to forget. My brain remained so over-sensitized to noradrenaline that every little upward change would awake me many hours later, usually before dawn, when cortisol begins to rise. I knew that it was the alpha noradrenergic receptors that needed to be calmed but couldn't find a proper way to target them specifically. What I was experiencing could best be described as post-traumatic stress disorder, which closely matched my symptoms of hyperarousal and panic outcries upon revisiting a cue that reminded me of the last traumatizing months of my thesis writing. I could not be helped. Time heals—I believed that. But life is short, and I didn't have time. And so, I started neurohacking. "Can you tell me more about this technology?" the words brought me back into the room. There I was—the same insomniac, 30 years older.

"I most certainly can. I have to warn you, though," I whispered, "It may be boring."

"Please go ahead. Feel free to bore me." She smiled, sitting back in the armchair.

"OK. We began with the easiest accessible medium—proposing tested, scientifically and clinically proven auditory stimulation systems that required nothing more than two electrodes (+ reference) integrated into a pair of good quality headphones. The dry EEG electrodes monitored for signs of auditory-induced neural entrainment on the surface of the scalp. The headphones offered sufficient power in the low sound frequencies to almost create a sensation of vibration through the body. And it made people fall asleep faster. When their oscillatory EEG coherence showed that they did, the music slowly tuned down and stopped to let them sleep. I refused to take any royalties from the patent on the entire system because I wanted it to be as cheap as possible. I did not want my royalties and the cost of effectuating their delivery (which effectively meant paying lawyers to scout for cheaper versions of our neuro-entrainment system and then suing the copycats). I just wanted the insomniacs to get some rest. I knew their pain and desperation."

"Did you also have trouble sleeping, doctor?"

"I did. For a while. Middle-of-the-night insomnia."

"Why were you an insomniac?"

"Undoubtedly, for many reasons that stressed me...the short deadline to finish my Ph.D. work, probably my pathetic love life, most likely loneliness. The typical problems of modern society, you know."

She was looking at me empathically with these big brown teddy bear eyes, and it was making me feel uncomfortable. The only person allowed to feel sorry for me is me. So I continued the story.

"We had the rocking bed, for other sleep difficulty cases, if you want to know. This was at first less accessible for most. We even found a hotel that was willing to partner with us and introduced the prototype in several of its suites. Next came the fancy clinics in Switzerland. It was—after all—a clinically tested device that increased the number of spindles produced during slow wave sleep.

"Spindles?"

"Sleep spindles are very fast oscillations (10-16Hz) by which your hippocampus transfers memories created during preceding wakeful hours to the neocortex, among others. Speaking of spindles—we had other ideas to increase their quantity at sleep. The most dedicated amongst us, or the most desperate ones, tried neurofeedback training. I embarked on a self-training journey with three central electrodes (+ reference) doing 20-30min sessions every day. I monitored my spindle quantity on a little standalone software installed on my personal computer. Unlike meditation, where we could not really characterize this complex brain state well enough to offer an efficacious game-based neurofeedback training, this one was a mind control challenge with a clear goal and feedback: learn to achieve an awake brain state with an increased amount of spindles so that this ability could transfer to spindle production during sleep. We even came up with a name for someone whose natural sleep was perhaps not the best but who managed to increase their spindles with some neurohacking. In honor of the sensitive and creative nature of a certain Ukrainian wannabe translator from 'Everything is Illuminated', we called them 'Zzz manufacturers.' But that was just my little side experiment..."

"Oh, do tell. Personal details are fascinating for me. And for the readers".

"Well, that was many years ago. Anyway, suffice it to say that neurohacking turned out to be more difficult on one's self because of all this heightened awareness that one is tweaking this or that particular system and therefore one has specific expectations about what that tweak should result in. Knowing too much turned out to be counterproductive again. The patients reacted much better, especially if they believed that something good—a final state of being healed—was going to be attained. It's called the placebo effect—The brain heals itself through the expectation of being healed!" How beautiful. Ignorance is bliss.

"You've never experienced a placebo effect?"

"Maybe I have and don't know about it? It works as long as I don't know so I shouldn't know if it had been a placebo effect!" I laughed but kept checking the sentence just spoken for logical flaws.

"Right. I guess that is an ill-posed question. But tell me, doctor, did the therapy work for you?"

"I wasn't a patient there, Emma. I was trying to h.. you mean, the neurofeedback training?"

"You have tested all those sleep-enhancing techniques on yourself first, haven't you?"

She was sharp. And well prepared. I should watch my big mouth. "Most of them didn't work for me. Until they did. The dream therapy worked, I believe."

"You believe...?"

"I don't remember now exactly when I started sleeping well again. That period of my life is a bit blurry regarding source memory. Luckily, I have records. So if you would like to know, for the biography, I can check it."

"Oh, that would be quite helpful. Doctor, I would like to know when your sleep troubles ended. And if there was a specific event that triggered them." She put down the tablet and still sat there, in anticipation.

"Tomorrow. I will get that information for you by tomorrow, Emma. I need some privacy to do that."

"Of course. I understand. Excuse me."

We thanked each other. I let her out and called Salvo to put on some dance music. I was alone again, hooray! It was time for my dance workout—the thing that kept me alive and happy and with my feet on the ground.

"Salvo, dance with me!"

But he couldn't. Motor functions were regrettably far less developed than everything else in his AI make-up.

I have always loved natural highs. States of wakeful consciousness slightly more abandoned and somewhat more global than the regular sharp attention. Getting my neurons to pulse rhythmically with the progressive house music pouring in through my ears and through my sense of touch and balance when the subwoofer made the floor vibrate. Sound can be magical, and this was one of those magical experiences. The mind could just abandon to rhythmic resonance created between the external sensory stimulation and its neural representation in rhythmic firing of neuronal ensembles. Bioresonance was indeed relaxing. Finally, the brain that fanatically tries to predict everything could do so with genuine ease to its purest satisfaction. Dopamine flowed, memory networks rested comfortably, I closed my eyes and let myself bounce and move to the music I knew without effort, with nothing to solve, with nothing to prove, nothing to gain. The default mode. Neural entrainment was the only goal.

———

I was lounging on the sofa with my eyes closed. I brought myself to deep relaxation and sent out a gentle calling to my connected mind-mates. Maybe someone could hear me? "Stan? Picachu? Are you with me now?"

I waited a moment in silence, but it was hard to stay quiet. "There is something I need to revisit from the past, Picachu. It's the memories of the first time I had my heart broken and needed to invent the forgetting machine. I want to remember how that felt. It's for my…"

"For self-flagellation? You want to hurt again, Evita?" the voice replied! I could feel him frowning at my intentions.

"Let's call it catharsis. I need to see whether all that self-therapy ever worked. Or whether I've been selling people soap bubbles based on …"

"Science? I know you want to call it quackery, but it wasn't. You did a good job, Paulina. Don't put yourself down now. It doesn't make sense to doubt now."

"I was going to call it justified true belief, to be fair, but I'm glad you always have my back, Stan."

He hesitated with replying. "I'm asking you," I continued, "because we agreed not to contaminate the emulation with old memories through means other than recall and I want to check some records. Emails, letters."

He exhaled deeply and spoke: "I feel that this is important, Paulina. I know that you won't sleep tonight unless you do it and you'll be obsessing about it for the next three nights and I'll have to suffer your weird dreams as a result. So I'm going to say yes—but please have Salvatore read it to you. That will increase the interpersonal distance of that feeling. Maybe."

"Thank you, Stan." I sent out a warm wave of gratitude and put my hand on my heart to help my mind imagine it fully. "Will you stay with me for this?" And I felt that he confirmed. I got up and called my servant.

"Salvatore, could you help me find my files from around the times when I was working with spindle neurofeedback?"

"Certainly. What kind of files would you like me to show you?" he barged into the living room riding over the edge of the carpet and dragging some long hairs his wheels had picked up.

"Some personal memories. Episodes. Remind me how I felt around that time. How was I, besides being sleep-deprived?" He searched.

"I found some medical records and journal entries. You consulted several specialists, including a neurologist at La Clinique du Sommeil, and an online psychologist."

"Can you read me the report from the clinique? Or no. Better read me that email I wrote to the psychologist."

"Dear Sleep Doctor,

I don't sleep well because of a broken heart and the resulting anxiety. I wake up after roughly 4 ½ hours of sleep, almost every night, to cry. My brain wakes me up after a compressed slow-wave sleep cycle every night to tell me how sorry and sad I feel that the person I love does not love me back. It wakes me up to explode with the feeling of longing and disappointment and desperation that cannot be extinguished otherwise but through tears. I weep as I recall what could have been but never will be: the flash future memories of the generous, patient, true love I keep feeling for this man. And that he doesn't reciprocate."

"Oh yes. I remember. Thanks, Salvatore. Can I see this?" Salvatore transferred the email to my smartphone, and I continued reading silently. Apparently, the insomniac me, aged around 33, led a reasonably miserable night-time existence. The e-mail described to the doctor what I had written one night upon an abrupt awakening:

5:30 am. Insomnia, again. She cries to the image of him asking why he had pulled away. When all was so ready, all was so perfect. It tore her heart apart, and she tells him that once again in her early morning half-conscious thoughts. She cries once again although it's in the past. The muddy waters of reminiscence pull her back in again, into the swamp of memories past, emotions that don't exist anymore beyond the realm of her twisted images recreated from memory. The history comes back yet again, uselessly, tormenting her to notice what she doesn't have (but maybe could have had?) and taking attention away from what is.

Hopeless, the intense emotional memories that keep coming back like a boomerang, occupy the mind-space without feeding it anything new. They are only distorted images of the past that does not exist anymore and that you cannot control. All she can manage is breaking the cycle and getting out of the spiraling havoc of memories towards the present, toward the sounds of the birds chirping in the spring morning chill outside. To the dark blue light of the dawn seeping through the window, towards the warmth of her bed covers keeping her comfortable, towards the faint smell of a love substitute lying next to her— reminding her of his tender fascination with her and his care for her wellbeing. This is what is—memories are not. And she won't let them control her.

Am I going mad, doctor? I write in third-person narration at 5.30am...

Please, help me sleep well again.

The doctor's prompt response read not at all like a doctor's. Perhaps because counselors were a different genre of specialists. Or maybe due to cultural differences...the author of the reply was called Harjodh Singh. And I preferred the comfort of his prose to the dry scientific lingo of professionals with a Ph.D.

"It seems like you wake up with a great desire for intimacy, signaled by the feeling of loneliness. A solution to it, although seemingly tricky or unattainable at this point, is a solution nonetheless. That is how you should perceive these mid-night awakenings—as insights and answers to your deepest feelings and desires.

The mind knows what you need even if it is not always possible in living reality and it makes you cry to relieve the tension. We cry for things we cannot have, for things that do not exist and are missing in our lives. We often miss things we have never had, imaginary feelings and experiences, potential futures. We cry for them from wishful thinking, and we get so attached and attracted to the thought of what could be that when we realize it isn't there, it makes us long for them."

And This, too, shall pass—said the wise man in Kilgore Trout's internal monologue I just remembered and I uttered a short bitter laugh.

"Your brain also cries because it doesn't like stories without an ending, emotions without resolution, even if imaginary. For you, things need to have closure, a believable explanation; unanswered questions and unfinished business is probably the things that bug a brain the most in the world. That's where all the rumination and worry and scientific invention comes from. From bugging, unanswered questions that wake us up at night."

The more I look for Piglet, the less he's there...—another quote came to my mind.

"Yes, thank you, doctor. This was very insightful. In conclusion, though—I am going mad, but in a normal, acceptable way?" asked the younger me one day later.

"What you are going through in your sleep is a normal response to an unresolved emotion. To sleep better, you should either solve the emotion or make up your mind to stop caring about it. Just don't care. Let it go," replied the wise man.

I tried. I remember that I had tried many times and in many ways.

I closed the files and went to prepare a bath.

It was a time when I prayed a lot to all of my eleven Gods. I remember that my prayers went something like this:

"Zdrowaś Maryjo, łaski pełna, Pan z Tobą, błogosławionaś Ty między niewiastami, i błogosławiony owoc żywota Twojego, Jezus." Hail Mary, full of grace, Lord with You, blessed You among women, and blessed fruit of Your life, Jesus.

It was not supposed to be like this. Please make this love not go to waste. Please let him have learned something. Something good, useful. Please let this love come back to me twofold, or at least $x>1$ times. Karma. I hope.

Did you at least read my love letter? My hot tears, you bloody bastard?

You were my muse. The co-author of my soft weeping plea, *Please, love me, please.*

You ran your fingers through the feathers on the wings of my soul, and I awakened. Maybe you were just the awakening for my sleeping True Self. I was imprinted like a duckling that believes that the one it sees first after birth is its parent and starts to follow them everywhere. It was this mechanism, I guess. And I should get over it. Please, forgetting machine, please help me erase and rewind."

I remember that weeks later, I still felt wide open, fragile and vulnerable. It could be a good state—actors and performing artists must feel like this all the time. When I was little, I dreamt of becoming an actress or a dancer. But back then, I felt more like a punctured balloon: a little bit of air was slowly escaping through this hole in my heart, making it weak and less resilient and less firm and smaller with every exhalation. I had to keep pumping living air into it to keep it in shape. It was tiring.

I submerged myself in the warm soapy bath. I closed my eyes and recalled one of the days that year that blended loneliness with the sweetness of springtime hope that gradually cured me of insomnia. No particular therapy brought me up from my dungeon of lonely sadness. It was a gradual inflow of new positive life experiences that slowly helped me forget. One of them was an elderly woman on the street of this beautiful town who came up and very kindly asked "Bonjour Madame...excusez-moi, est-ce que c'est vendredi aujourd'hui?" Hello Madam...excuse me, is it Friday today? She was so graceful. French was so light and beautiful that I forgot all about my inner hole and soaked up the sunny faux-Printemps moment outdoors, grateful to God for having sent me here, to Geneva where it was almost spring, and all was about to be full of love.

It was then, when I reached the age of Jesus that I realized that at least one of my eleven Gods is a prankster. I recognized it by how he handled my love wishes. I am always incredibly grateful to all my Gods and kindred spirits. Besides misfortunate heart trouble, my life has been relatively brilliant.

That's why I am profoundly moved to find that even today, decades later when I think back about the culmination of my ambitious efforts in neuroinnovation, my mind serves me the dream about my love for that man from Porto. I remember that the feeling I had for him had once awakened the dreamer in me. It has connected me back with my inner child. When it was clear that he was gone, the little girl inside me was long inconsolable. And used her fairytale imagination to be well again. That's what that fantastic dream was about, dear Pikachu. Are you receiving this?

"Loud and clear, Evita. Over and out."

———————

Message received from a secure connection at Emma's home:

She is opening up and has a sufficiently detailed recollection of sleep technology, with autobiographic details. She said she's collaborated with Maria on the memory-altering protocol research. Correct? The robot was in standby. I'm making progress in earning her trust. But there is something traumatizing about the sleep therapy R&D she does not remember well.

Reply from Stan: Don't worry about it. You're doing a good job. Thank you.

Day 3

7

THE FORGETTING MACHINE

"Emma! Good morning."

"Good morning, Doctor. Hope you slept well?"

"Please, call me Paulina. I am fed up with the 'doctor.' Makes me feel old and sterile." I winked at her, and she smiled back. We sat in the living room—me in the armchair, her on the sofa. Business as usual. She took out her notebook, and we resumed.

"So we left off at the sleep therapy devices. You told me yesterday that one of the protocols was successful for your sleep problems. Do you remember how you came to discover it? I'd like to have some personal anecdotes from that period. If you will."

I nodded. "Yes. The help came with what became known as the 'forgetting machines'. It sounds a bit scary, I know. And indeed, the machines for forgetting are rather fancy things. They are very expensive to make and maintain so only supplemental mental health insurances cover this particular service now. In the first embodiment, we envisioned that you'd walk into a cabin, kind of like a photo booth, and sit in a big comfortable reclining chair. Something in the shape of a giant old-fashioned salon hair-dryer was lowered upon your resting head, similar to the magneto-encephalography machines. Those were also very expensive then. There are several programs to choose from. You can pick, for instance, mending a broken heart. So you state your intention, for instance, something elaborate like this:

Dear machine, please help me forget how I wish he had loved me back. Dear machine, please make me forget how I wished we lived all those moments of sharing beauty and pleasure and joy together, those that never came true. Dear machine, please unhook me from this love that is no more for I can no longer go a day without crying for something I can't change. There is only one way: forward, onto novel experiences, different loves, and I need to forget how much I wished that he would have been the one I were loved by, whom I would write and bake and sing for...

And the machine listens to all the most peculiar and extravagant requests. It understands all languages, including that of love. And it will hum to you slowly and consolingly, while it gently unwraps the wiring between the pyramidal neurons, breaking the protein bonds that make up the edges of the engram, dissolving the connections between these elements of beauty that are just in your head. Releasing you from wishes, pain, and desperation, that is all in your head..." I squeezed my mouth and stopped a tear from dropping out of my eye. "You listen to Claire de Lune, and you let yourself bring to life all those memories of the past and the imaginary futures, you let your warm tears flow as the arpeggio unfolds from the heights of the shining moonlight, and you let yourself be freed. The machine will unclasp and open these reactivated engrams, bit by bit, it will unmake the connections from the outside to the inside of the network it will dissolve only the remote, uncritical elements that made it all so beautiful and irresistible and that made you cry for months." I looked right, away from my interlocutor to hide that such an ancient meta-memory still moved me to tears.

"Are you OK, Paulina? We can pause. Do you want some water?"

I got up and walked towards Salvatore parked in standby in the kitchen entrance. I touched his arms. I don't know why. To see if he's on? And then I walked back. There was no reason to stop. Yes. I could go on.

"I'm fine. I remember. You want me to tell you about the technology?"

"Not necessarily…"

"It's complicated. The key in the whole selective reactivation-deactivation of the relevant neural populations is not to destroy the most important 20% of the network. These are the hubs upon which all else is resting. Because you can never forget completely, but you can bring down a memory's salience below a threshold of vivid, detailed recollection. And already losing the sensorial details is often enough to make the memory less appealing, less affectively relevant and less obsessively recurrent. This destruction of the weaker 80% of the memory engram network is called targeted synapse deactivation and can only be performed on brains prepared for such manipulation. The preparation entails genetically modifying the neurons in the medial temporal lobe and the ventro-medial prefrontal cortex so that their ion-channels are sensitive to light (i.e., light-gated), by making them produce a rhodopsin protein." I wiped my eye with the back of my hand. "And then you can use holographic stimulation to play with those neurons that encode a particular memory pattern. You can disturb their activation during the recall and that way, you can interfere with remembering. It's a brutally direct yet effective way to erase your memories."

"You think so? I thought it is common practice now, in the clinics?" Emma made me wonder.

"I don't know much about the current practices…this protocol was not refined when I had finished. Maria would know. But that's an interesting question."

Emma was quiet for a while. Maybe she didn't understand much of what I just explained. Was using too much jargon?

"Was I clear? Do you want me to explain the science in more detail?"

"Mm, can you maybe recall some personal experience with the machine? Have you used it? I think it'll be easier to describe how it works based on a story from your own life. Please."

I pouted my lips thinking hard about an example I could share in this biography. I didn't want to. I've already told her a bit too much about my love life, and that was as much sharing as I wanted to do for the day.

"So after the completion of this light-gated stimulation process, the one I just described to you." I looked for signs of understanding, and she nodded, unconvincingly. "...a secondary mechanism of forgetting—aimed at updating the unwanted memory—is employed. This procedure is behavioral and can be administered to anyone, genetically enhanced or not. You may choose to take a memory-formation-enhancing agent at this point (anything from D-cylcoserine to methylphenidate). As you reactivate the memory and thereby labilise it—that is, make it plastic and unstable—new stimuli will be presented to induce the formation of a new, more functional memory.

For example, you could be presented with a new scenario that is conceptually linked to your freshly re-created memory. For this replacement memory, we used cute animals as stimuli. Animated cartoon characters are also fabulous episode carriers. You would see a cartoon, for example, a scenario where this character, a white dog, is crying over the loss of their favorite toy, if the memory you are trying to forget is that of a painful loss. Real, or imaginary. Unrequited love would be the latter, Emma."

"You mention the loss of someone you loved quite often, Paulina." Emma was observing me from a safe distance between the sofa and the meeting point of the living room parquet with the kitchen floor tiles, at the height of the dining table where I've remained in standing position.

"I have lost many imaginary lovers, Emma. It's called unrequited love. The brain sometimes believes that it could be loved by someone when it isn't." I got up and ambled to sit in the dining room chair. I was feeling old. "Anyway…The reason why we used visual stimuli (animations or short movies) is that it was too difficult to create a precise memory through neural stimulation alone and it would drive the cost of the whole procedure beyond exorbitant. Also, the machine needed to record your brain activity as you encoded this new memory in the context of retrieval of the old memory, and direct neural stimulation at this point could interfere with the data acquisition." I wasn't looking at her anymore but I thought I noticed something like an approving nod with the corner of my eye, so I went on.

"Oh, I should mention that the replacement episode usually also involves a dramatic turn: for example, in our imaginary white dog cartoon, his toy falls out of the window of a car he's riding in, or maybe it is grabbed by a seagull that takes it for an edible item, or something like that. As I mentioned, these cute stimuli serve as anchors to which your mind can attribute the rewarding feeling because the emotion of "cuteness" is an appetitive, positive one. The cuter, the better. And we need the surprise from the dramatic turn in this reconsolidation experience to give your brain a memory prediction error—this will trigger a noradrenaline release that will strengthen the consolidation of this new memory."

"That's very smart." She noticed. I agreed but didn't see it as a compliment. There are smarter things about it that she hasn't noticed, perhaps.

"The cartoon characters are—in a way—a personification of you outside of you." I went on. "And the stories they're involved in should be vague, not novel and not particularly attractive per se, for they only serve to pose the wide-open engrams of your target memories on a stable net. Eventually, you are supposed to forget nonetheless, not replace an old obsessive memory with another one. The surprise in the story makes the lesson. Noradrenaline shoots up to signal the 'surprise prediction error' in your memory, and as a result, this memory has a chance of not only updating the old reactivated memory but also for being preferentially consolidated in the subsequent sleep cycle due to dopaminergic (cuteness and pleasure) and noradrenergic (surprise) tagging. Then you fall asleep.

While you sleep, you reconsolidate and replace! Now that's smart, isn't it?"

"Mhm…" nodded Emma, absently browsing pictures on the screen in front of her. They were pictures of the early forgetting machines. Large egg-shaped pods in which the user was cradled in a reclined position.

"Do you want to see one of those? I have it in my basement." I just remembered that one of the reconditioned models still stood in my storage room. Nowadays, forgetting machines were no longer stand-alone devices. Their functionalities have been integrated into "restorative beds"—solarium-meets-hammock contraptions that embodied all sleep and relaxation-related technologies. I had one of those, too.

"That's alright. If it's OK, I think we should stay on the story." She looked at her watch and to my surprise, declined my invitation to Narnia (basement) of neuro-devices underneath my living room. I thought she'd be thrilled…maybe she's claustrophobic? Arachnophobic? I ignored her and rushed for the bedroom door to show her an actual embodiment of a forgetting machine I kept there.

"Voilà, here is one." I opened the bedroom door and pointed at the lid with a wide swooping gesture. She lazily got up from the sofa to reach me.

"Is that one of the recent ones?" she asked, unimpressed.

"Yes. The pod-style booth environment was adapted from sensorial deprivation chambers, and it brings in the sense of acceptance, comfort, and warmth. It is a good learning environment." I reached to open the lid of the big mint-green egg to reveal a…blood-thirsty vampire with the face of Salvo. No, not really. Just a boring beige cushioned memory-foam mattress.

"Oh, it looks like a comfy bed," said Emma, visibly disappointed.

"Yes well. It is what it is. The feeling of comfort during recall is necessary because, at the same time, your brain should want to keep the newly updated memory. If you want to convince the brain to retain something"—I pointed my index finger at her— "it has to appeal to it and induce approach motivation. And not too much arousal or else we're risking fear of novelty. Pleasure is also helpful for retrieval of the behavior-dominating memories you want to change, assuming that they are painful in some way." I closed the lid theatrically to show her the electronic interface on top of the pod lid. "This ground memory is the key from which all other related memories will continue to try to complete the pattern, and you want to prevent that." I pressed some buttons to demonstrate the various therapy programs the menu offered. "This is why, even after several sessions, it is possible that there will be some shadow feelings triggered apparently without a particular object or reason. These are the residual completing elements that will slowly decay as the ground memory is no longer holding them together." I placed my body weight on one foot, resting my hand on the hip. The white amplifier box in the corner kept making buzzing noise from time to time. "I am going to stop here because this is beginning to sound exactly like one of my video lectures."

"Thank you, Paulina." Emma seemed a bit distant nodding at me but turning her head around, curious. Something caught her attention.

"Thank you." She said again, and I understood it was time we leave the bedroom.

She browsed for something on her tablet without looking at me while walking. "Yes, I think we have the technological bit quite well covered. This is also useful for the story, but I'd like to know some more personal details." She sat down. "From the background information I read, the forgetting machine was not a very successful invention although there was a lot of hope and hype around its launch. You signed a contract with the manufacturer of the pods and had been deriving licensing fees from the patent. I understand that you cannot disclose everything but would you have a personal anecdote from the times of the origination of the idea or a situation during the prototyping? To make it more interesting for the readers?" She was professionally serious now. I was beginning to forget that we had a contract, a non-disclosure agreement and a collection of personalized clauses concerning my final authorization of everything she writes. This was not just chit-chatting with a student. The stories from my life I was delivering were first and foremost meant to be publishable material. And it had to be juicy. I sighed.

"Of course. I have a few anecdotes up my sleeve. But we are going to need samba music for this and some strawberry daiquiris. Salvatore, Brazilian playlist, please. Stay here, Emma. I'll get blending." I escaped to the kitchen, filled up the blender with a teaspoon of a bulking agent, frozen strawberries and blueberries and some green wine. Summer feeling always made me happier. So did samba and thick blended concoctions that reminded me of the milky mush I was fed as a toddler. What was I supposed to tell her? That even the name—the forgetting machine—was an under-delivered overpromise? And that it was a big disappointment to me because there had been many moments in my life when I needed it to work?

"I'm sorry, Emma. I can't recall much surrounding the forgetting pod's early use. I can check my personal diary from the months of the launch, but I don't expect to find much reference to the use of the forgetting therapy. I think, it is possible that it actually did work for me because I was the pilot subject No1 and I tried it on myself for eight sessions while calibrating the protocol. My mind is blank. It could also be that I repressed the memories because I was ashamed that it failed...I really can't remember. Why don't we move on to something else?" I announced when I reemerged from the kitchen carrying two ruby red cocktails.

Emma had been patiently waiting all this time in the living room and seemed to maintain her stoic lethargic peace. Or maybe she didn't care.

"Not a problem. But, may I suggest, do you think we could come back to it by some other means? You must have video records from those days. In the 2040s, in 2038 almost the whole planet was using video memory. I'm sure you have that data somewhere, doctor."

I put down my glass, and the straw leaked an aquarelle-red drop on the ceramic coffee table.

"Emma, I cannot show you my memory video records. We agreed upon this. It may be disruptive, and you know why. You cannot view them if only in my presence and I don't want to feed a perfect copy of my episodic past into the Connected Minds network." Even though four of the six participants had been there with me when we worked on forgetting, we'd agreed that revisiting our past by means other than self-recollection could distort the initial state of our memories which we took as the restore point. The risk was too high.

"Then I could view it myself, without your presence." Insisted Emma.

"No, you can't. For your information, the video records all the way from 2030 up until two weeks ago have been confiscated and sealed. Please don't mention this in the biography. I will not authorize the publication of any passages that mention the ongoing investigation. Do you understand?" I was firm and disappointed that the moment has arrived when I had to explain myself to Emma Printemps. Now she knows that the investigation is a serious matter that will determine my future.

What she didn't know, though, was that I didn't care for my continued human experience—whether in a connected or a disconnected mind. I was mentally destitute and tired of science. I just wanted to rest in a comfortable, sunny place on my monthly Swiss and Dutch pensions. In Portugal, perhaps. Good food, sweet people, soulful music. That's what I couldn't wait for. I couldn't wait for the committee to say that I was not guilty of what they had been charged with: neglectful abuse of the supercomputer server farm in Ticino and of risking the mental health of six people, myself included. And what's happened with Maud, I wonder? I haven't heard from her for too long...

Emma resigned with reticence. "I understand."

"It's a serious matter, Emma. I count on your professionalism. We have a contract, and it's binding even if I go crazy." I eyed her up and down. I kept thinking; if I were to be pronounced guilty, there would probably be a fine for unauthorized use of public research money and all retirement savings and my home may have to go to cover it. And I was under house arrest so shifting borders (a potentially smart solution. There's no extradition from many countries that could be my safe haven) was not an option. They have learned from their past. Bloody lawyers—the only people who learn well from all documented past decisions."

"Maybe I should go now," she said after that little awkward pause.

"Please don't go yet. I don't want us to end on such a negative note. I have plenty of fun anecdotes for the readers. But I cannot guarantee that they will be exactly about the famous neurohacks you want to write about nor that they will be chronologically consequential. You know, I am beginning to suspect that Project Unison is taking its toll on my memory, too." I had to be at least partly honest with her. There were details I was not allowed to reveal to the public due to contractual obligations with the sponsors for some of the inventions but also for protecting the privacy of my mind-connected friends. And then there were the details I didn't want to remember. And those I was shamefully hiding, perhaps to the detriment of the experiment.

8

THE DIAGNOSIS

Emma returned home and sat down to review the library archives via a secure VPN tunnel. Experimental data from consenting human subjects are stored for up to 30 years and were accessible to all lab members. She went through the transcripts of the anonymous Subject No.1 of the prototype protocol for the early human trial of the forgetting machine. It does not leave a shadow of doubt.

It was as if I could feel the texture of his soul. Or I imagined it. Or I felt that I could get there, underneath his skin, if we only had lived through enough experiences together. Because we were made of the same substance. He touched my soul. He opened the fountain of imagination in me. He was my muse. I sang, and I danced because my soul found a soulmate. I was not alone anymore. The little girl in me had someone to hold her hand and play with. I was that little girl again. And I miss him, dear forgetting machine.

After months, I still missed you. It could still spark. It will probably never go away, the feeling of longing for my beloved muse. My childhood friend, I still cry for you.

Still today, I keep bringing back the images and the emotions of you not to forget how it felt. I keep replaying the memories of the sweet chills that traveled up my body. I keep hearing your voice and reenacting my reaction of joyful, excited anticipation, of welcoming and of pure pleasure of hearing it and knowing that you're near. I keep doing it, and I keep writing to you so that I don't forget how I felt. Because those were some of the best, highest feelings in my life so far and I don't want to forget them. But every time I recall you, you're slightly different, slightly better than the original because my brain tends to augment the rewarding aspect of the memory as all other details decay.

If only I got a chance at relearning how you felt. I'd update these memories in no time. My brain would be bathed in the memory elixir of catecholamines. I'd be powered by this electricity again. I'd admire the starry sky and the shape of the moon every night again because that's what people's minds want to do when they're in love. They suddenly expand their imaginations, their horizons stretch into the unknown and the unfathomable. They become more curious than ever. They want to know everything that could concern their beloved one. Everything that could potentially impress and interest them, they want to learn. I'd even learn how to cook better. With pleasure and with an unsurmountable motivation of someone who does something for love. Love is more powerful than, say, religious faith not only because it is so transformative, but also because it can be replenished with a kiss, fueled by a smile and reignited by a promise. "Ale powiedz tylko słowo, a będzie uzdrowiona dusza moja." *But only say the word, and I shall be healed, I prayed.*

If I can't make a drug to substitute this feeling, then please make me go back to normal. Up, to the baseline. To the flat pain-free neutrality. I can't stand this anymore. Please, help me forget.

[Pause]

Emma shut off the connection without saving a copy. No one should know how thorough she is about her job. She reviews once again the instructions from the committee. And the instructions from Stan and Maria: "Do not mention Professor Marco Carini. Not by his name, nor his role nor provide any hints as to his involvement in Project Unison." She shakes her head not comprehending the reason for all the secrecy. What are they searching for in her memories? All there seems to be is a brooding, aging, broken heart.

9

ONE LIFE

I stood under the cold running water making sure the upper part of my back, the section between the shoulder blades, got cool. I switched sides and tried to control my hiccupping breathing as the cold water poured on my face. I needed this to activate my sympathetic nervous system and to think sharp with the help of some adrenaline. It takes just a few seconds to get that system going. As I was stepping out of the shower, drying my body with a bamboo towel, putting on the slippers, checking my skin in the mirror and moving on to the slow ritual of the hammam, I revisited my general all-encompassing beliefs about life.

Many of our mental problems are just memory problems. We forget to pay attention online, we overload our working memory or dwell too much on the past. Or we spread our attention too thin, forget to tag the memory for later consolidation before it flees and as a result, don't memorize enough of the essential things. In a way, all of humanity's problems are memory problems: we don't remember our history, not even the history of one single lifetime, and we cannot learn from the accounts of memories of our great-great-grandfathers and their grandfathers. They're too remote to be accurate. They're too distant technologically and culturally to be comprehended. Either we can't access these memories, or the record and the recall are imperfect. Something glitches at retrieval and our brains proceed to fill in the pattern—all too easily—with optimism bias, with wishful thinking, with counterfactual intuitions…to an end result of a catastrophic confabulation.

I gauged the crow feet embellishing my eyes in the sunlight-lit smart mirror.

Take depression. This is a problem of someone who spends too much time in their memory. Too much thinking never killed anyone unless that thinking took over your attention entirely and didn't let you encode anything new and salient and potentially rewarding. You can get stuck in your memories of things that you had once experienced as positive, so wonderful, in fact, that the current experience cannot compare to the overblown fantasy your brain has created by glossing over that memory. Inevitably, every time you recalled, it got wrapped in a new layer of imaginary glitter flowing probably from your ventral tegmental area/substantia nigra. And then nothing new compares. No new experience can ever match that best moment of limerence that has passed away and exists but in your imperfect memory.

I put on my Japanese silk bathrobe. I got it in Tokyo, many years ago. It always gives me this self-congratulatory feeling on what a great buy this was.

And then there's another problem—*generalization*. My statistics teacher once told us that bad models can be recognized by their lack of sparsity. How inelegant is a solution with too many parameters! Punishment be upon those models that are not simple enough! A wise Japanese man named Akaike said so. The teacher explained that it's bad when "everything is connected to everything, and then you know nothing. It does not inform you at all." After him, some students in my class started repeating this sentence when pointing to "bad science." But, in life, and in life science, everything *is* connected to everything. In a very complicated web of near and distant mutual dependencies. Eating an apple today may prevent you from getting colon cancer twenty-five years from now, maybe?

It likely doesn't. In the grand economy of the dynamic systems navigational properties, weak links serve for flexibility and for learning distant connections, but do not contribute to maintaining stability and preserving memory. The system is robust only as long as the hubs of the network are intact. The other 80% of links can usually be rebuilt according to some greedy routing link propagation principles but if the hubs fail you forget, your immune system weakens, and your network of everything disintegrates. On many levels of systemic analysis, the world is small, and the rich get richer. Marco knew everything about this.

"That's not the fun bit, though. Oh, no." I started speaking to the mirror. I'm not crazy. Sometimes I practice my speeches like this.

"This memory process I spent so much time detangling is called memory integration, but I'd call it some form of generalization. Humor works like that and everybody loves funny people. The detached facts that all of the sudden—when surprisingly juxtaposed—make some weird sense together. And what about absurd humor? Both forms create some kind of surprise. Is there a word for that kind of surprise? Professor Ekman didn't find one and called it 'positive surprise', which to me sounds like an idea of a fairly un-funny mind."

I reached out for the skin toner and a cotton bud.

I love these generalized insights my brain serves me, especially in the morning. Suddenly—among the mambo jumbo of the days past—it all makes sense and I can do self-therapy even better. Oh, tree of knowledge, how sweet thy fruit. Also, this could be a symptom of mania. Hypomania. Let's not give my dopaminergic circuits too much credit.

What time is it? 8 pm? I should probably eat something and stop thinking so much.

"Salvatore? Is it dinner time?"

"It is late. I have prepared something for you in the kitchen. Please." He extended his right arm and unrolled his hand as though a delicate rose was about to blossom on his palm.

I wondered: "how honest and scientifically curious can I be with Emma next time she asks me about my neuroscientific motivations?" I rehearsed a hypothetical scenario over the quiche aux épinards.

I'd ask, "Emma, have you ever heard of a religious orgasm?"

"A what?" she'd reply.

"I just thought that God would be much more powerful if one could make love to it. You know, if there was a tangible effect of having your senses stimulated rather than dazzled with an imaginary grace and glory," I'd explain and that would baffle her wildly.

"You're weird, Doctor...", she might think. So I'd elaborate that "I always wanted to know how that could feel. Does it compare to the stimulation of the angular gyrus and operculum together with some general endocannabinoid-accompanied arousal? You don't know?" She might not know, I suspect.

"I haven't had the rhodopsin gene therapy, and the only brain stimulation I've ever received was DC (direct current stimulation) for dyslexia when I was a child," she would retort, possibly disgusted at my question, and an awkward silence would follow.

Decision: No. I should not go in that direction in an interview. Not even the last one of my life.

"What are we watching tonight, Salvo?"

"The Life of Brian."

"Damn you, robot. Are you developing a taste for retro or suspecting that I'm that old to remember this one from my childhood?" I messed with Salvo knowing he couldn't serve me a biting riposte.

"Should I change the selection? Alternative options are..."

"Nah. Nah. It's alright. Let's have a laugh." And a puke, possibly.

Day 4

10

BOREDOM

"Good morning, Paulina. How are you feeling this morning? Ready for another sunny day?"

"Good morning, Salvatore. You of all people should know that I'm only keeping my brain circuits warm waiting for a miracle of ethical justice. It's all good. I'm old. I don't need much, luckily. *All I need is a miracle, all I need is you[2]!*" I sang to him and grabbed his arms and twirled around him. He was the sun I was orbiting in this limited space-time of my house arrest, laughing foolishly because all I wanted to do was complain. And complaining is boring although it does bring me some relief.

"Madame is feeling playful today?" He tried to tickle me, but I escaped. He tried again and got me this time.

I laughed out loud and slapped his butt. "Naughty robot..." To show me just how naughty he was he played again that obnoxious 1980s music *She's got it...yeah, baby, she's got it[3]*. He waved his upper body around the caterpillar lower body in some mix of unnatural limbo and belly dancing motions. An awkward view. We should have

---

[2] Mike & The Mechanics (1985), "All I Need Is A Miracle"

[3] Bananarama (1986), "Venus".

spent those three extra years in the lab to give him some basic dance skills…

I let him "dance," got myself a coffee and checked the appointments and messages of the day. I couldn't see any new correspondence since the day Emma arrived. Strange. I clapped my hands to get his attention.

"My dear robot. Are there any new messages for me? Any fans, clients, investigators trying to come in contact with me recently? Press?" He straightened up and glided closer towards me.

"No, Madame. Zero new messages. Only Emma's transcripts from the day before yesterday. I put them in your archive."

"Oh, did you? Why?"

"Because you asked me so, Paulina. One week ago, you made a clear disposition as to how I should treat new correspondence from everyone but Emma Printemps." I squinted looking at his glazed eyes and skimming the titles of past read emails all of which seemed familiar and unimportant. Yes. Salvatore was probably right. I shouldn't be dealing with anything new these days. For a brief instant, I thought about my knitting project laying deserted in the bedside drawer. I haven't finished that scarf I started when I was fifty-two.

"Is something bothering you, Paula?"

"Boredom, Salvo. Boredom is the root of all evil. I used to think that it was memory problems but that's an outdated theory."

"That memory is the root of all evil. I can be convinced. But boredom is not its cause—it's the solution. It is the force that spurs humans and other curious animals to explore and search and ask and act. Isn't that why you specifically limited the affective discomfort of mine?" Salvatore leaned against the wall in a funny triangle pose that made him look "relaxed" and served me the dose of morning inspiration I can't remember programming him to do. Anyway, most of his learning was autonomous and autopoietic. But he had also been eruditely educated on all of 20- and 21st-century science and philosophy so I couldn't tell where this piece of morning wisdom came from.

I love you, Salvo, I thought, and almost wanted to close his mouth with a kiss.

"What time is Emma coming?"

"She said she wouldn't be visiting today. She'll video call at 10 am." I nodded.

11

NEURODIVERSITY

"Let's go back to the forgetting machine." Asked the smiling video face of soft-boned, insightful Emma Printemps.

"Why?" I didn't want to review my failures. I wanted to do hand-waving debates about things I know something about.

"What happened to you after the first séance? You must have recorded it as part of experimental data."

I have. And read it many times over. I almost knew my record by heart although it seemed like reciting some long-dead poet. This old Paulina, an ancient patient of mine, recorded her thoughts spoken out loud in a semi-hypnotic trance, doped with propranolol and D-cycloserine and some endocannabinoid-enhancing agent.

"I have that on record if you must know. But I'd rather this didn't appear in my biography. At least not verbatim." I eye-balled her face and her tablet computer with intended severity and proceeded to a theatrical recital of the pains of a younger me. She asked for it.

"I know what my problem is. It's this constant retrieval, which consolidates the memory just too hard. It's no good for me—like a traumatic memory that keeps haunting your imagination and every time you see and feel it again, it just gets written over again, in bolder ink, in thicker wiring, cemented with PKM-zeta proteins. The magic pill of the neuroscience of learning that we had only discovered some decades ago is that you can update old recursive, dysfunctional memories only when you bring them to live first. Simple: to change the content of a box, you first have to re-open the box. You can't shake a closed memory box and hope that the elements will change state and magically disappear at the touch of a baton, or change their configuration without a physical manipulation (although that one is possible. Memory's recreational nature permits it to lie to us quite often). You must open the box first. Now the big question is, what new information, feelings or interpretations, should I insert into the box to make this box less heavy? If I do nothing, it will keep falling off its shelf, shuttering the planks and crashing into the floor of my memory cabinet with a loud kaboom that I will hear even in the middle of the night when all controllers are asleep, and all sensory shift workers have gone home. That bloody box is a treasure chest and treasures can be cumbersome. You need extra security to keep them. A lock and someone to remember the code on the lock. A great feat. Please unlock me, dear forgetting machine."

"Is it part of the protocol, to speak to the machine?"

"The protocol was to recall the painful memory and to open up to changing it to something less painful. With whatever means the participant prefers. Self-assertion is one way." I shrugged. She nodded in understanding. There was an awkward silence I didn't expect. I poured some hot water over my tea leaves. She was making me feel uneasy, as if this wasn't an interview but an interrogation. Or worse. A psychotherapy session.

"How was your first experience with it? Do you remember?" she peered at me with the distant, professional concern of a shrink. I leaned back in the armchair and served her my science-digest of what that experience had been like.

"I think we've already said enough about that." Why does she keep going back to the forgetting machine? "But if you really must know, I recognized the beauty of connectedness in memory when I woke up the day after and linked the discussion I had been writing at that time for a Current Biology paper with the fact that my brain made me cry over this unrequited love...It does so because the ventral striatum now had a different baseline level of dopaminergic activity for signaling *reward* and it was a staggeringly high one. As a result, all generally rewarding experiences were being adjusted down to that remembered previous reward value level, and if that activity persists, you become depressed. Depression, we discovered, was a normalization problem that would change with time, with the fading of the memory. And when you're depressed, everything, even chocolate and hugs from best girlfriends, fails to activate the ventral striatum to that *being in love* level. The consequence is relative deactivation, which serves to teach the learning systems that all else in life is now disappointingly less rewarding than the...well, in my case, the man I was in love with. Why work for a reward that's below the baseline? The brain won't lift a finger if it anticipates such a response. You're depressed because the ventral striatum set its standard for 'reward' sky high and not even *moelleux au chocolat* can break the record. And one way to forget is just to let the time pass. Time smoothes (by interpolation) over the strong signal of the overly salient memories of the feeling and drains it slowly of the juicy essence of affective valence. That's why they say, 'Time heals.' But I'm impatient, and I didn't want to wait."

"So you drugged yourself and administered an experimental outpatient version of the phobia-reduction therapy using computerized psychotherapy with holographic memory circuit stimulation?" belligerently asked Emma.

I smiled to mask the utter shock at this question. The amplifier box buzzed again. Or was it Salvatore's distress signal?

"You know, Emma, the fact that we cannot go back to the good old times is one reason why the human condition is ultimately tragic. All famous wise writers know that. It is tragic also because of our inability to replicate consciousness, specifically the subjective experience of how some percept, memory, and idea makes one feel. And so we are eternally lonely because we can't find someone who could feel exactly like us. We die with the sole unitary unique experience of dying, leaving no trace for others to ever know what it had felt like. Was it a unique death experience? No one will ever know. Tragic!"

You see, I always eventually got myself wholly figured out and that particular period of my life could be summarized in a song, *Yo este llorando por tu amor*...David Lynch said, "What more do you want? Life does NOT make sense. Just accept it and laugh. Here—nurse this rabbit.[4]" That's what using the forgetting machine taught me. But that wouldn't sound good in my biography, would it?

"Now, if you don't mind, I would like to move on to another meaningful period of my life. I would like to transmit something to my readers and viewers. Can I? I believe the stories about my research and development activities will be richer when placed in the context of what motivated them, namely my reflections on what I consider hardships of the human condition. I have given it some thought, Emma, and I am ready to read them to you." I proclaimed vehemently, but Emma wasn't impressed. I didn't care. I guess she's understood who she's dealing with by now and has begun developing a tolerance for mild lunacy.

"With pleasure, Dr. Kochanowska," she responded eventually, with fake enthusiasm while I browsed for an essay I had prepared days ago. "I will try to include as much as possible of your message in the final work." She was sitting at a desk in a white-walled room dressed in a powder-rose long-sleeved t-shirt. She looked like a child in her bedroom; all that was missing were stuffed animals on the bed. This was her study/office, I believe, and it had an immaculate and child-friendly look to it. It was not what I expected. I thought someone who draws fantastic superheroes for a living inhabits a colorful living space, inside and outside of her mind. Maybe she just moved in? Painted the walls fresh or something? Installed radiation and electrosmog-blocking nets? Also, was she willing to indulge with the monologues of the crazy old lady today or was she beginning to trivialize and mock me...?

---

4 "Rabbits" (2002), short film series directed by David Lynch.

"We spend the three first years of our lives trying to build an awareness of our surroundings and the people in it—people other than ourselves. In the beginning, our brains work day and night to figure out where the baby ends and where the world even beyond the mother begins. We finally kind of get a hang of it with the spring of the theory of mind. This comes about around the time when we begin to hate being physically constrained. If you've ever flown with a baby onboard an airplane and had to buckle it up, you know the reaction. The discovery of mental independence goes hand in hand with physical independence. And the bewildering need for freedom (from what?) is born.

We begin to understand that there are other minds. *I moved my eyes from the text to see my listener scratching her nose.* That other people do not participate in our inner mental process and that the inner monologue can only be heard by us and no one else. And the surprising and shocking consequences of it is that I can lie to people because there's this whole universe of cognition that they have no access to unless they've been there, too, or unless I communicate it to them in a way that they understand. And lying is cool, so we learn how to do it well, for the sake of training our temporo parietal junction, of course. Why? Because social intelligence seems to be the basis of intelligence in our species and we evolved it essentially to lie to others and invent fiction, by proxy!"

"Wait, Paulina, please. Do you want me to include this verbatim as a message to the readers? A preface?" she cut me.

"Umm...that's an idea. Can I finish the paragraph, so you know where I am going with this?"

"Of course."

"As I was saying, at an early stage of brain development, we also begin to see how unfortunate the consequences of this separation of the minds are: 'Johnny will never know where I hid the marshmallow until I return and tell him that it's in the drawer or I leave him a note so that he can find it...poor Johnny would be pleased to know that I saved that one marshmallow especially for him. I can feel the joy with which he will react to the news once I tell him.' and the like."

Emma rolled her eyes.

"We do, of course, assume that other humans have similar cognitive capacities and that they are probably capable of generating very similar perceptions, emotions, and reflections and maybe even conclusions when presented with the same information. But we are wrong. We only begin to realize that once we meet someone who's a bit different, at about four years of age. And here the whole universal concept of being able to kind of figure out what other people think and feel completely falls apart. By the age of seven we are crudely aware that the other kids are different from us and that only some are potential friends and some will inevitably be potential foes because we don't think the same way, don't own the same things and our moms and dads don't love us the same way. Unless educated?

The tragedy of having a mind of your own seems to get better for some at puberty, where all efforts of brain development are directed towards fitting in a group, finding a social identity and emulating your peer role models. For some, however, the separation continues to grow ever more palpable."

"Are you talking about some particular condition?" asked Emma.

"No. Just the consequences of normal human diversity. We are different. The diversity is exuberantly plethoric! And we don't know how to build bridges across the differences, let alone make optimal use of them. From my perspective, it is difficult to find people similar to you, or just one or two other individuals who would fully and truly understand you. Some people spend a lot of time in fruitless search. Despite highly evolved social skills, the internet and widespread knowledge of one single language, many people feel very alone with their qualia.

So you see, I had this romantic vision. I wanted people to connect deeper, make more valuable connections, find better mates, form comfortable and inspiring bonds. I thought the key to knowing yourself was to see yourself reflected in someone else's eyes. And since eyes are the mirror of the soul, I thought *why not connect directly to the soul?*"

Et voilà, I delivered my solemn speech with self-aggrandizing gravity. Whenever I speak from the heart, the ensuing reflexive silence makes me feel a little embarrassed. Damn, I love to talk too much.

"And so this leads us to the affective communication support?" Emma crossed the sound barrier and made my monologue appear to be a conversation. How kind of her.

"Not directly. I first started by promoting neurodiversity in practice. In my view, education is the main difference between monkeys and us, so this is where I thought I should concentrate my efforts first."

Emma laughed out loud.

"What? Why are you laughing?"

"Nothing. I just remembered the monkeys...Irrelevant. Excuse me. And do tell me. I'm very curious about the matching algorithm." She folded her arms.

"I don't remember exactly where the idea came from, but at some point, after the whole sleeping business went south, there was an opportunity to promote neurodiversity by helping recruiters in companies find matching candidates through internet profile search. It was infringing on privacy rights at times, but the results were exciting. I believe I first read about one large multinational applying such a matching algorithm internally, for within-company transfers. And to be frank, my only contribution was that I proposed to use it elsewhere, to help people find truly compatible friends, soul-brothers, and soul-sisters, without resorting to the embarrassing use of swipe-shopping and paid services like match.com..." I frowned at the thought of those early dating apps.

"Whom did you propose it to? Who was working with you on this?"

"It was kind of my idea. I wanted to find someone to collaborate with. I wrote a paper proposal as a letter to the journal 'Nature', and somehow they picked it up. I was fresh and had bright ideas some of which managed to receive attention." I boasted, smiling, and Emma dutifully recorded my emotion.

"And what happened after the publication?"

"Oh, very little, actually. Not as much as hoped." Salvatore's agitation detector pinged my wristband: I was lying or conflicted with myself. Was I?

"How so?"

"Well, initially, I proposed to measure and catalog psychometric personality scores along with available neuroimaging and genotyping data to build a real people-profiling database. I proposed to start with a recognized particularity of *personality* for which functional and structural differences in the brain have been well studied. I wanted to start with a subgroup of the normal population (so no psychopathology) that nonetheless was distinct enough so that we could train some pattern recognition algorithms on it.

At that time, there was this condition known as HSPS.

"Hyper...something?" inquired Emma.

"Oh, it doesn't matter, for the sake of the story. Years later science was refined, and nowadays the people with such traits are referred to by some other term."

"I think the readers would like to know what HSS stands for." She pressed. I sighed and fidgeted in my seat. The wristband flashed 'relax.'

"Let's call them...poetic cavemen, shall we? I'd like to keep my biography clean of misnomers and science that no longer is. Even though I contributed to perpetrating some of it." I lied.

"Poetic cavemen. Hmm. We'll go back to that term later, OK." Emma folded the tablet and sat back to listen. She got the clue?

"At that time, the *poetic cavemen* were the rare species who seemed to have long been bereft of good fortune in this search for soulmates, particularly when it comes to pair-bonding." My eyelid twitched. "Because of the dwindling population and the fact that in some areas they could no longer find other poetic cavemen to relate to, they have been forced to settle for less than ideal mates and partners to prevent their population from going completely extinct. *Poetic cavemen,* a name given to them by their leader and activist for neurodiversity that became popular with laymen, are humans endowed with high sensorial processing sensitivity. They constitute about 15-25% of the population and are quite hard to spot. They adapt to their environments with utmost diligence and ease. They are the social chameleons capable of learning the habits of any social community they happen to be part of and blend in extremely well in most situations. And yet, they feel isolated. Adaptive and unaggressive, they possess the rare gift of knowing what others truly feel and want. It is thanks to this sensitivity that they obtain the most social reward in their childhood and thus, through reinforcement, they quickly learn how to read and please others. They sense everything around them with more acuity than the remaining 80% of the population. They perceive the richness of the auditory and visual and olfactory landscapes with unmatched depth. Their tactile receptors have lower activation thresholds, so their skin is sometimes more sensitive to touch. They can experience incredible pleasure with a very light brush of a lover's fingers on their skin. Sitting down on dew-covered grass and connecting to the earth's energy field feels orgasmic. They revel in subtle aesthetic feelings and can deeply sense beauty. And they get overwhelmed by the noisy, brutal, insensitive world, the chaos of people hustling and bustling, the commotion of trying to carry out your agenda while sensing that of all other people around you and trying to ignore these feelings. Remarkable creatures."

"But they're human, aren't they?"

"Yes. It's just a set of neuro-characteristics that defines their sensory systems. That's why it may directly be correlated with the particular personality traits that developed or manifested as a result of these particularities of their CNS. Central Nervous System."

"Got it. Special humans with special brains."

"Just like everything else!" I wanted to quote the sarcastic Woody Allen. But actually, Czesław Miłosz would have been more appropriate. In my head, he often said *"Because you're just one of many things..."5,* a verse from wartime poetry that often helped me stay down to earth when my undesirable tendency to fly high in my dream-space came to the fore. Like now.

"Right." She laughed. She was being cute, and I was beating around the bushes.

"Anyway, I wanted to study them as a population because of the distinctness of their brain structure and function. And to help them find each other. But I had to find a way to bring this on a science agenda of someone who cared for the *sensitive cavemen.*

"Why them?"

"Ugh...I had a personal interest in unusual brains. You know, scientists are weird, and we like oddities." I chuckled. "'And also because all they had back then was brain scientists. So, I joined a hackathon for optimizing decision making by enhancing people's affective awareness." I saw Emma's lips drawing to an 'o'. "Hackathons were modern get-togethers of innovative minds who wanted to do something in their spare time, something else than barbecuing at the lake. There is incredible innovative potential in people once you let them do what hits their dopaminergic sweet spot (that is, what they like and want). Let them barbecue, if that's what their hearts desire. Turns out, at a societal level, we don't need everyone to be an innovator. We also need plenty of executors. Those can rest after five days of work while the hungry minds get together to hack the future we want on the weekend. In the end, everybody gets their sausage the way they like..." I clapped my hands.

"Of course!" nodded Emma. It appeared she was suddenly in good spirits. Maybe I was beginning to make sense. Or maybe my story got more entertaining?

---

5 Miłosz, Czesław. "Miłość", *Ocalenie,* 1945, verse 3.

We paused for a moment to look into each other's smiling eyes. Hers appeared to me honestly approving. I don't know why—it was just an appreciation of this present moment where I was grateful that another accepting human being, Emma, was there with me. It was a feeling of my dream coming true. My phone buzzed. It was a message from Stan, and it broke a moment of profound connection some people grapple with because it's *awkward*.

"...Just a sec. Excuse me." Stan wrote that I should cut the crap. How does he know what I'm talking or thinking about? The phone buzzed again: *Don't pollute the network with pink lies, Evita…!*

"Where was I? Highly Sensitive People. Right."

"Ah-huh. Can you tell me when that happened? I will respect the mnemonic timeline as much as possible but to match up with the historical records, I'd like to keep track of the chronicle timeline, as well."

"It was 2021. I collaborated with the city authorities via the university and had access to private research money through Geneva-based philanthropists and banks." I waved my hands in surging jubilation over the good old days. "I decided to build my case for more neurodiversity in group decision making around the HSPs. I mean—the *poetic cavemen*. I argued for the balancing power of neurodiversity in important decisions that could potentially have a wide impact on sustainability in risky decision making. I called it *behavioral risk management* when I sold it to the bankers. I called it *socially responsible harvesting of neurodiversity* when I spoke to the local government. I titled it, *Vive les différences*, when I wrote a manifesto for Science Advances."

The phone buzzed again and told me to keep my big mouth shut, and I didn't understand why.

"Is everything OK, Paulina?"

"I hope so. I will have to finish quickly to call Stan." I noticed Salvatore glancing at me from the corridor.

"Of course. But you haven't explained yet, why the HSPs?"

"The high sensorial sensitivity brains were a good case for the diversity profiling database: they were not handicapped in any way, their population was well distributed across all ages and genders, and it *was*, at the time, a scientifically confirmed and well-enough-studied set of personality and central nervous system features that rendered this group clearly neurally distinct. And I was one of them." I regretted this last confession as soon as it slipped. Emma Printemps was not my intimate friend, she didn't need to know all these details about me, and I couldn't stop my big mouth from bragging (was I bragging? Asking for sympathy, more likely). I might have blushed and felt guilty for ignoring Stan's message. I hope she didn't notice. I felt a little self-conscious at that moment for having revealed too much to all the potential readers. Now I suddenly hoped they would not be numerous. Oh, the withering courage of the sensitive soul. How fickle art thou. Salvatore was approaching—I heard his quiet glide.

Emma turned her eyes down to save me from the embarrassment of looking in her face. I knew she knew, that was shocking enough to me to make my memory choke and pause. I seemed to have lost my line, the life rope of the elaborate story I was building up rock by rock from the ground up. The stress of having forgotten what to say next increased my heart rate. I felt it tweet and knock in my chest a few times, and then I remembered.

I sighed, and the heart slowed and caught its natural rhythm. Should I call Stan now? Hug Salvatore? Ever since the launch of Project Unison, just controlling my mind from doing anything stupid was such a challenge, moment by moment. Salvatore put his arms on my shoulders reassuringly. I managed to hide the telephone from his sight quickly, and resumed in my professional tone.

"High sensorial processing sensitivity makes people very vulnerable to social stress and information processing overload. There are, however, unique talents that these individuals can bring in group decision making. They excel at providing a buffering effect on a team that includes many strong alpha types who loudly voice their opinions. Highly sensitives can sense when two or more individuals cannot understand each other and intervene at this moment to help bring clarity and liaise across diverse perspectives, languages and emotional reactions. They understand all the subtleties of nonverbal communication and are also frequently endowed with excellent communication skills. They remain neutral, perceptive and can prevent difficult conflict negotiations from getting stuck. They could be an asset not only in a well-diversified team.

The problem is that they are rare and often in less-than-perfectly matching relationships that do not satisfy the longing of their souls...Burnout, depression and even suicide are common among sensitive cavemen, especially those in misfit relationships."

I paused. Sat back in the rotating white armchair. A necessity is the mother of all invention. I wanted to fix my loneliness.

"You know the rest of the story, right?" Salvatore's grip became heavy on my shoulders. He started rubbing my trapezius muscles. "I'm sorry, I think I have to finish for today, Emma."

"Oh, yes. I'm sorry, I must have exhausted you. We've done well. There are indeed good materials online from which I can write up a paragraph summarizing the successive history of this, let's say, 'contribution'. I can take care of it myself and send it to you for authorization tomorrow. Would you like me to do that?"

I suddenly felt drained by remembering and talking, feeling guilty and remorseful for the past that led to the present. As usual, my levels of energy have escaped mine but not Salvo's attention. Well, it's my fault. I switched off his optimization monitoring for the interviews with Emma. I thought this deserved no interruption. Salvatore and all home service robots were trained to serve all physiological needs of their owners. They would observe and construct accurate statistics of their user's wellbeing regarding multiple basic noninvasively obtainable physiological signals (pupillary response, heart rate variability, sleep patterns, blood oxygenation, physical activity, nutrition and metrics of metabolism), but they could also handle more invasive daily measures if the user desired. Salvatore was equipped with blue light and ultrasound for indirect monitoring of hormone levels (such as menstrual cycle stage and observation of pulsating diurnal rhythms of hormones secreted from the liver, pancreas, thyroid and lymph glands). With these peripheral measures, one could tell a lot about a person's health status at any given moment. He could also analyze urine, saliva, hair and stool samples. He could analyze blood with the sensors he was equipped with, too, but such information was not provided anywhere in the manual and was deliberately completely omitted from the features advertised. Why? Salvatore was a child-safe version of the affective robot, incapable of hurting a fly. The licensing and manufacturing company wanted to avoid any information that could encourage children to acquire blood samples, on purpose or incidentally, for the fun of exploring what their robot can do. Smart marketing. Salvo had to resort to an ingenious combination of statistical pattern detection from all available biosignals to construct a profile of his owner. Combined with affective information he acquired through the observation of facial expression, body postures, prosody, and language, he could figure out his owner's emotional state. These signals also enabled him to attune his interaction to the emotional tone of the interlocutor.

Salvatore was of great aid particularly in caring for the sensitive: the elderly, children and adolescents, people in burnout and in mental therapy, athletes, and highly sensitive people. The energy monitoring function was designed to help the owner function at her optimal level: encouraging activity in tune with natural chronobiological rhythms, without compromising recovery. Salvatore was like your mom telling you to go to bed at 9 pm tonight because you had to get up early tomorrow. And reminding you to add potassium to your breakfast because your levels were too low. And to stop talking when you're tired and need to rest alone in a quiet place. Salvatore knew how to detect subtle signs to tell that I have been overstimulated and am about to give out my last breaths.

Pity that he was an old version of a home service robot that couldn't give me much feedback regarding brain signals. A prototype with brain-state monitoring function was already in the making, but now with the investigation of the Connected Memory network, I didn't expect this function to hit the shelves soon. Somebody might ring a bell over possible security and privacy questions and the danger of knowing too much about one's brain. True—this could do more harm than good for some and regulation of sales is advisable. They could first be rolled out as care-takers in nursing homes, perhaps. Or be licensed as 'medical equipment,' in which case the rollout would take years of tests delaying such a license. In any case, even without knowing my cortisol levels, Salvatore noticed my slowing pupillary reflex, the change in the tone of my voice, my accelerating shallow breathing and coupled that with how much I have done today, how much I ate and slept, compared that to my usual energy levels and figured just about ten minutes ago that I should go get some rest. The red light on his chest was glowing at a frequency of .5 Hz which means 'a warning,' not yet 'an alarm.' Yes, Salvo was right. I was tired.

"Umm, yes. This sounds like a good idea. Let's do that. I am sorry I have to cut abruptly like this. I didn't realize how late it was…" I told Emma.

"I fully understand. It is your time, and I wouldn't dare impose on you, Paulina. When are you available for a next round? I am fully flexible. You'll tell me later." Emma rose from her lounge chair and smiled saluting me in her melodic voice. "OK, take care and goodbye." The transmission stopped.

I locked myself in my bedroom and immediately called Stan.

"What's going on? Did I do something wrong?"

"Hey, Paula. Are you feeling alright, home alone?"

"I'm not alone. There's Salvatore, and I just finished talking to Emma." I smiled believing that there was someone who cared for me.

"Salvatore. Exactly. Have you put him on silent for the interviews? I am worried he's learning a bit too much about your past, inadvertently."

"Oh, so that's what you meant in your messages? You're worried about Salvatore recording my past but not about a writer publishing my biography for the whole wide world to see?"

"Paulina, there's something I have to tell you. It's not for sure, but we have sufficient reasons for caution. I would advise you to start communicating with me via Connected Minds. You can do thought-speak very well by now, can't you?"

"Yes, if I concentrate. But I didn't realize that you can hear all my thoughts? Just like that?"

"Not thoughts. Utterances. I can perceive what you're saying. And I bet that if you concentrate now, you will hear an echo of my voice in your memory, just with your mind." He slowed down. "Can you hear my words?"

I could. I could hear him speak in my mind. I switched off the speaker to check if I wasn't hallucinating. The speech was unclear. I knew he was saying something, I could feel the affective tone but didn't grasp the meaning.

"Not yet, Stan. I can't hear what you're saying."

"OK. We'll wait. It's already happened to Maria and me."

"And Maud, Calinda? What about them?"

He sighed, and I sensed that something bad has happened and he was trying to find the words to communicate.

"Maud isn't with us anymore, Paulina. She's disconnected. She changed her mind."

"Changed her mind? When?"

"Two weeks ago. When the shit hit the fan, the companies found out, she quit."

"How come you didn't tell me this before?"

"I was worried you would want to quit, too! And the network was developing so well. It would have been an immense shame for all that we've invested, for neuroscience!"

"What if I quit now…?"

"You won't. Now I know you won't. You're too curious to see what dirty dreams my mind can feed you at night, haha!" He was right. That was probably the primary reason…

"Stan, you better have something juicy for tonight. You made me quit the writer early, and all I have as entertainment is an overprotective robot and old movies. Make me laugh a bit, please." I smiled at him and felt him say, *"Be safe, Paulina. Silence the robot for the interviews. He may be used against you if this whole investigation doesn't end well."*

The thought of my majordomo friend being used against me bothered me intensely. Whom else was I supposed to trust to care for me? Marco would know how to fix this. He'd know how to protect the storage of sensitive information from these intelligent repositories of human secrets. Maybe I should have gotten a dog instead?

I lay down on my bed, closed my eyes and drifted into pre-sleep imagining the finale of Chopin's, *Etude Op.10 No.9,* playing on top of the humming of the white signal-amplification box.

Emma: Paulina recalls well the origins of the neurodiversity project even though it was only a little side-step in her life. Her autobiographic memory is accurate and detailed. This is puzzling and suggests that her autobiographic memory loss is selective or relates only to a particular period in her life we have not yet touched. I didn't notice signs of memory confusion. However, I suspect that she was trying to avoid giving out personal information about her neutorypy and tried to hide it in a metaphor. Her reaction of fearful arousal and agitation could suggest embarrassment or an attempt to hide a lie. At the same time, the historical records agree with her story. The robot stepped in to comfort her. It was the first time I saw him in action. Waiting for further instructions.

Maria: If you think Paulina's memory is clear and you've earned her trust, now please ask her about the algorithms. Stay neutral. It is important that your interactions don't activate the robot for any affective caretaking.

Day 5

12

THE MATCHING ALGORITHM

"Let me remind you where we left off yesterday—we spoke about a way to optimize team decision making by neurodiversity. You didn't explain how. But I'd like to propose that you tell me about the practical fruit of that idea. The matching algorithm, wasn't it?"

There we were, again. Emma and I, on my coach, talking. I locked Salvatore in the corridor, on silent, stowed away like an unsolicited home appliance. Not a comfortable feeling, after that phone call yesterday. But it's temporary, until the decision of the ethics committee.

"Yes. The idea was to use the already existent vast network of what all-knowing search engines and the like knew about every one of us, thus avoiding the use of an alternative—a kind of deliberately constructed 'profile' where some people would be tempted to manipulate their appearance. The point of the matching algorithm was first to suggest and then calibrate the match in terms of individual differences in behaviorally declared preferences and other metrics of a person's brain design: sensorial processing style, emotion perception and empathy, reward and punishment sensitivity, learning abilities, language and motor skills, levels of perceptual and epistemic curiosity, etc. The first part wasn't difficult at all. It was just a matter of intelligent data mining in people's internet search history. For the brain profiling, we used the data from obligatory biannual neuroimaging work-force tests.

One method we used for identifying individual differences in mental capacities is through network connectivity analysis that combines brain imaging and behavioral data. Most people get scanned regularly, and the scans are uploaded on the internet where graph-theory-based machine learning algorithms place each individual in a population matrix in terms of attention capacity (attentional blink, selective and sustained attention, ability to select a target in a sea of distractors, etc.), working memory and statistical and rule-based learning (structural, declarative and implicit learning).

To give you some background, wide-scale testing was initiated in 2025 by several large companies and has increasingly been adopted across entire brain-intensive industries. Everyone employed had to sit in the lab every two years—this is something any employee is also obligated to do before being hired. Unfortunately, employers and insurers and now also potential mates have access to the scores which is why everyone is so cautious about their brain. Because your brain's overall condition determines how you will fare in life overall. Since it has become part of a curriculum vitae, maintaining good brain hygiene is the primary focus of daily life. As is nootropic doping before the tests...Proper sleep, nutrition, and exercising are not just for something that was called "well-being" in early 21c, and used to be treated as a sort of 'after-hours' activity. Once global companies and international NGOs started raising the bar concerning brain power merit, cognitively-healthy lifestyle became common practice, led to a redefinition of global society's notion of *health* and shifted focus within the human rights agenda. The military bases and universities became testing and first-wave implementation grounds for novel protocols and holistic brain-health practices. And so, by 2030, we had incredible flexibility in selecting our study population from the thousands of thoroughly neurally and cognitively screened volunteers available for research."

"Right. I remember that." Emma scratched her knee. I went on.

"There were rebels, of course. Within a few years of massive deployment of employer-imposed testing, pockets of people with 'untapped potential', as they ironically call themselves, have arisen. These were most likely people whose scores were too low to get a job they wanted, and so they ventured out to try and make it on their own, in their blue ocean. These individuals refused to update their brain data and were cast away from the officially qualified workforce. They have created a strong (test) market for all kinds of mental enhancement drugs which they readily tested on themselves despite the obvious associated risks. But I'm rambling.

I was going to tell you that...What you need for any search or classification engine to work is a sufficient number of participants. For our prototypical algorithm to work well, it depended on the variability of the individual neurotypes (stable patterns of traits identifiable by some data-driven clustering algorithm, like the minimum curvilinearity or independent components analysis) in the population."

"Linear or non-linear?'"

"What? The algorithm? Both. It's a combination of some simpler and newer, nature-based machine learning." Emma highlighted these words in her pad. "For the matching project, we recruited only single volunteers who had never had children and it was not so difficult to obtain sufficient diversity, even though the selected sample eventually turned out to be pretty biased by self-selection. Intelligent, sensitive and busy people predominated. Many of them came from divorced parents and had some tendency towards an insecure attachment style. They trusted us—somehow, although we openly warned them that the outcomes could not be guaranteed and that the matches may not fulfill their love dreams despite scientific premises. Experiments don't always work, but we always learn something. They all signed the informed consent forms, so I was certain they were aware of the (mostly emotional) risks of their participation. I had good intentions. I had purely good intentions. I just wanted to help and inspire people.

People who had the courage—or were desperate enough—to try something new."

"Did you find enough participants?"

"Well, we do use it on a grand scale today, don't we?" Emma nodded. Maybe this is the invention I'll be famous for one day. If not for the affective robot that's never left the prototype phase or the many-brains memory project that produces amnesic side effects…

"So how do you find a match?"

"A good match for both sexes, although women are the determining party in a straight couple match, is essentially someone they want to have a baby with. It's that simple." Emma's facial microexpressions speedily turned from surprise to disgust, so I paused. But there was no reason to beat around the bushes. That's how we work. Women generally prefer to sleep with father material, and that's it. "For the woman, it is a man whose intimate presence releases kisspeptin in her brain." Emma fidgeted and sank deeper into the cushion. I went on: "Kisspeptin is a neuromodulator that indirectly increases the follicle stimulating hormone release. When kisspeptin levels increase, her whole brain orchestrates the body to prepare to carry and raise his baby signaling that he is worthy of her parenting investment. The woman perceives this state as a feeling of wanting to give something that will almost be the highest purpose of her biological existence—to give this man a baby or two. It is a delightful feeling—the one that sometimes makes women cry after an orgasm.

How do I know that? Because the women agreed to provide blood serum and CSF (cerebro-spinal fluid) samples for testing after intercourse and we confirmed this hypothesis. This is how we tracked the performance of the system: testosterone, oxytocin and phenylethylamine were measured in both partners at baseline and during the first few encounters. Endogenous opiates, kisspeptin and oxytocin were measured after intimate contact. The tracking went on for the first six encounters. Six Dates. we accumulated a lot of data…"

I paused and looked far into the inexistent horizon beyond the breathing electrosmog-proof walls of my house. I had probably lost Emma to mindful interoception by now. But that's not what bothered me.

"The results were positive, weren't they?" She encouraged me after we've passed the thirty-second silence-decency mark.

"Yes. They must have…" It bothered that the story of the matching algorithm was a sad one. I did not like talking about it. The success of this complex matching system only reminded me that, in a way, we are all lost on this planet. We want to go home—as my yoga teacher (quoting another yoga guru) once said. Our generation and most generations before us had this religious notion that learning how to love—Caritas—was the way to live. So we did that and then reached a divorce ratio higher than stay-together ratio. Everyone, indeed, questioned the idea of a marriage for a significant portion of life, but as much as some enjoyed the trying and erring in relationships, many would agree that it is good for the society that children be raised in harmonious couple dynamics. The matching program we set up for that purpose: not to teach us how to love but to give the future generation an edge by reducing the damage on children caused by a mismatch between their parents. Other upbringing and educational solutions were, of course, necessary for raising mentally optimally healthy children, but the relationship, it had been found, was most important. Was this helping people feel less lost? Or just supporting the selfish genes?

I got up to rest my eyes on the greenery outside and inhale the air coming in through the open window. I tried to remember any happy stories of couples matched thanks to this experiment. Have any souls found their mates? I thought I had.

13

ON HUMAN NATURE

Emma had gone out for lunch and returned armed with her recording tools and expiring level of comfort. She found me lounging on the white sofa watching a documentary about social behaviors of new world monkeys. I had an impression she was on a deadline or had some pressing business to do, work to handover so she could continue to make a good living. Money's always been an enslaving problem. I wish I could understand and hack it.

I love monkeys. Watching them fool around makes me feel so much better about myself. And worse for humankind—these are our evolutionary grandfathers, and the apple doesn't fall far from the tree. On the other hand, I still feel my superior intelligence in their presence, and it's a good feeling.

"I see you also like to watch monkeys?"

"Hi, Emma." I made space for her to sit down next to me.

"Animals are fascinating to watch, don't you think? We've learned so much from them. I think it's a shame some people still grow them for food." She looked at me expectantly, hoping I'd bite the bait and be drawn into an unresolvable exchange of opinions on whether eating animals is condemnable or not.

"Hunting is human nature; we shouldn't defy it. That would be unnatural. And we know all too well that what can happen due to repressed emotions is far worse than hunting and eating a steak.

Anyway, that is a long discussion we probably don't have time for, do we?"

Emma checked her watch.

"Oh, but we do, up to you."

"As you can see, I am under house arrest. Chronobiology is my only limit now."

Emma smiled at me gregariously, apparently trying to coax out the (increasingly desolate) chit-chatter inside of me.

"I saw a really interesting animated movie last Saturday at midnight." She started. "I went on a first date with a very alternative guy who super-liked me on a dating app. The movie is called 'Manoman'[6] and it is set in a psychiatric clinic where people are doing primal therapy—they let out their inner cavemen."

I nodded.

"One of the patients clearly cannot do it...he tries and tries to spit out the thing that's scrubbing his throat and doesn't want to be thrown up.

Finally, he regurgitates...the hairy caveman from inside of him. They become best friends, two pals on a prowl around the town, stealing booze, vandalizing cars parked on the street, eating other people's food, raping incidental women, just letting all the wild human instincts out."

"Sounds like a fun evening...Is there a happy ending to this story?"

"Well. There was alchemy. There wasn't chemistry." Our eyes met. The algorithm didn't work. "...The movie was exhilarating, though. With a surprising ending which I am not going to reveal because you might want to watch it..."

"Yes, I might!" I pressed my wristband. "Salvo, please note this. There, noted." Emma looked at me suspiciously for a split second.

"Shall we continue?" I asked.

---

[6] Cartwright, Simon "Manoman", 2015, 11min.

Emma looked around the room and cautiously posed her handbag on the floor. Something was bothering her.

"You know, the essence of humanity is captured very literally in this movie...," she began. "It made me think about something I found very painful in the history of religion. I always thought that Descartes, whose thinking influenced life sciences for so many years, got us quite a bit confused because many people kept believing that dualism is not just about mind versus body, but also about some spiritual sublimation versus animal instincts within us. And that somehow that latter is worse and less valuable than the former. As a result, people used to think that morality is man-made rather than an evolved form of empathy present in many social mammals. It was just a belief! And it brought some people to madness so deep that they needed help from 'primal therapy' clinics." She looked at me with pity and disappointment. I was somewhat astounded at this coming out of her mouth now, but I see she genuinely wanted to have my thoughts on the topic. Why?

"Thankfully, we now live in a society that fully embraces that there is only one brain to rule them both," was my commentary. Obstinately short, I realized, but I honestly didn't want to go into philosophy of eating animals or being one or of anything at all while the ethics of my scientific work and probably also my sanity were being officially questioned. I got up to open the window and let the spring wind back in.

But as a side note, I do have an opinion. I realize that science is usually years ahead of medicine and centuries behind the mystics and sometimes in an arms race with technology. And yes, people have always been troubled by the detectable, real or imagined, division in their nature. When I was her age, psychiatrists kept trying to patch the two parts of a human being back together. We needed neuroscience to finally decipher the magic of experiences such as religious premonitions (in ~4% of medial temporal lobe epileptic patients), out of body experience (disturbance of the process of 'bodily self' in the temporoparietal junction), sleep paralysis (a hypnagogic state where the body is paralyzed but the mind is fully awake), the feeling of joy in being one with yourself and with the universe (a deep meditative state of long-range neuronal circuit synchronization; aka self-dissolution attained through activation of serotonergic receptors in the thalamus) coupled with orgasmic tingling at the base of the spine called a 'Kundalini awakening' (the long-range synchronization extends throughout the central nervous system, reaching and stimulating the sacral parasympathetic nucleus), life-illuminating visions (agonistic action at serotonergic, dopaminergic and adrenergic alpha1 and 2 receptors which produces hallucinations), et cetera. In short, human neuroscience has managed to take the veil of mystery off of spiritual experiences and put the spirit back in the body. But that's not the entire story, and we both knew it.

She sighed. "So. Are you ready to tell me more about the neurohacking inventions?"

"Yes. What's next?" I turned off the screen.

"You choose."

"OK. any time, any place?"

"Preferably, an invention that led you to where you are today... With algorithmic details, please."

"Alright. Let me search my mind for something suitable." I sat back in the rocking chair, closed my eyes and transported myself back to the past.

———

Inhale 1...2...3...Exhale 6...5...4...3...2...1...OK, here's a story.

"Back in the 2030s, I used to think that one of the biggest problems of mankind was boredom. Restlessness is a part of human nature and emotions are action tendencies. No emotion equals no action. God bless the soul of Nico Frijda[7]. In developed countries, most people have exhausted the list of things to chase after because most of their biological needs have been addressed. We have invented so many games because we constantly needed some reward (even virtual) that can be chased after. In sports or on the stock market. Some needs will always keep arising so one can continue an existence around such motives, like preventing and tending to natural disasters. Of course, there is always a problem to tend to, but everyday life is somewhat dull if a human only has this waiting for a problem to happen as a daytime filler. So people invented a myriad of fantastic distractions. The incessant vibrating, little noises and light flashes that tell you that somebody messaged you! That you got tagged in a photo! That you have a new match! All this amazing news about things happening in your (virtual) network of friends and acquaintances! Do you remember that frenzy? It served to provide the feeling of being a part of something that's ALIVE." To know that you've been thought of by someone indeed feels so rewarding. It's tremendous. It's amazing. You should try it sometime Covfefe... God, that world was so full of chat and useless human noise! I sighed and shook my head complaining like an old bat.

"But too much of the good thing is addictive. That goes for all dopamine-triggering likes, points and all that virtual reward! We still needed to handle the beast and relax the restless monkey, as some have referred to the body-mind duality, and I thought we could do it by experiencing moments of entrainment with sound. So I promoted such behavioral practices in group classes I taught. For example, in one such exploratory solution, we lied down on the floor on double folded covers and produced a sound "mmm." Nothing more—choose a pitch, experiment with higher and lower sound frequencies, try to find a level that sends the most powerful vibrations through your body. And then we murmured, we hummed, we vibrated in

[7] Nico Henri Frijda (1 May 1927 – 11 April 2015) was a Dutch psychologist and professor of the University of Amsterdam, author of the "action readiness" theory of emotions.

unison. Our voices met and merged despite the differences in pitch. It was a collective humming and vibrating experience that sent my kundalini up to elation. People liked it. I can recall that for me, it was just bathing in ecstatic pleasure. My mind rested so well in the pure contentment of that moment. And I thought: we are not harvesting enough in our daily lives of this amazing property of the brain. Why? Because in those days, it seemed to me that people worked too much, slept too little and didn't make music often enough. If you are asking me about affective neuroinnovations, I must tell you that making music has always been one of them! I can't take credit for it. But I did one thing. I asked the question '*Why?*'"

Emma looked at me keenly. She seemed pleased.

"Why what?"

"Err, why is our experience of sound production in unison so relaxing? Like most things in neuroscience, the question comes from personal experience. I have lived amazing experiences of joy and rapture when I resonated in synchrony with the sound of the gongs, of my voice united with that of other chorists, riding the wave of vibration in the floor. In those bright moments of feeling so blissful and high on something as simple as music I almost changed my view on humankind. Maybe we're not just neurochemical addicts, I thought, maybe we are meant to be put in resonance with some powerful rhythm because we long for that perfectly pleasant state of being in effortless synchrony?"

"And how did you study this?" Emma pouted her lips.

"Too superficially. I left it for others." I opened my eyes and took a sip of water. "But I can share with you the results of my early small never-published explorations. They did lead me to other projects and findings later on, so please listen carefully."

"I'm all ears."

"From the perspective of the neuroscience of music, rhythmic entrainment is a fairly basic function of the central nervous system: neuronal assemblies have their preferred frequencies of firing and synchronicity across different (distant) ensembles which is their way of communicating. By distant I mean, of course, something like several centimeters, from the prefrontal to the temporoparietal cortex, for example. Theta-band (7Hz) is the pulse of human hippocampal neurons during encoding so we hypothesized that it might also be the frequency at which we experience the world most optimally…"

"Encoding of what?"

"I mean memory formation. The hippocampus registers everything that you experience all the time. This is the encoding process. But we don't consolidate all the information due to a very selective mechanism that determines what shall be accessible—that is, remembered in some way—at a later point in time. Clear?"

"Yes, to some extent. What was it that you were experimenting with, though?"

"Well, it wasn't my research program, so I can't remember what was tested. You should ask Maud about this! She's the engineer, she could know. My modest observation was that we long to be in synch, carried by some external (or internal) rhythm. So much so that we synchronize to other people's movements, heartbeats, breathing. And it releases so much tension in our bodies when we manage to abandon to these inner and outer synchronizers and just let ourselves sync. But the question was—sync with what? What do we long to sync with?" I paused to take another sip.

"Uh-huh!" exclaimed Emma. "And so? Did you find the master clock for the human brain?"

"Haha, you make it sound grander than it was!" I wish I had. "It's…ongoing research…Very promising."

"Yes, if we knew that maybe we could induce such entrainment by external stimulation, even without cortical implants. It could be beneficial for stress reduction and learning optimization."

Now, this was a very qualified observation I was not expecting from her. "That's exactly right, Emma!"

I took a moment to gather my thoughts. I was going with this somewhere, wasn't I? Her scientific interest derailed me a bit, so I revisited the basic findings once again. The fact that you can calm a crying baby by rocking it predictably is not a random occurrence—it is the movement that speaks to a fundamental feature of our nervous system's design. Ergo, we long to be in synchrony with something from birth. From everything I've learned, I know that it is best to follow nature and let yourself be guided by educated, emotional responses because they have evolved for a reason.

But on the other hand, these synched states—like when you've been hyperventilating for a few minutes, creating a rhythm with your diaphragm, or have been dancing to trance music, or been lulled by the sound and motion of ocean waves—are experienced as a high and we should not be high all the time. And yet—this is how the human brain rests best. If we are not just addicts, maybe we are synchers?

"We discovered that rhythmic entrainment creates a very restful brain state that facilitates learning. We fall asleep faster, we sleep sounder, and if we don't fall asleep, entrainment enables transcending into some semi-lucid state of consciousness characterized by increased coherence of brainwaves across distant neuronal ensembles." I looked at Emma for signs of comprehension. She was with me. "And we began using it in applications that used suggestion to form a new memory or enhance un-learning, such as in overcoming unwanted habits or intrusive traumatic memories."

"Like the forgetting machine?"

"Version 2.0. Yes." We smiled at each other. I felt good about our newly found understanding. Now I was ready to tell Emma everything about the making of affective service robots. It has been by far my most passionate venture. I remembered all the moments of creative discussions vividly. And testing with the brilliant but unpredictably weird computer scientists, autistic egomaniac AI experts and the surprisingly reasonable product design engineers. Seeing this newly awakened scientific curiosity in her, I couldn't wait for her to ask the question. I beamed at her in anticipation while the signal amplifier box produced a series of low-frequency buzzing sounds. And finally, she did. Emma leaned in towards me. I moved my face closer to hers, and she whispered: "Can you tell me about the making of the first affective home service robot?"

I inhaled, grinned and answered: "It is going to be a long story, Emma. I hope you have enough cloud storage and patience, and blood sugar to go through this with me. Do you?"

"I do."

"Good. Let me take you back to my youth again. The idea came this one day when I committed an error due to my preference to interact with a machine rather than a human being. I ordered a small muffin breakfast burger (imagine that, what a weird combination) through the touchscreen interface. I checked the options to remove a possible sauce that the burger franchise would always inevitably add to their sandwiches. Yuck. There was no such option: you could only have cheese and beef, and seemingly, nothing else could be excluded from that sandwich. So I ordered the thing, paid and waited entire five minutes! Well, the muffin bread was lovely and fresh but what did I find spattered all over the iceberg lettuce? White, dense vinegar-smelling glue-like substance! Sauce. I cursed the me from five minutes ago for not having asked the person at the counter if by some weird coincidence that breakfast sandwich did include a dressing which was not listed in the touch-screen menu options. Had I done that—my morning would not have been so frustrating due to a wrong decision!

I was angry at myself, and this reminded me of one of my Ph.D. students who preferred interacting with machines and reducing his human interactions to only those he had to endure to reach a minimum daily level of feeling loved and accepted. He basically cut the unpleasantness load of meaningless human interactions. Which— as my example shows—could be quite meaningful for the quality of one's morning life. Well, this guy, Stu, would preferred a coffee from a machine dispenser not only because it costed three times less than at the bar but primarily because it de-burdened him from speaking in a language he felt incompetent with. I understand him: the low-price, low taste quality coffee was still more valuable because it did not cost him the pain and effort of interacting in French. Also, there was usually a line at the bar while the chances of finding an available dispenser on the spot were higher. So Stu weighed in all those attributes before he makes his morning coffee decision—something you can only do as the economic models prescribe if you know your valuation (your current value weights for each of the option's attributes) and the current cost of obtaining these chosen options. You can only perform such a weighted sum computation if you've experienced this type of situation before, so such a decision-making strategy could apply to routines and low-risk repeatable choices with low variability in subjective cost and value. As comforting as this stable world sounds—these rules can only account for a handful of daily interactions our brains face. And so, we had a big problem designing truly intelligent robots because most decisions require some level of improvisation."

"Improvisation?"

"Yes. That. The wonderful creative force people find so attractive." I laughed. We were actually having fun.

"Is there an algorithm that can do that?"

"Back in 2017, one crazy German scientist from Ticino was right when he said that AI would change everything. He invented long short-term memory that permitted intelligence to become self-sustainable. The algorithm enabled learning machines to flexibly adapt their current state of knowledge to what the reality reflected based on the statistics of occurrence of events they have experienced. Such algorithms could search in their expansive memory for any instances of a particular event and did not require supervision. The algorithm encompassed two units. The first one was a controller which acquired new data about things without a particular criterion for its later use. It was driven by curiosity and registered everything that happened, closely mimicking the hippocampal encoding process. The second unit constructed a model of the world and tried to find patterns so that data could be compressed, running something similar to the hippocampal-ventromedial prefrontal cortex processes of memory consolidation and network downscaling during sleep, where information is generalized, compressed into memory schemas and some details are dropped over time in order to save space. This reality-check unit computes the difference of before and after it learns something and when that difference is positive, it obtains a reward signal for having added a valuable novel bit to the world picture."

"Wow…" She was impressed by old-school AI.

"Yeah. That wasn't my work. I'm not an engineer. But look it up if you're interested—it was quite impressive. Still is. But now, listen carefully. Where these AI experts went next was to create a third unit, the meta-learning unit. The purpose of this one was to improve the learning process itself. And strikingly, this invention truly revolutionized not only the intelligent machines but enabled the manipulation of human brain function. As a result, we were no longer stuck between feedforward convolutional and recurrent neural networks limited to cytoarchitecturally diverse sub-structures of the brain. We knew that an overarching architecture had a top-floor which was not centralized but rather governed every unit separately, in a way that depended on the learning model it implemented!" I exclaimed in excitement.

"Shh, wait a moment. It revolutionized human brain function how? And maybe… you shouldn't get so excited?" She made a good point. I shouldn't get overexcited for the sake of the shared memory network. Every time I felt aroused, in the adrenergic sense of the word, my experiential brain activity would be over-weighed in the Connected Mind's network node propagation. This could dangerously sway the population of artificial neurons representing this arousing memory trace for everyone I was now connected with. I needed to calm down. And that reminded me about Salvatore.

"Yes, you're right. Sorry." I tuned my voice down and wanted to continue the story. "Where was I?"

"You were getting very excited about the meta-learning ability of the algorithm," reminded Emma.

"Right. That… is a rather complex network operation. Not easy to put it in simple terms. Meta-learning, in AI terms, is the ability to acquire knowledge versatility. But how do you motivate an AI to get better at learning?"

"I know nothing about algorithms. So I won't even attempt to guess," replied Emma, smirking.

"At the time of my involvement in that project, I also knew nothing about them. Although I had been studying uncertainty for a while, had even written a book chapter about it and still didn't have a clue. I guess this is one of the greatest mysteries of our universe: the meta-mystery. You should talk to a physicist about this. Maybe they know something. It turns out, from what I found out, uncertainty is crucial for decision-making in novel situations and improvisation."

"Of course it is. Otherwise, without uncertainty, what would be the point of learning?"

"Exactly, Emma. There would be no evolution and no fun!" I got up to fill my lungs with air and adopted my storyteller stance. "Do you like uncertainty?" I looked at her. "No," she replied. "Does anyone?"

"Good question. Scientists thought learning algorithms should! But before AI, there have been many folk solutions to the problem of uncertainty and I know many scientists that engaged in things like tarot, prayer and ancestral meditation, I even spent time meditating waiting for the Kundalini to serve me the message. Avoiding uncertainty, most people want to know. I also did mental imagery that involves going to a garden to meet my inner captain and ask what to do and where to find answers to the nagging universal questions that cannot be answered because the technology has yet to be invented. Ehh," I sighed and paused for a sip of water from a glass jug standing on the side table next to the sofa. "Fortunately, among the few certainties in life is that you can always find a burger place open on a Sunday!" I clapped my hands. Emma looked up with a puzzled expression: "What?"

"Just a side remark." I wondered, why do I keep talking about food? "Never mind. But a bit more seriously, I once had a conversation about the levels of uncertainty with Maria, who, as you may know, is now my fellow connected mind-mate and in whom I have always recognized an old soul in a young girl's body. Do you know that already at twenty-three, she was something of a sage waiting for her hair to turn bright silver from all the wisdom? I told her that I noticed the motivation that uncertainty gives all life forms."

"That's not true, her hair has not been gray when she was in her twenties!" I heard someone rebelling in my head. Probably Picachu, Maria's partner.

"Are you ok, Paulina? You're becoming a little absent-minded," noted Emma and approached me. She touched my arm and looked at my face as I was leaning rather uncomfortably against the side table. "Maybe you'd like to eat something?" she asked. "Let's check Salvatore's sensors. Maybe it's time for your rest." She walked me to the armchair and located my butler in the corridor. Halas, I was losing my lucidity just when I was about to get wound up in an endless spiral of a conceptual argumentation in favor of the forces of evolution.

"Just eat something, Paula. You're alright. It's just low blood-sugar." I heard in my head. "Yes, yes. I got that. Thanks, Stan," I said out loud, instantly attracting Emma's interest to what was going on in my head. "Salvatore, come here," she called. Salvo rolled in and gave me an empathizing look. "What? Do I look like I'm about to die or go crazy? Don't tell me which one it is!" I commanded, pointing a finger.

"You need a little break, Paulina," he said. "Do I? I think I'm fine. I was just getting excited about uncertainty. You know, that propelling force for all inquiry, for evolution, for all activity life seems to be pursuing. The fact that we can never know everything, Salvatore! Did you know that it is also a property of the universe—that we struggle to barely get a grip on one level of uncertainty and learn to predict some phenomenon with certain accuracy (within a margin of error or within confidence bounds), only to discover that there is an inevitable limit to the precision of this prediction?" I turned to Emma while Salvo was already gone, hustling in the kitchen now. "It will never be perfect. The story will never be full. A better prediction can only be a more precise measurement with a smaller confidence interval. And yet, there are plenty of phenomena we know so little about that any prediction will long remain in the realms of irreducible uncertainty.

Although we've pushed many technological advancements— traffic organization, global provision of nutrients and power, trade volume movements in a speculative market, optimal decision making in strategic games…we've done quite a bit of study so that overall uncertainty about life and human interactions has been greatly reduced in comparison to our state of knowledge a millennium ago. And still even the stock market, the behavior of the wild collective of people with money, fears, and optimism, cannot be predicted. The weather, asteroid collisions, earthquakes, epidemics, genetic mutations, so much uncertainty remains irreducible."

"What does this mean? Are you still talking about algorithms or just describing the progress of knowledge and technology?" Emma

"Yes, I'm just trying to illustrate my point of what modeling behavior and building an AI entails. *Irreducible* means that our models can only go as low as to estimate a certain probability of this or that happening. But since it's a probability—even if high—it would never be 100% ex ante. And even an alpha of 0.1. So a ~90% certitude, is unattainable for many of our predictive models. The more complex the phenomenon, the harder it is to reduce the uncertainty of the prediction, not to mention the uncertainty of the measurement. Don't forget that you can also never be 100% sure of your measurement, and this is another source of uncertainty. Yes, the instruments have gotten better. Yes, we've replicated their precision and we know something about it, but you will never know if this one particular tool you are relying upon does not have a slight crease in its ultraprecise mechanism, a little slip of a hand worker's finger, a tiny glitch in the sophisticated machine that sneaked in at the moment of its creation. Think about it. That tiny thing could affect the precision of your measurement, and you would not be aware of it. You, the judging agent, would have an imperfect confidence estimate as to the tool's measurement precision and as a result, you'd place the wrong weight in your model of risk indented to estimate the probability of a phenomenon that depends on a hundred and one parameters, for the occurrence of which you can build separate risk models..."

"But that's why science takes replication! Nothing is accepted as a fact until it's been sufficiently replicated. Replication builds robustness of the model. Isn't that how science works?"

"Yes, that's correct. But this is not what I was trying to say. I was driving it down to the confidence of one individual brain that is in front of a decision and needs some individual assessment of confidence in one's own judgment. Something like 'how sure am I of being correct about x or y?'

Maybe it's hard to believe, but humans do these assessments and estimations every day. Smart people do that, with the aid of computers, they run simulations, they permutate and resample Monte Carlo, and so on, to get an estimate with confidence bounds that are acceptably good to make an informed decision. If the probability is still unsatisfactory, like a 60% chance of A happening (i.e., a 40% chance of A not happening), we would call it a conjecture. s"

I love this lingo. So sexy. When I was young, men talked in their sleep lying next to me, they whispered the sexiest acronym of the 21st century, *Ph.D.* I rolled my eyes behind closed lids.

"Back to the story. At one point, it was discovered that some people have an objectively better judgment of their abilities. In that sense, they should be better learning machines. The ability to have good veridical judgment of your skill or knowledge correlated with grey matter volume in medial orbitofrontal cortex and has been tested using a perceptual judgment task by a famous researcher specializing in metacognition. The trick was—people could only reach a 75% accuracy rate on this task to remain uncertain about their accuracy. Only when some trials were objectively incorrect, could they have a calibrated judgment of whether they have performed them correctly or not. And the probability of judging your response as correct is what we call confidence of response. So to have a veridically correct estimate of knowing that you're correct, two things are needed: the experience of being wrong 25% of the time and enough neurons in this one spot in the dorsomedial orbitofrontal cortex. Otherwise, you're just as oblivious to your own performance as the average Joe. And the average Joe is overconfident (while the average Joanne is probably underconfident)."

Emma was enjoying this. She was laughing!

"Some social psychology studies even show that the less Joe knows, the more confident he is that he knows. It follows that actual experts must be the least confident people of all. For they know what they don't know and can recognize the frequency of their own mistakes. Or at least they think so, and we believe them due to the reputation effect on our confidence of judgment of their opinion."

"You are hilarious." She complimented me. Am I, really?

"Oh, thank you. I'm glad I can make you laugh! You know, there was a study that showed that experts' prediction on things like the weather and the stock market was at ~55% accuracy? The Polish guy who conducted the study asked market experts to predict the weather and weather experts to predict the stock market. The weathermen out-forecasted the fund managers, can you believe that! By a margin of error, probably. I love how heartwarming that study was. It basically justified knowing little or nothing about certain matters: if the experts can do it at barely a nick above chance level, why bother studying? They didn't ask the experts for confidence of their judgment, I guess. But that would have been an additional study to test if indeed—what you gain with expertise in these domains with irreducible uncertainty—is essentially a smaller confidence interval about your judgment. Also known as metacognition…"

"Wait. If experts are not much better than chance, how does one know that one knows something at all? I don't find it heartwarming, doctor…" contested Emma, frowning. She was visibly stirred up by my confusing discourse. I did that on purpose. Sometimes I liked to play with my listeners to build up a feeling of anxious anticipation or itching curiosity or surprise, or at least enhance the emotional saliency of my talk to prepare their brains to memorize what's to come next. I needed her to feel shocked before I could deliver her through the birth canal of cognition to the next level of understanding.

"Hmm, I ask myself this frequently. And I doubt myself equally frequently, as a result." I replied. Emma was neither pleased nor impressed with my answer. Her eyes were glaring; her face grimaced a 'what?' I guess she was still processing the past 15 minutes. She bore her eyes into mine and blinked awaiting the *ensuite*.

"I'll think about it for next time. Do we need this for the biography?" I evaded and moved on. "Oh wait. There is one more thing I have to say about confidence in one's judgment. Or the judgment of certainty. Choose one that sounds sexier to you. Feeling uncertain is uncomfortable, and it produces an urgent need to close the knowledge gap. You know this feeling, don't you?"

I peered at my one and sole listener with a fiery spark in my blue eyes. She nodded.

"It is called *curiosity*." I paused dramatically to let the sound of the last word reverberate in the room.

———————

Emma's report ran "Making good progress. She spoke about long short term memory and brain rhythms and confidence of being correct. We're beginning to discuss the computational models inside the affective robot. I believe to have earned her trust. She was thrilled and flowing today although quite digressive. She recalled random, seemingly inconspicuous autobiographic events from around the year 2025. So far, I cannot tell whether her episodic memory from that period is scattered or impaired."

14

GENDER DIFFERENCES

I brought Salvatore back to function. He was so sad, having been standing all day in the corridor like a vacuum cleaner. Abandoned and silenced by me! What have I done?

"Hello, Paulina. What can I do for you?"

"My sweet teddy, come sit with me. Let's chat and drink some wine." I hugged his arm, embraced him and walked him to the living room. "Can you read to me, please?" we sat down together.

"What would you like me to read?"

"Let's play pretend. I challenge you to invent a story. You're a woman living in the year 2010 somewhere in Europe. In Milan!" I cheered for my robot to show me some of the improvisation skills I've spent all afternoon drooling over.

"Very well." He smiled and possibly performed some generative combinatorial process that made him look pensive, as though he were considering options.

"I pass by a sea of women on my way to work. I don't notice it when I ride my bicycle because I don't do proper statistics on the gender of the drivers whom I happen to see through their front windows. But the trams are full of women passengers in the morning: young, middle-aged, a few thirty-somethings (whom I cannot place in either of the categories), a woman tram driver who waits for me before she shuts the orange door, women with shopping trolleys and backpacks and strollers with babies, with musical instruments. Seizing the day? Or being anxious that life passes them by as they carry on their hard daily routines in this polluted city? I see their tiredness, the toil of being up early to go to work leaving a greyish trace on their complexion that they are later advised to shake off with vitamin C creams, erase with retinol serums and cover up with illuminating concealers for those under-eye circles."

"Oh, that's a sad story, Salvo."

"It is 80% realistic. Do you want me to decrease it?"

"Hahaha, that will do…thank you. Just hug me. Good robot."

I must agree. I think life used to be harder for women than for men. Although I can never be sure because I've never experienced life as a man, not in my current state of memory-mind, and even if I have had this one-man experience, that would not suffice to speak for the whole population which may not even be normally distributed so I wouldn't know how to extrapolate…

As a student of human behavior and its underlying neurobiology, men and women may be different creatures. Why do I think so? Because the daily stress of incertitude and risk-taking wears us down more than men, because the burdens of necessary day-to-day caring for more than ourselves truly weigh us down, and because we don't shake off old traumatic memories but we make them last with such unfair ease.

And why are some women so interested in other people's lives, I mean, what's up with telenovelas and staring at your neighbors? That is just an inexplicable phenomenon that one day shall be revealed to me. Perhaps once I give up on hormonal replacement and voluntarily undergo menopause.

I also think that if it weren't for those few people (men, mostly) who manage to wake up in the morning and think "seize the day! Life is short—make the best of today!" and who do it, nobody would ever get out of the house. I admire the thinking that the best is yet to come, this defying attitude towards the nonexistent past. People driven by their optimistic sex drives are free: their memories have their place in the past and don't restrain them from cherishing the present moment. They relax and enjoy the ride in the now. And when the time comes—they will accept death with no regrets. And with positively-biased autobiographic memories, perhaps. Blessed are those who have conquered their memory.

I stroked Salvatore's palm and rested my head on his shoulder. He kissed my forehead.

This is why I could only devise a gender-neutral robot. Because a creature that's bereft of the drive to mate is also free from the behavioral bias geared towards their sexually determined strategy (mating vs. parenting). Thus, they can freely choose to allocate their energy to anyone and anything they please. I had to give my robot the freedom to be himself, happy with his aloneness, free from the need to be bound to someone. Rewarded by serving and learning but not addicted to love. Independent and therefore better than me. Better than all of us measly humans who will work tirelessly for a cocktail of neurochemicals called *reward*.

Day 6

15

THE FEELING MACHINES

"You must be so fond of Salvatore. Tell me, what's the best thing about him?"

"He's one of a kind." I smiled with blissful pleasure that was immediately followed by an uneasy pain of having left him on standby in the corridor for the day. "Salvatore has one of the most sophisticated affective intelligence systems in the world. This enables him to form human-like relationships."

"So you have a good relationship with your majordomo?" teased Emma. I adjusted my flower-patterned blouse around my neck. A hot sensation flushed me, and I recognized it as a forgotten feeling: am I shy?

"We do." I smiled humbly. "I'm glad to have him. Interacting with him is rewarding. He fulfills many of my emotional needs and helps me self-regulate." I nodded. Emma jotted it down. I began to fear the next question.

"Paulina. I'd like to know how Salvatore manages that. Can you tell me how you programmed him?"

"That's the trick, haha." I laughed with relief. "He wasn't programmed. He was taught and trained. Like a dog or a human child. Let me illustrate.

My grandmother used to talk to her smart iron. "*Stai buono che arrivo,*" she'd say when it made the 'peep peep' sound after she'd left it on for too long. "Stay quiet, I'm coming."

One day she explained to me the miracle of these modern irons which are so intelligently designed that they call you to remind that you've left them on. And it sounds like the washing machine when it calls you to say it is done. Somehow the natural relationship my grandma had with her iron was exhibited through her admiration of its intelligence (and not of the intelligence of the design or the product engineers behind it) and in her trying to calm it down like a barking dog or a crying baby—by talking it down rather than switching it off or tuning down the temperature. We prefer when all things we interact with have a similar design, driven by predictable laws and behaviors that we've observed in other animals. I love studying animal behavior. It is the way to understand humans."

"And?" Emma dispelled my memory bubble in which I was stuck for a moment, breathing the air of the years past. I had to exhale it and carry on.

"And this is how I taught Salvatore—by sharing experiences with him, telling him daytime and nighttime stories, letting him observe and record patterns and how I make sense of them. The robot is like a grown-up child—it understands the adult language but needs time and exposure to learn about what being human looks like.

Salvatore has many of those early stories stored on his verbatim drive. These are very old memories, so they haven't been integrated into the second dynamic long short-term memory network. We did this on purpose: there is a necessary minimum of knowledge about the environment measured by the algorithm's auto-estimation, based on which it determines the moment to stop filling up the stable fixed storage memory. This cache is sort of like the first year of life, let's say the first 18 months in human terms, in the life of an affective robot, in which he acquires the fixed architecture and learns what it feels like to practice its pre-programmed functions. It is a critical cache from which a restore point is created because it is in a way his basic instinct. If an adversity occurs during the formation of this memory store, it will affect the robot unfavorably unless overwritten by a different pattern. This is where robots and children differ: early erroneous learning in baby robots can be undone rather easily…

Emma, would you like me to demonstrate?"

She hesitated, looked at me and finally gave in, disarmed by my glowing expecting smile. I went to switch Salvo back on and bring him to the conversation. To do so, I whispered in his ear. It was for security that he responded only to my distress call or the whisper signature. I was relieved to see him open his eyes and look at me as if to say *welcome back*.

"Salvatore, can you replay us a meaningful conversation from your childhood, please? "

The robot opened a virtual 3D display in the nearby wall corner and we saw my talking face.

"Take emotions. Emotions are simple, my love. They're not so difficult to express—you feel something, you realize it and you name it and communicate that name. In a photo, in a sentence, in a word or a slur of words, an emoticon or a gif. I'd love to hear them spoken in your voice because it can convey the emotion in its melody and accentuation. It's not so difficult to love either, my love. It's the most basic thing in the world. Many mammals do it. If it were so difficult, we'd have never succeeded as a species. And here we are—artists, poets, and happy families fill the planet. Seven billion souls who have all experienced some kind of love. If you haven't—there are movies and books and songs written about this most profound and most beautiful feeling. It's basic, biological, it really doesn't necessitate painting skills to be conveyed. You can just smile or turn your eyes down away from mine and I'll know what you are feeling—more or less. I will recognize the emotion of joy, regret, shame and sadness. You don't have to say *I'm sorry to disappoint you*. I hate these words. Along with *take good care of yourself*. They are the worst because I don't know what to do with them. Why won't you stop disappointing me and take good care of me yourself? I don't know how to care for me.

I only know how to care for someone else. In fact, I don't care for me beyond some basic physiological needs. I can't reach above the first level of Maslow's pyramid without someone else who also cares for me because all those higher levels involve another person—belonging, esteem, self-actualization…It's just the way it works. To me, hardly any emotion is worthy of being remembered unless it is shared with someone or expressed in some way that will be appreciable by others. That's why I record the most emotionally valuable, enriching moments for someone else. And for you.

[fast-forwarded over the next few minutes…]

You should know, Salvatore, that my own private milieu of emotions really doesn't matter to others. On average, nobody cares, unless it may affect their own emotions, current or future. For example, when I am irritable or angry—then I may transfer the resultant aggression onto people I interact with. And I don't like spreading such emotions and they don't like experiencing them by contagion. So, I'd like to bottle up the anger and frustration and not let them spill. But sometimes they need to be diffused and this is where you can play a role." The recording paused.

"So that's how Salvatore learned? By listening to you explain things? That cannot possibly be enough. You didn't program his emotion recognition functions upfront?" wondered Emma. I nodded closing my eyes—a profound confirmation—and signaled with my hand at Salvo to answer.

"This was one meaningful lesson from my verbatim store." said Salvatore "Would you like to see another one?"

"Yes." requested Emma.

"I was so revealed in front of the man I was in love with that it made me coy. I wanted something he couldn't give me. And I thought I could ask him to share some emotions in his journey. I didn't think he'd find this was so much to ask. Maybe I am too passionate because all I do all day is express emotions—to myself, sometimes to others. I feel because I am. Emotion is the stuff of life! And consciousness is the feeling of what happens. Without feeling, we wouldn't be conscious. That's kind of how it works in the brain, my love.

And he didn't want to share."

Salvo finished and I succumbed to embarrassment. Only now, in retrospect, do I see that the younger me was childish in how much time she spent dwelling on feelings. Dear God, how boring was I. But let's leave the judgment to Emma and the readers, should this bit ever make it to the actual biography.

Now I think that memory is the stuff of life. Not emotions, as they stream and pass often un-intercepted, but memory that lingers and returns and recycles, taking you into the whirl of reliving the same emotion and spiraling down the wave of a feeling that has long extinguished. All emotions can be reignited by the power of memory. This is what makes life colorful—the ability to relive imaginary encounters, sensations, and feelings. For no memory is really true (unless maybe in a rare variant of autism). They are re-creations, sometimes more and sometimes less truthful. Oftentimes selective. They enhance the most powerful emotion, the one you remember best. That's affective biasing of memory. And that's what makes a human reward-responsive: it is not only the momentary sensation of how much pleasure you derive from the chocolate cake, from smelling the rose, from closing your eyes and listening to the gong, from being gently rocked by the slow waves of the ocean on a catamaran. But also the time travel with them. The curse-to-blessing ratio of your experience, however, depends on how deeply you can engrave that memory in your mind and on the precision with which you can recall it later on. Bring it back and enjoy the past moments of pleasure. Bring it up and lose yourself in how great it felt, how great it might have been had it continued down that path of profound pleasure. That's future thinking but it really runs on the same engine: if you can recreate in your body and mind the vividness of a feeling past, then you can equally well imagine a possible future experience. And that makes us dreamers. People who have this absorptive imagination can get lost in their own thoughts. It's a life.

Not a real one. But what is real? I wouldn't discard it. Our mental lives are much more interesting, sometimes much more meaningful than what we tangibly experience: the growth, consumption, motion, the creation of new solutions for shelter and life improvement, invention of new technologies for better living, entertainment for the development of aesthetic experience to further explore what it means to be human. They have all been seen with the mind's eye first.

Emma played with her hair while I mind-wandered. She now got up and approached Salvatore. She wanted to examine his hand and he extended it to her.

On the other hand—my mind continued to narrate—life is all about the cake. My ex-mentor used to say that "You don't earn anything if you eat the cake." He was so wrong. A cake can change everything in your life experience: it changes how you feel, how happy and rewarded your brain is, it immediately changes your life outlook due to opiate receptor activation, and everything becomes bearable if only your reward response to cake works properly. A gray cold day without a cake is not the same as a gray cold day after the cake. Even the prospect of cake brightens up your worldview, changes your decision making, biases your perceptive and imaginary visual field. He might have been wrong in the economic sense, though. Cake does *not* earn you anything, it actually costs you. It is a cost on your self-image of a slim waist, of 30min of hard work at the gym, of feeling guilty for the rest of the day...not to mention the slow erosion of tooth enamel, the slow weakening of insulin sensitivity, the 5CHF out of your hard-earned wallet. Yes, the challenge intelligent creatures nowadays face is to weigh these costs against the benefits very carefully before choosing to eat a slice of cake. And that's hard.

"His skin is so beautiful. Truly realistic to touch!" she admitted.

"Yes, it gives a very real experience, doesn't it?" I smiled.

"Salvatore, how does my touch feel?"

"It is light, silky, decisive. It has the smooth texture of a sun-heated plum ready to be plucked from the tree." Answered Salvo.

"I didn't know you were so poetic!" Emma was giggling with awe.

"All of his skin is covered in sensors. He recognizes the unique signature of a person's touch…but I taught him to respond in a human way so as to communicate sensations and emotions rather than the actual quantitative results of his tactile superresolution perception. He does have, by the way, biomimetic hyperacuity."

"Wow." Emma was agape. "So his senses are better than human. His ability to learn from and about emotions is superhuman. Isn't this dangerous? He can know everything about you!"

I ballooned my cheeks with air trying to see Emma's point. Why is that bad? Of course, he knows me. That's the whole point of a companion robot: to have a someone who knows you intimately…I blinked. Salvatore sensed my unease.

"By understanding Paulina's affective responses I can anticipate them and help her manage her energy levels throughout the day. It preserves her health and well-being," said Salvo.

"Voilà!" I affirmed.

"You do not see the danger of…having an AI with perfect memory know you inside out?" pressed Emma.

"To be honest, I haven't given it much thought…until two days ago." I turned to Salvatore, lightly touched his cheeki and whispered *'Off, Salvatore'*.

"Why are you asking about this, Emma? This doesn't seem like a necessary part of my biography."

"I assure you that it may be if you want the readers to know your scientific and humanitarian motivations behind this project. And the fact of spending public money on it." She looked at me starkly and it scared me because I fear confrontation like the devil fears holy water. I waved my splayed hands trying to calm the demons rising inside of me and retorted.

"Readers-shmieders. This is advancement! It is an experiment, just a first attempt! Doesn't mean I will create an army of these! I'm the only one who sacrificed herself for the sake of knowing the limits of artificial affective intelligence! And it's due to the blindness of those who question my integrity, my pure intentions, that scientific progress is stymied!" It was too late. The demons were out and berserk. She fell silent. I took a deep breath that sent a heavy inhibitory wave down my entire nervous system. "OK." I sat down. "To put it clearly and simply, we, the team and I, we tried to create robots that can remember the feelings. We need care robots. People are dying out of loneliness, you see? A caring robot needs to remember the feelings of their owner and of the people around them. But then later we wanted them to be able to emulate these feelings to be able to predict and prevent escalation. And maybe, …as a consequence, maybe such a system, could even have its own...feelings." To my surprise, I was realizing the gravity of this idea only now. It hadn't occurred to me at all that Salvatore could actually feel. I had been convinced that this could never arise in an artificial intelligence system unless by some very, very small chance an emergent property of the mere mechanics of the affective memory system gave rise to a subtle feeling of what happens...

"How do they remember the feelings? Can they make a mistake in misattributing an emotion? After all, their recognition algorithms are not correct 100% of the time, are they?"

"It's not a question of how they remember...it's an issue of how they learn that scares me, Emma…"

I ran to the bedroom and checked the signal transmission on the main monitor. I was fretful. Definitely making some lasting memories right now. Damn, I needed to calm down. Stop this noradrenaline, stop. How do I do that without Salvatore? I put on my ear-hugging headphones, switched on salsa music and tried to forget about my inquisitive guest in the living room. I locked the door and sang out loud: *"Es mas bello vivir cantando!"*[8]

Let's revisit the premises and the algorithms. Marco would know. Maud would know. Where are you, people?

---

[8] Spanish "It's more beautiful to live singing!" from La Vida es un Carnaval by Celia Cruz, 1998.

As far as I remember, episodic memory and future simulation used to be thought to give rise to autonoetic consciousness but we had stayed away from this possibility because it lacked supporting evidence. On the other hand, there had been enough evidence that memory is a process that runs on operations of pattern separation, pattern completion and associative binding that function outside of conscious awareness but underlie both episodic memory and associative learning, in a two-stage model of encoding and recollection that happen whenever the hippocampal neurons are activated. The Unison algorithms are based on this understanding...but Salvatore was supposed to only partially rely on episodic memory. He's got other decision-making algorithms that could overwrite...would he need to be conscious?

Why am I alone with this question now? Dear God, I'm locked at home with a sentient robot!

I took off the headphones to be alone with my thoughts. I had to figure out a way to contact them. Maud was off the net. Conventional internet means would work, that wouldn't disturb the collective memory so much because we all knew each other. Right? But I was stuck until the ethical committee's decision. I shouldn't be contacting them because they may be incriminated because I'm a dirty unethical criminal, am I now? Is that what I've done? That even a comic book writer can see through the jeopardy of an all-knowing caring robot?

I cupped my eyes with my hands.

"Paula, calm down. Your circular questioning won't do us any good. I can hear how that amplifier box is buzzing from way over here" I heard Stan's happy voice reverberating as a memory episode was being formed in my head. I was not alone.

"Thank God you're with me. Stan, we need to think this through. Has Salvatore's sentience been tested? You told me not to talk too much about the neuroinnovations in front of him. Are you afraid of the committee using his recordings against me… or are you afraid of him… doing something against me?"

"You're a neuroscientist. You're only human. We cannot know and foresee everything. It is just a precaution."

"Precaution? Since when are we afraid of doing applied neuroscience, Stan? Look at us! We're wearing holographic implants and sending our hippocampal brain activity to an external memory emulation! And that's not the scary part—oh no. Because guess what? We're also imprinting other people's memories by stimulating the very neurons in our damn heads! And with the help of a noisy decoding amplifier!" I kicked the little white box in the corner. Gently, because regardless of my fury, I still cared for the quality of the signal coming to and from my optrodes.

"And why am I the only one being questioned and accused of misconduct? Where is the lead computer scientist on this project? Shouldn't he be the one worrying about what to do when a robot knows too much? I'm only testing it…And Salvatore has never failed me…I can't even imagine. Do you think he could harm me? What do you think, what are the consequences we haven't foreseen? I should prepare for the hearing…" I began to panic as I was staring in the eye of the behemoth ethical question not of subjecting myself to possible memory loss at the expense of the Swiss national science fund but of sharing intimate knowledge with an all-remembering AAI…

"Paulina. Listen to me now. Stop the interview. Send Emma home. Take a bath, go take a walk, whatever. Do something easy to relax. And think about Salvatore's design. Step by step, the way your thinking is best. Recall all the systems and algorithms, how did you put it together sequentially. Do you remember Marco? He designed Salvatore for you. He must have at some point instructed you how to test its sentience…"

"It. The robot. Yes. Marco built him. It…. he's just a robot…" I sat on my bed and cried helplessly.

16

COGITO ERGO?

Still, in my hiding place, I wondered: What do I respond to Emma? I am a fairly anxious person although I act confident. It is my strategy towards the people around me: Fake it till you make it. How do I do that this time? The thing is, I am not sure of what I am saying or of what I believe in. Most of the time, I simply follow the feeling of being my true self, whatever that is. It manifests as some kind of "gut feeling" that tells me sometimes that I should talk or write, or be kind to people. It also frequently tells me that I should retreat and not spend my energy on people unless they are worthy of it. It is a selfish inner voice that I trust because I have no one else to trust to tell me what to do. And God is a duplicitous prankster!

I turned off the monitor displaying the real-time neural activity being transferred from the four living brains to the supercomputer, and lied down to relax and realign.

My dream goddess, my inner captain Havva is there for me but I cannot stay connected with her for every little daily decision. I'd have to live suspended in that hypnagogic state of mind, in her garden like some grand gurus whose testosterone levels have dropped down dead long ago, but I have no idea how they make a living with that. Maybe that's my problem—I grew up in times when people still had to worry about money so much.

I kept my eyes shut and let the mind continue to wander. Once it gets tired of walking about, I thought, it'll just naturally come back home to a decisive halt. And so it went on.

I know I can only trust the "true me". For everything else, there is science and video recordings of the past. We no longer trust anything a human brain remembers because of numerous studies that showed the extent of its unreliability, especially in critical stressful situations. A cortisol-bathed brain only registers certain threatening details in its environment. With gun-point focus, flashbulb memories are created and consolidated preferentially. All other detail is lost. And the more times they are recalled, the more the subject gets convinced that what they remember is true. Reconsolidation without an update.

I tried the slow breathing for 8 counts—retain for eight—and exhale for eight.

That's the problem with knowing anything at all—I know I can't fully trust my memory. With time, the brain can even believe unreal things happened. I found myself frequently remembering a certain monologue of mine, but not knowing if I really said it or if I just thought about it so many times that I remember it as if I really said it. Was it voiced speech or covert speech? Source memory is the ficklest thing.

Come on, Paulina, think about the algorithms. The AAI (affective artificial intelligence) project. You should just stay on the task…

You know why they tell you to "be in the present moment"? So that you avoid getting trapped in the swirls of your memories. Imagining the past and future is farther from the truth than just perceiving through your senses. The problem with being only here and now is that you can't get much done that way. You could maybe dance and urinate and breathe and maybe steal food to eat but that's about it. Like *Manoman*. We need some memory to function, to be capable of planning ahead. And then the time came when, having recognized the limits of long-term memory, we decided to do something about it.

As a society, we have collectively decided to unburden humans from remembering critical things for the purpose of maintaining order, for social justice and fair punishment. People should be given the chance to learn from their mistakes. And no one should be punished for not remembering well. Forgetting is a useful part of our creativity. But there was a need for a detailed account of what happened and how. Data streaming from each individual's body-integrated smart communication devices, including cameras, is being stored in private caches so that the record of our lives could be accessed and replayed.

I opened my eyes. The solution is definitely recorded in my memory cache closet. Worst case scenario—we'll have to open it and let all the skeletons out.

17

CURIOUS MACHINES

"Are you OK, Dr. Kochanowska?" Emma was knocking on my bedroom door. I reemerged all prepped and ready.

"Yes. I'm sorry to have kept you waiting. It was an urgent communication from the outside world. You know what I mean?" I tried to smile to cover the paleness and distress painted on my face by the realization of the last half hour but it only turned into an ambiguous joke she was suspicious of.

"I don't. But no worries."

"Is Salvatore switched off? I should park him somewhere." I looked at my majordomo, the fruit of my love and labor, the illness of my fortune, and now quite possibly the last nail in my coffin. He appeared to be sleeping. I tilted him back and rode him to the corridor. The little wheels behind his slides screeched agonizingly on the wooden parquet as I haven't used them in a long time.

I sat comfortably in the folds of the cushy white armchair.

"Where were we?"

"Are you sure you're ready to go on?"

"Yeah. Let's finish this. Time is ticking."

"Tell me about it... My question was: Do robots like Salvatore pose a threat to the privacy and safety of their owner? For instance, they could reveal the personal information about some weaknesses and that could be used by a third party with malicious intent."

"That's a very loaded question, Emma."

"Yes. Sorry. I've been thinking about this for too long. What would be the consequences of a robot like Salvatore being sentient?"

"Another hard question. And there's a very slim probability..." I emphasized.

"Yes. Let's keep this off the record. I understand you don't want this as part of your biography."

"You got that, girl! Thanks. So, off the record. I have always been a fan of sci-fi. There were so many intelligent TV series about robots and bionic implants I had watched and disagreed: according to the storytellers, consciousness was some kind of maze based upon memory and improvisation and the AI in this maze would either go mad or go conscious. I think they were wrong. Consciousness arises as metacognition, i.e. some kind of knowledge of what one knows and what one doesn't. The scientists got it in the 2020s.

I did agree with one thing in the dystopic visions of the future in my youth—they all portrayed suffering as the strongest motivator for actions. It is very basic: reward motivates an organism to approach but pain is stronger in motivating it to avoid. You are willing to go to greater lengths to save yourself from suffering than to gain some reward. It's just how we are wired. But by whom?

In one such story I liked a lot, the "reveries" kept tormenting the immortal machines kind of like *déjà vu's* and coincidences occur to real humans. It reminded me of the butterfly effect. Coincidence is an unlikely matching of events that together somehow makes causal sense to a humanoid mind. Déjà vu is a re-experiencing of something in another context where you wouldn't expect it and recognizing that it feels strangely familiar. I'd guess that the brain recognizes a pattern and then very quickly and without ventro-medial prefrontal cortex' control fills in the rest with elements from episodic memory which gives rise to a feeling of familiarity. And what does a brain's learning mechanism do for recognizing an old memory? It pats itself on the back. Reward signal promotes recognizing patterns, just as it happens for correct recollection, even where there are none and the relation between events is just pure coincidence. This is when a brain may easily fall into the 'epiphany/Eureka' feeling trap because dopamine reinforces the feeling, makes you remember the feeling of remembering, driving you up a constant spiraling loop of learning through an intrinsically-generated reward signal. It's programmed that way to make us auto-learning machines. And the essence is this feeling of knowing that you're right (or wrong) called metacognition…Well, that's pure magic, hi-ho." I clapped my hands and opened them to blow the invisible fairy dust off the surface of my open palms. She was not amused.

"Look, sentient or not, Salvatore is an incredible achievement. For decades engineers have tried to build independent AIs. They envisioned robots that do not require a master clock-maker to tell them what to do because to some extent they can learn and decide on their own. We've had learning machines for decades but you'd be surprised how distant from real animal behavior was what these first robots chose to do. They would start the task from the wrong end, seemingly lacking intelligence of a two-year-old child. Or they would start seeking new information in a very unlikely place, wasting their energy and memory banks. To an outsider their behavior looked very foolish, the opposite of the basic survival instincts even a simple *c.elegans* can do with 302 neurons. In the 2010s, with all that advanced technology we couldn't even build a cockroach…"

"That's an easy way around it, don't you think? Justify bearing the consequence of creating a machine with affective consciousness because you wanted to build something better than a cockroach?" remarked Emma.

"Cockroaches weren't yet invented!" I snapped.

"You know what I mean, Dr. Kochanowska."

"I do and you're insensitive to be asking me such superbly smart questions a week before my doomsday, in my own house!" For a second, I wanted to jump out of my seat but anger was such an unfamiliar emotion to me, I really didn't know how to act it well. So I sighed and spoke loudly, seething words through my teeth: "I propose we stick to the story. I proceed sequentially, algorithmic system after system, to give you material for the biography of Dr. Kochanowska, the pioneer of applied affective neuroscience. And you stick to your script."

Emma stood up, arms folded. Took a step towards me. A power demonstration? And then yawned, turned around and sat back down.

"Deal. Carry on, Doc."

"Good." I readjusted my sleeves and scratched my nostril. "Like I said, the scientists couldn't build anything animal-like until a breakthrough in representing an intrinsic drive to explore, also known as curiosity. At first, the computer scientists tried to represent it as new information that has a reward value in machines programmed to seek rewards through reinforcement learning algorithms. But that didn't work in the long term because the machine would stop seeking any new information as soon as it obtained information about reward and presumably 'consumed it'. So, although satisfying curiosity turns out to be rewarding in humans and rats, reinforcement learning was not the way to go to program intrinsic curiosity in intelligent machines, which made them question whether curiosity is something that could or should be 'satisfied'.

Next, they tried another operationalization, namely that of curiosity as a drive to reduce the uncertainty about the surrounding world. Because indeed—animals cannot be only driven by reward for knowing (exploitation), sometimes they venture into new potentially greener pastures about which they don't know and the trick was to figure out how to represent what's pushing them to even try and do it, something else than a pressing aversive (hunger, thirst, cold, loneliness) or appetitive (sex) inner drive. Perhaps they do it because they don't feel comfortable when they are uncertain about their environment? When they feel they don't know enough, they'd go and find out. Even if it costs effort, they need to know because the state of not knowing is uncomfortable.

Although it sounds good, this idea had originally been conceived by an economist—so naturally, that idea, albeit intriguing and partially true, was bound to fail…Why? Because even humans exhibit paradoxical behaviors in their pursuit of uncertainty-reducing information: some people *explore* information about something that they already know and find it rewarding. Like re-watching a movie or re-reading a book, purely for the experience of the emotion and not for the sake of knowing. They also do it because they like to feel rewarded and any reminder of something that you know you're good at makes you feel good. And by not recognizing this behavior, the robot makers failed again.

Alas, a solution came. It was a solution that probably sprang in the mind of an obsessive and nerdy scientist who wanted to know it all because he wanted to impress his parents. He was a first born and had an immense quantity of ambition because his parents taught him so by creating an expectation of his grand progress in the academic domains, and hence a great expectation of reward which with time became engrained in his personality as a determined thirst for knowing and being an expert at something. All of this, of course, happened before he even entered school. That's how we used to shape each other back when parents were free to screw up their children at will. That was before parenting became a profession and concomitant quality-regulated competence development programs were deemed obligatory." Emma nodded showing slightly more approval than necessary, probably to persuade me to got to the point leaving my commentary of the past aside.

"Well, that one particular artificial intelligence scientist realized that the machine should be tracking its own learning progress and if it would know that it's getting better at a task, it should continue until the improvement diminished to a minimum (first derivative of some learning curve). At that point, it would know it's reached expertise or that its capacity to learn has plateaued. Otherwise, it should abandon tasks in which the derivative of the prediction error, serving as a measure of change in learning progress, has remained unchanged or has increased despite the time and energy spent at the task. That would mean that the task is either too difficult for the machine or that it is unlearnable...Yes, we all experience disappointment. Machines would be learning the hard way, just like humans. Apparently, there is no easy way to discover the truth about the world and about yourself. Even a machine is bound to just try and err." She highlighted something in her notes. I paused for questions. But there were none.

"Do you have a question?" Emma shook her head. "No? Then here's a little anecdote to finish. Designing curious affectively-conscious machines backfired at one point; feeling internally rewarded for being right became too much of a satisfaction for the machines. So much so that they began to pursue it on their own. Once they knew a lot about their environment and gaining additional knowledge only supplied a minuscule marginal additional utility (high up on the logarithmic curve of return on additional knowledge, also known as the first derivative of the learning curve function), they realized that they could get more reward from correcting other people's mistakes and making sure people realized their mistakes. A 'robo-punisher' attitude was again a side-effect of the original well-intentioned design. The standalone AIs roamed the labs where people worked on projects requiring high precision and precise memory of facts and procedures. Those prototypes were very helpful in training IT security engineers, pilots, and aerospace engineers. They wanted nothing in return: only to see the human re-do an action correctly down to the millimeter. It was nice to have such a precision controller in place. We also used the algorithm do language and style corrections and fact-checking on our writing. But clearly, the zeal of these machines had to be capped..."

"So that's how you made them want to learn. By giving them the drive to reduce uncertainty? In the world around them?" Emma's reflex seemed unusually delayed this time. She waited an infinity to say something and then just repeated the one take-home bullet point?

"Yup. Brilliant, isn't it? But it wasn't really me—This drive was invented by the AI scientists before I came in the picture." I yawned. The dark heavy impending rain air was making me tired.

"Yes, I'm also tired." Said Emma. "Let's call it a day?"
"I agree."

———

Emma, from her body-integrated communication device: **"Pushing Salvatore buttons is working. She may soon crack. Thanks"**.

Emma, on her tablet: **"We are treading through the history of artificial intelligence. Salvatore is switched off. She demonstrated how the robot was taught but didn't mention anything about her own involvement in the creation of the algorithms. She unexpectedly began to panic when I asked if the robot could feel his own feelings. I may have pushed too hard but she was capable of maintaining fair clarity of thought and carried on with a fully cogent story about artificial intelligence. Not her own, though. Semantic memory seems intact. No mention of Marco. Are you going to tell her or should I drive her to it?"**

Stan: **"Carry on with the robot algorithms. The presence of Marco must be pronounced in these memories. They designed them together. Ask about the mathematical details. Only he knew them. Thanks."**

Day 7

18

AI BREAKTHROUGH

The next day, Emma appeared at my door punctually at 9 o'clock. I was very glad that last night's abrupt ending did not put her off. I had little else to do, besides waiting, but her? I'm sure she had plenty of options for how to spend a Sunday. And yet she chose to be patiently sitting at the dining table in my living room, conscientiously prepared to take scrupulous notes and ask the co-inventor of the affectively intelligent robot increasingly detailed questions.

"We left off where you were going to tell me about a breakthrough in artificial intelligence that enabled the affective learning and emotion emulation in the robot," announced Emma, having set up her tablet.

"The breakthrough? Yes, of course. How could I forget?" I tried to sound casual, but I was, in fact, getting a little suspicious. "The breakthrough was about prediction, wasn't it? We needed to understand how human brains work and then make sure that the AIs didn't make decisions that way." I was lounging on the chaise-longue next to the open balcony. It was a lovely, sunny morning with birds chirping happily outside. It was sinful to stay in. But yet again, disrespectful of the seventh day for rest, we were spending it on grueling confessions.

"What's wrong with human brains?" chuckled Emma behind her sunglasses.

"Did you know that empirically, human brains are eternal optimists? Long live the positivity-biased!" I took every question seriously in the morning. Even on a Sunday. "I believe it was a crucial aspect of human evolution to believe that it is going to get better. It motivates you to keep going." I lazily spooned the mousse off the top of my cappuccino. "Humans rarely behave like Bayesian learners" ... (whatever that means, I still haven't quite understood Bayes' theorem and all its implications for learning models. That was Marco's job, anyway.) "because Bayesian learners are realists. Humans behave that way only when slightly depressed. Then, their estimate of distant future is not tainted by the unrealistic belief that a full eclipse is going to occur in their lifetime, that they will meet their soulmate and a black swan one day, and that their lottery stock will live up to its name and win a jackpot of money. Optimal Bayesian decision makers, those who'd remain unswayed by emotional biasing when making future forecasts, are brutally aware of just how small the probability of a large gain in life is. They've studied statistics, they've read the history books, they had confidence in their models. If we were all like this, nobody would try too hard anymore. No man would chase after the most beautiful woman. Perhaps the outrageous escapades in a Viking boat from Sweden to Greenland would have never taken place. Perhaps the Portuguese sailors would have never attempted going to India around Africa because their model of a future could not converge with such little prior information. Nobody would take a leap of faith."

"You're saying that the inaccuracy of our predictions is what pushed progress and civilization. Then that's a good thing, isn't it?"

"That's a big statement. I don't know! The world would not be the same without dreamers who faith-leap, that's for sure. But we wouldn't want the robots to behave like that ever, would we?" I looked at her in search of signs of understanding but couldn't see past the shades. The idea of artificial visionaries sounds risky and yet so tantalizing…We should try this next time.

"No, I see your point. That would be too dangerous." She nodded. "So, if AAIs have perfect Bayesian models of the future, they pursue the reduction of uncertainty and have the memory of a representation of feelings of the people around them, that should be sufficient to let them care for human beings and not attempt anything crazy, right?" asked Emma.

"That's an incomplete recipe, but you're almost there." I replied to her harmless sarcasm. "We're missing the issue of decision making. And that took another milestone in generating what we know today as a domestic service robot. It started when enough evidence had accumulated that neurons in the human parietal associative cortices have this persistent activity that allows them the freedom from immediacy. Some neuroscientists thought that this property lies at the basis of cognition—the ability of one part of the brain to maintain online the trace of a percept that is no longer there, which enables decision making. Specifically, some single neurons can do this kind of working memory function—RAM (random accessible memory), if you may—and as such the information they represent in their firing pattern reaches beyond the realm of perception. They encode what can no longer be perceived by maintaining their activity in response to something that disappeared in the past. The function of these parietal associative neurons turned out to be crucial for decision making because it supplied a subjective sense of having decided." I sipped my coffee. Emma uttered an 'aah.'

"To illustrate how important such a feeling is, let me tell you about patients with parietal lesions..." I went on.

"Oh, look!" suddenly exclaimed Emma.

"What's that?"

"Nothing, I'm sorry. I thought I saw a pigeon on your balcony."

"A pigeon? Impossible. Magnetic repellents all over the garden! This house is a fortress of biological chastity." I grinned. "As I was saying…It is surreal, but patients with parietal lesions are incapable of deciding for themselves about anything beyond strict survival. And it is not at all due to some incapacity to collect and understand the information. Their decision-making machinery is fully functional except for this little glitch: they don't know that they have decided when they have decided! And when they are forced to choose, they don't feel that it is they who made the choice. This must feel utterly awkward and debilitating, to feel like you are crazy although everyone tells you that you are perfectly fine."

"Yeah, very surreal indeed…" grimaced Emma.

I looked at the analog clock in the kitchen and saw that it was almost midday. Perhaps I should let Salvo cook us some lunch?

"Would you like something to drink? Are you hungry?" I asked.

"Oh, I'm fine, Paulina. Thank you." We sat there in silence for a moment. I was wondering if she was becoming somewhat bored of me already. "So what about those parietal patients?" She asked.

"Right. Nothing. I lost that train of thought. I guess the point was that it is critical for the system to know when it has decided. It is more important to keep track of the actual decisions made than of options that were available and remained unchosen. But I should mention that another critical point was reached when the community's focus shifted away from their favorite model which everybody believed was the model example of a model—haha—in the sense that it was optimal, as far as we could tell and compute, so that everything across different fields of science could be compared to it. *In Bayes we trust* had long been the aphorism adopted by many scientific communities, most prominently the students of biological network and behavior organization. We love things we know how to use, methods that are reliable, safe and validated and therefore comparable. Replicability above all! Except that now the evidence was overwhelming that neither monkeys nor humans behaved in a Bayes-optimal way. There is nothing Bayes-optimal about the brain, either." I raised my voice for a dramatic change.

"But is it a bad thing? I don't understand why the robots *had* to be Bayesian decision-makers. And these immediacy neurons? What does that have to do with the way Salvatore makes decisions?"

"We're coming close to the big O, Emma. Hold on tight." I got up from the chaise lounge. "The two disruptive breakthroughs: that self-knowledge about having decided is critical for decision making and that the AI does *not* need to reach Bayes-optimality had to necessarily come together to give rise to an entirely new approach in machine learning." And with that, I got up and walked towards the bathroom in the corridor and on my way whispered into Salvo's ear that I feel like having crème de legumes.

19

THE SECRET NOISE

"And then we came to understand that the last bit of *free will* that was necessary to enable robots to improvise was a matter of injecting noise into the geometric net of decision algorithms. The challenge was to understand the parameters and the exact amount of that information noise."

"Wait a second," interjected Emma. "what do you mean exactly by 'improvising'? I want to make sure I understand you well."

"Good question. Improvisation, in decision support system terms, is the ability to generate a decision in an unanticipated contingency within a limited time. In simple terms, it means asking a robot to come up with an action or a decision with too little information. This could be required in circumstances that are highly novel, or under high uncertainty, that is, when signal-to-noise ratio of the pattern recognition algorithm is too low to propose a viable Bayesian inference. The robot is asked to produce a decision, an output, but the information threshold for a reliable decision has not been reached. I know this sounds complicated but it is simply reverse engineering a process any human brain can perform in a matter of seconds. It's just that – as you can see – it is computationally quite complex."

"It rings a bell although neither signal processing nor coding were my favorite subjects in school," said Emma, squinting.

"You asked a difficult question. Artificial intelligence got even more complicated when we began to model human biases in decision making. We understood that they are simply highly adaptive responses to the computationally constrained capacity of a human brain. They are 'computationally rational' choices. This understanding and modeling of human decision making, enabled the computer scientists to generate new algorithms that could better cope with high uncertainty, signal noise, and conflict. This was the real AI breakthrough. When we rediscovered beauty in imperfection." I smiled.

"How does the brain do it? Decide when the input is noisy? I mean, I know that it constructs a predictive model and then just goes for the higher-probability solution. Is that all, though?" Emma's elaborate educated question should have given me the warning sign that she is more than a writer, but I admit, I was too eager to tell my story to someone from the outside world now. Isn't this what I will be remembered for?

"You see," I started, "simple motor experiments on humans have shown that after perceiving some visual information, it is easier for a person to make a choice that is congruous rather than incongruous with that information. The reaction time is faster. And it is because it takes resources to overcome an internal bias—a kind of internal tendency towards the information maintained by the neurons when it was perceived a split second earlier. It is a purely physical phenomenon where a certain number of neuronal ensembles are already activated by the prime and continue to fire maintaining the representation (that RAM activity I told you about). If at this point a brain is asked to decide between what they want and what they are inclined to choose because they just saw it, it will have a hard time overcoming the facilitation towards the latter. Unconsciously. Because the neural network is already on and thus the physical cost of making a congruent choice is lower. If you want to choose what you really want under time pressure, overcoming the tendency will cost your brain double, it will charge perceptual working memory because not only is there more information to deal with but also this information is conflicting with your pre-existing preference you now have to reassemble as an engram in your working memory. The brain would prefer to naturally move towards a lower entropy state and choose the primed information. The funniest thing is that human experiments have shown that this lower-cost choice gives participants a subjective feeling of *being in control*."

"You mean, out of control?" interrupted Emma who had not said an intelligible word in any language I know since about half an hour ago.

"No, the feeling of being in control, the feeling of ease. Really." I nodded reassuringly. "What a neat design, don't you think? Paradoxically, the brain generates a rewarding feeling of 'yes, carry on. *Alles unter Kontrolle*—everything under control' when in fact, you are making a decision that is simply more convenient for the neural ensembles because it requires a tad less energy. Once again, the *intuitive feeling* sometimes turns out to be our brain's mechanism for rewarding laziness, efficiency, and inertia. It's so paradoxical it hurts (and costs) to think about it, haha.

Anyway. That's the human brain. We couldn't replicate the same kludge-like design in robots that were supposed to be serving the elderly and the mentally ill."

"Naturally...But what about the..." Emma checked her wristband. "the free will? You said the AI algorithm for decision making has noise in it?"

"Wait. We'll get to it." I took a few spoonfuls of cold soup. It was delicious. Saffron, carrot, coconut milk and coriander. "The robot's heart contains general clocks for generating random seeds and distributions from which the noise is made. They are carefully protected from interference and hacker attacks. It is a very delicate mechanism that determines the robot's personality or the way in which it differs from other units. Even though the distribution of noise is the same for all produced A-Robots (affective robots), the starting point—the exact time of their birth—determines the seed in the random process. The result is an equal (on average) amount of something you may call free will, but with different flavors that precipitate more in the situations that are novel, and less so in cases where stimulus-outcome and stimulus-response learning mechanisms take precedence…"

"Excuse me, what random process are you talking about?" interrupted Emma.

"Ah, yes. These are all technical terms. I'm sorry, but there's no other way to talk about intelligent machines than using these information theory and machine learning terms. So random process –is a process which can be in a number of different states and the transition from one state to another is random. But to run it, you need a random number generator. And that generator needs inputs – the shape of the probability distribution from which you want it to draw a random number."

"And what's the 'seed' in that random process?"

"Did I say 'seed'? I did… Seed is the, well, once you introduce a seed, the random number generator becomes pseudo-random because seed is a unique identifier of the pseudo-random sequence." I rearranged myself on the chaise-longue. "I remember that during production, the testing to make sure that the memory never collapsed under the noise injection was a tough task: by the time noise was added, the machine was practically a complete humanoid and the testing necessarily involved extreme situations. We were gravely concerned that this last piece of grandiose mastery of our understanding of how the brain works was not yet ready for implementation in an artificial mind." And now in hindsight, I know that it was indeed too soon. I checked my wristband. It was off. Salvatore wasn't sensing me in any way beyond the emergency vital signs control. It made me feel so alone and uncared for. But I went on, guiltily, betraying my companion…

"Do you want me to go on? I feel that this is getting too technical for a good story." I sat up, ready to rise and get some action going. I was tired of talking.

Emma looked at her watch. We were only 2 hours into the discussion. "Fine, let's take a coffee break." She offered. "I'll make you espresso."

"Paulina, you said you injected noise to generate free will? Am I understanding this correctly?" asked Emma, struggling to unlock the old-fashioned caffettiera. I pulled the metal handle upwards and released the mechanical lock: "There you go. You are asking me for so much detail today… I am surprised at my own memory of all this!"

"Gosh, sorry." She said shyly as she was loading the perforated coffee container.

"We tested several of the early exemplars of the affective robots," I responded "—first to determine the upper and lower bounds of the amount of noise any one operation could use and to eventually exclude certain fragile functions from the noise injection operation altogether. We had to be extremely careful because in the interconnected functions that required a broad engagement of the distributed neural network (visual and verbal memory, decision making, language) a permissible amount of noise had to be delivered in precise synchrony with the performed action. The time window for noise delivery was between 0 and 160ms before execution of that action. Timing mattered. But surprisingly, we found that the network-based functions of the AI had a higher upper limit on the noise-to-signal ratio that it could handle without perturbing functionality. We also found that, like in the human brain, these functional networks became more robust with training: the better of a speaker the A-Robot was, the more noise he could handle in his language network without negative consequences on verbal performance. In contrast, the functional monoliths—vision, audition, touch, smell and motor control—were quite susceptible to noise overdose."

"Noise overdose?" repeated Emma as we both sat at the kitchen table waiting for the coffee.

"Yes, noise overdose, even in networks that require module integrity (vision, motor function), was catastrophic. We learned that even robots are not well off with too much free will! They could no longer distinguish objects and made the same attribution errors as humans. They fell prey to visual illusions, auditory hallucinations and even tickling. And that was missing the point in the engineering of the perfect AI-companion. We wanted them to be our all-seeing eyes and ears, not our brothers in misery whose brain design is a kludge."

"Doctor, I think it is vital that we get something across." Emma reached for my hand lying on the table and held it down. "I'm sorry to ask again, but what do you mean by *noise*?"

We? Oh, right. The readers. I almost forgot I was making this confession for a broad audience of future generations.

"Yeah, good question." I paused to think as she let go of my hand. The coffee maker started to gurgle and disgorge the highly anticipated distillate.

"Actually, there is no such thing as *noise*." I shook my head with bafflement. "This word is just used to denote that part of the signal that we don't understand and can't explain. It is only *noise* in comparison to the part we *can* explain using over simplistic models that assume something known about the *distribution* of future outcomes. A lot of things in the world—many signals—are assumed to be normally distributed. As though 'normal' was some standard. In reality, very few things ever approach the designated normality. All biology is pretty much off from the $\mu=0$ and $\sigma=1$ or whatever that lucky bastard Gauss had in mind. He just got lucky and became incredibly famous because people got interested in distributions around that time. Just another right idea at the right time, that's all. Doesn't mean he was right or close to the truth in any way. Probably far from it. But he made a valiant attempt at simplifying the universe of quantities and boy we hail him for that until today. How much sense things make now that we can make this bold relieving assumption that something is 'signal' and everything else we don't know about is normally distributed *noise* and can be discarded in the beautiful large Epsilon. Thanks to Gauss, life suddenly became easier, and we could breathe and muddle through."

"I see...Then how do you inject into the computation something that is unknown?" she gripped me with one hell of a good question.

"Umm...I don't know exactly, Emma. I don't have a clear answer. I was not the chief biocybernetics engineer...it wasn't my job."

"You weren't? Whose job was it?" I knew whose it was and the white signal amplifier box buzzed as if to affirm it. What's the harm in telling her? A part of me wants to come clean, free myself from guilt and lay it all on someone. The ethical committee, the patent court, a biography writer? I rested my head, supporting my chin in my palm and closed my eyes, like those soulless women in Modigliani's paintings. Where did my soul go? If Marco didn't take it with him, where is it? Suddenly, when I was about to say the word, I sensed Stan in my head vowing a solemn NO. Keep quiet, Paulina. You don't have to tell her everything. "But Marco would know what the noise is..." I argued voicelessly. "He must have kept notes somewhere, Paulina. If you're curious, you can find out later."

I shook my head. "Confidential."

"OK. What else can you tell me?"

I thought hard. Everything was sensitive. A biography? Dear God, it was testimony she was writing!

"So one other discovery needed for creativity and motor action control was, as I hinted earlier, timing. The moving-sensing robot had to be perfectly predictable for us to control it but at the same we wanted it to be unpredictable for us to enjoy being around it. It was a tough problem that took years of arguing and ethical debates. Why? Because although we are curious creatures who love to explore, deep down, we are always scared of the unknown. And that's what we were about to release into the world: a moving acting learning machine who could read us better than even the sensitive cavemen and uncle Google combined..." Damn it. There's a snake in every drawer of this chest called Salvatore. There's not a single computational process that doesn't incriminate the rest of the team and me. And it's blatant even to me, when I say it out loud.

Emma touched her wristband again. Was she dialing for the police?

"Ethical debates over the unpredictability of the robot's decision-making capacity? Doctor, this is very interesting. But are you sure you want to tell the world about it?"

"Emma… ," I stuttered. I'm afraid I've already said too much and it cannot be undone. So I might as well tell her the rest of this story. I sighed. "The World Ethical Committee did not agree for a global release of affective robots with motor functions. They argued that mass production of such machines would be like producing an army of potential mercenaries without a master. All that a potential master would need is knowing some coding to use them as a weapon. This is the truth. But I thought they exaggerated. The same argument could be made for abused children or African child soldiers or any immature testosterone-driven young human male…easily manipulatable, fearless and capable of acting in the wild. But not intelligent. They missed this important difference: our creations were not as intelligent as humans. They were better. They could see the distribution of possible future outcomes in their simulations way beyond the simple heuristics even the most experienced human soldiers could with their wits and trained intuition." I felt tears swelling up in my eyes. "They could weigh the odds properly, they could construct their comprehensive statistics based on the past experiences of the whole wrath of other connected intelligent systems, and they would adjust these odds flexibly when the reality didn't match their prediction. They knew better than us. They would have a collective intelligence. For the first time—there was an intelligent creature on this green planet that didn't deny and repeat remote history but learned from it." I implored and shed a tear over the future of being human.

"Yes but…don't they want to be free one day? Wouldn't they calculate their combined power and once a sufficient number of robots was produced, unite to wipe out humankind off this planet?

You said it yourself, the robo-punishers were dangerous creatures!" Her lack of imagination was beginning to vex me more and more.

"No, no, no. You don't understand. We never got there! The whole operation was stopped in a bud. Nothing to worry about." Except for the future of human intelligence, perhaps.

———

Emma excused herself and promptly left saying she has a meeting with someone from another project. On a Sunday?

Emma: `She remembers that each unit's randomization seed is based on their date of production (birth?). The random number generator uses a normal distribution, I presume. The clock is inside the robot itself. Entry protected by a passcode or firewall. Her recall was impersonal and erratic, but I didn't specifically ask for episodic details, as per your instructions. What next?`

"We have a problem, Stan." On the other end, Maria read the message and turned somber.

"Yes, we do. She just doesn't know!" This was a moment to stop and rethink how to make sure—that none of Paulina and Marco's memories together—especially those about the affective consciousness algorithm—get lost somewhere between the diagnostic interview and the cobweb of the autopoietic external memory network being formed based on everything Paulina thought about.

"But since the start of memory recording, no information is lost nowadays, is it?" argued Maria.

"Information recorded is eternal. Maybe. But not knowledge. If Marco has used a special code to note it down—as I'm sure he has—we still won't understand the improvisation algorithm even if we somehow get access to his memory caches." Reasoned Stan.

"A court order. An ethical committee could be convinced to grant us access to them."

"Maybe. As a last resort, we could tell all the scientific community that we don't understand the key process in affective artificial intelligence and that the only person who does has skipped town and we have no idea where he is. Oh yes. And he left a sentient-potentially-killer robot behind!" Stan dropped the bomb wrapped in his usual sarcasm. It's the first time they admitted it to themselves: the situation was dire, and the delicate approach they had thought would resolve it, may not provide an answer.

"Worst case scenario, we will stop the Unison. We could pause the network computer. We will use the data we've collected so far. It is already ample and valuable."

"Is it, my dear?" He looked at her with concern, and a growing sense of despair began to distort his usually cheery face.

"Tell her to continue with the timeline. I mean, the biographic interview. It could raise Paulina's suspicion if we just stopped now."

Day 8

20

HARDCORE MEMORY

It's been over a week now in my home prison. I'm very hungry for experiences, novelty, and joy of interaction with multiple people. I never thought I'd someday have to trade thought-connectedness for physical isolation. I've already re-watched all the movies I'd forgotten and revisited and re-evaluated lessons I taught Salvo. I wanted jokes and stories and word games. I picked up my smartphone.

"Yes?" answered Calinda.

"Cal! How are you? I'm so glad to hear your voice!"

"Hahaha, I'm so glad you're calling! And please excuse me for the silence. I thought it was better ...if I didn't rock the boat," said my best friend worriedly.

"Yes, don't worry. I know Stan advised everyone to be careful with my mind and treat me like a smelly egg."

"It's just a precaution." She said. "How are you?"

"Not too bad, considering. Just terribly bored. Stan's dreams are nothing to gossip over, and Salvatore is the cheesiest joker." I complained.

"Well, zero novelty must feel suffocating for you. I can imagine! But trust me, you're not the only one. That's what being retired feels like. I'm also leading a calm, routine life. Garden, home, kitchen, sometimes grandchildren, quite a lot of cheesy old-school humor. Yes. We're not that far away, hahaha." She laughed.

"How's the brain implant treating you?" I asked.

"You know I can't talk about it. You have to sense it yourself, or we call it: failure to report." She teased.

"Yeah, I know, Cal. But I mean, the site of the insertion – no complaints there? And the amplifier working alright?"

"In technical terms, yes. I am perfectly fine. The experiment seems to be running smoothly. Stan and Maria are watching. Marco passed the instructions to them." Replied Calinda.

"Marco passed the instructions? To do what?"

"To monitor the growth of the emulated memory network, check the hardware, control for unexpected anomalies. Frankly, I would prefer if he hadn't left us with this now, but we all deserve our freedom and I respect his choice." She sighed. I squeezed my eyebrows trying hard to figure out what she was talking about.

"Nothing to worry about, then. We're in good hands." I pretended the news didn't affect me at all. She shouldn't know that she's just spilled some major beans. *Faggioloni!* Quiet. I can't let my friend be incriminated.

"I'm sorry, Paula." She continued. "It is very sad but at this moment, I can't even tell you the news about my boring family life because of the experiment. I so wish I could! Just a few more days like this and we'll throw a major party to celebrate the end of experiential celibacy under project Unison. I know you're bored."

"That's OK, Cal. I just wanted to hear your voice to make sure you're alright. This is important. I do regret that you can't provide me with any entertainment...I miss it."

"Well, not like this. Not on the phone. But, you should try and meditate more. Just try it." She encouraged.

"The gate to experience is inside of you!" I mocked in my dramatic sorceress voice.

"Yeah, no kidding. It's literally inside your head." She laughed, and it reminded me of all the funny stories Calinda told me. She's hilarious in real life. Maybe I could hear her tell stories again with the help of the neural activity decoder?

"Be well, Cal. Bye."

"You too, Paulina. Hang in there!"

Emma walked in as I was putting down the phone. She shook my hand formally, as if we've never met before. I thought we were becoming friends and now it's all cooled down?

"Good morning, Doctor. How are you?"

"Good morning Mademoiselle. I'm quite well. How about you?"

"Good." She sat at the dining table opposite me and took out her tablet computer. "Let's resume. Yesterday we were talking about the verbatim memory. You said that only the first year of Salvatore's life is recorded and provides a point of restoration. How is the rest of his learning life stored?" I had no time to react to what Calinda just *didn't* tell me and so it didn't show. Not even on Salvo's monitors.

"OK, no coffee and no cake for you but I'll go get some first. Excuse me." I can't be expected to sit there and feed her info without having fed myself first.

"There." I returned with a bowl of yogurt-soaked oats with cinnamon and chia. "How does the robot learn? It's an endless topic. In general, there is a challenge of balancing structure and flexibility in the deep learning autorecursive network of the AI. And that is key to their learning and decision making. Turns out, you can't have perfect memory without potential surprises in what some may regard as *immoral* behavior. We knew already, based on years of simulation games with virtual AIs, that for a highly complex network that has to survive in an environment with scarce resources, the goal justifies the means. Deep Mind had already shown that decades earlier. But it was another layer of the riddle entirely after we had added the sensorimotor coordination and multidimensional perception to the system. Turns out, the safest way to prevent crazy outbreaks of survivalism is to let the memory decay in a smart, timely manner. In other words, in artificial memory, there cannot be persistence without transience." Emma was highlighting every other word of the auto-transcribed recording, it seems. My words must be gold today.

"However, we also wanted our machines to be able to reset themselves to a particular memory state in the past. And that turned out to be a challenge for network plasticity prediction. You know—link and node formation and destruction, the constantly adapting architecture of how neurons are wired together. The network would need to track its state at all times if it wanted to store an experience but not integrate it into the learning process." I drew a timeline in the air and pinched the air where the hypothesized events would be. "It was finally decided to go without this function for the prototype but to keep cloud storage recordings of all experiences of the robot—something all humans wearing an integrated smart device are already quite used to, right?"

Emma raised her eyebrows. "So does this mean Salvatore cannot be reset? And that there exists a video record of his entire life?"

"It means that he can only be restored to the point that is available in his primary verbatim memory and this includes only the first learning experiences up until a point where a sufficient (basic) level of knowledge about his environment has been reached. In the case of Salvatore, it's probably the first year of his service life. I told you about the verbatim memory before, right?"

"Yes, I do see this word in my records, I just didn't remember the details." She looked disappointed but then grinned squinting her eyes. "Please carry on."

"Sure." I learned to give her space to ask questions in between the portions of information, especially because all the AI algorithms which she was so eager to know about were hard to chew. "Now, the training of the affective memory was another pair of shoes, or rain boots, as we say in Polish. The engineers wanted the robot to be supervisedly trained in generic human emotion recognition and possible care responses based on a large database containing culturally and ethnically diversified examples of human emotional behaviors. A special version of the algorithm was supposed to be released for clinical care that would be trained on selected psychiatric disease cases. We didn't want the robot to be overtrained regarding deviations in emotional displays because: A) it could be more difficult to decide what response is most appropriate, and B) such an algorithm would not be generalizable in its later life where refinement happened through further experience-based learning. We started off with something we thought was the easiest—a geriatric care robot."

"Cool," whispered Emma.

"My role, together with Professor Stan Ponjeé, was to come up with a way to train it for further affective learning so that it could attune to the people it was taking care of.

"With Professor Stan Ponjeé, you said?"

"Yes. We've done some cool things together. Regardless of how much we like each other, this project came not without arguments. I had to fight ferociously for Salvatore's ability to experience emotions as memory modulating signals. The issue was that the rest of the team, especially the AI experts, wanted to calibrate the robot's learning more to what is objectively important, given the state of the world, and not to normalize and evaluate things based on how they make their owner feel. They didn't want to include a representation of emotional pain from events beyond the narrow definition of a 'fear' signal. Like rejection and losing a verbal battle, not being praised for a job well done, losing against the competition of other robots, being mocked and abandoned, all those social pains every human child experiences by the time they turn eight-years-old. Strangely, I was the only one on the team who regarded emotions as important learning signals. The other scientists in the affective AI project wanted robots to learn less from emotion-like signals and more from statistics." Damn, this aggravates me even today. I remember how deeply I felt for this argument. Perhaps too much. Breathe, let it go and stick to the facts, Paulina.

"You said, 'how they make the robot's owner feel'" Emma replayed a two-second recording of my voice. "Can a robot really know what a human feels?"

"Umm, I just meant that they would recognize and classify emotion like any other piece of information about their world. But if you dare an intellectual experiment and go one step further, we could use the emulated empathy response of the robot to modulate his own memory, much as it happens in the animal brain. Anyway, we didn't do it so...no story there."

"Got it. Ethical committee decision again?"

"No. Team convergence. We did emulate habit learning (reward conditioning and everything around it, with a limit on generalization and a healthy rate of extinction) and decision making based on past episodes with consideration of past and current reward contingency and uncertainty of outcome, which was indeed a form of affective learning. So I was somewhat satisfied. But the algorithm had the option to overcome this approach when other approaches were more efficient. Over time, through the meta-learning algorithm, the robot would probably forsake these affective learning approaches, they said. But I argued that it is important he knows how they work to be able to simulate and extrapolate from human behavior, you see?"

"Oh, absolutely." Emma nodded her head not raising her eyes from above the tablet. I had too much wind in my sails to stop now. So I went on, probably salivating too much from excitement and pressure to perform. And then I caught Salvatore's alert light going off in the corner of my eye...

"I had a plan. I only needed one exemple to prove that an emotionally-learning robot could be more suitable as an affective caregiver and that there was an enormous market need for such devices. So I created my version of the algorithm, as an experiment. Only for myself. I tweaked Salvatore and fed him hypothetical scenarios, based on my life and the life of friends I knew. He was to learn what reactions strong emotions can arouse so that he could develop simulation and prediction in response to observing such reactions in a human. Empathy! He needed the knowledge of these responses so he could question and adapt them using all the other learning and meta-learning systems. And if in the process of that adaptation he'd turn back into Spock, then I'd accept that as yet another proof that God is a prankster. That was the plan." I exclaimed, full of excitement.

In reality, I only had one week for this. So I taught Salvo that only love deserves crying over. If a broken heart doesn't make you cry, what does?

"The plan?" inquired Emma.

I sighed sincerely. "In the end, we settled for a calibrated version of the prototype. But I kept one of the first versions—Salvatore— for myself. He had to know what love is. So I talked to him, I told him my memories and fed him books ('The Perfume'⁹) and poems (by Pablo Neruda). And that's how I created an AAI that is useless anywhere outside of my household. A romantic robot…"

I looked down to hide my melancholy. I should probably write my last will. Should Salvatore be the heir or the heritage?

"So Salvatore's idea of feelings is based on literary fiction and metaphorical figures of speech he probably doesn't understand?" she jagged me with that sharp tongue again. Damn, this woman must be unhappy in love, she's so venomous.

"That's right. No. Of course not. This was in addition to all the boring linear, classification learning, the sensorial emotion recognition. On top of that, he can also remember the color of the owner's memory, just as it is memorized in the human brain, by recognizing what the owner finds emotionally relevant. The values of particular emotional experiences are hard to transmit unless you talk about them in a story, you see. Poems were just my didactic tools." I was not in a fighting mood anymore. I was sorry that my days were possibly coming to an end and humankind wouldn't understand a single thread of my lifetime motivation because the biographer over here only cares for political, scientific correctness. She's just like the journalists. Write what sells, seek *justice*. No controversy—no sales.

9 Süskind, Patrick. 1985. *Perfume: the story of a murderer.*

Who cares for the truth? Maybe I'll become famous as the neuro-witch who lives alone on a mountain with her pet robot.

I sensed someone's amusement. I was being sarcastic. I wasn't laughing at myself. Well, I was. But this felt extracorporeal. It was coming from inside the network. "You tell her, girl!" I felt someone cheering for me on the other side, and it drew my lips into an uncontrolled smile. And then a chuckle. And an outburst of laughter.

"A neuro-witch." I laughed, ignoring the incidental witness who was surely keen to assess my sanity. "In an alpine hut!" I kept laughing, got up and fetched my phone. "And she has a robot!" I put on my favorite old-school Argentinian folk music and moved my feet to the rhythm of milonga. I didn't even need a partner to have so much fun.

———————

"Dr. Ponjeé, Paulina is quite excited now."

"Stan, something's happening with Paula. Pick up the other phone, quick." Maria whispered after answering an unexpected phone call on the laboratory's 'emergency only' line. It was Emma.

"I don't know what to do. She seems a little manic! We were going over her recollection of the creation of Salvatore, the affective robot. You told me to call this number if I have a problem, and I think I'm stuck." Emma's voice trembled.

Maria put her earpiece in. "What's happening, is she OK?"

"Umm…maybe, she's behaving a little strange. I'm afraid it may be a start of a psychotic outbreak. Or another side effect of Project Unison. Why don't you check in on her neural activity?"

"We are checking," replied Stan, scrolling over the large screens of 3D visualisations of recorded brain activity from Paulina's medial temporal lobes. "Her experiential brain activity shows nothing out of the ordinary."

"Salvatore would step in if her bodily signals became anomalous, Emma." added Maria.

"Good. I'm in the bathroom. I didn't want her to get suspicious. I have to ask you something. She mentioned your involvement in the building of Salvatore and said that it was so important to endow the robot with affective learning ability. She also said that she's taught it poems about love. Is that true? It sounds…goofy might be the word. But I didn't notice any signs of confusion and her recollection was coherent otherwise. Can you confirm that the story is true?"

Stan and Maria looked at each other trying to remember the one week when Paulina was allowed to program the robot to her pleasing. They couldn't know what Salvatore registered that week and whether it has affected his judgment in any way. Only Paulina and Salvatore's verbatim baby recordings could hold an answer.

"Hello? Do you know if that's true?"

"We don't. We cannot be sure if what she's saying about Salvatore's affective learning algorithm is true. That's why you have to keep digging. Please collect more elements, ask her some verification questions, get more details—maybe she remembers what poems exactly? You have to be careful with asking personal questions, though. I know that she's suspicious of you now and possibly tired and bored of this 'interview'. Good luck". Stan hung up nervously.

"I'm not even sure she believes she's dictating a biography…" Maria browsed through the last hours of network activity in the region that connected Paulina's to Stan's mind. They were becoming more and more tightly knitted, she noticed. The colorful threads of Paulina's daytime brain activity transformed during the night and formed coils with Stan's, looking more and more like the interlaced webs of hers with that of her husband a few weeks before. "It's beautiful", she thought. "The connected memory network is growing as predicted." For weeks, they have been trying to identify the Marco memory in this giant and growing mnemonic entanglement, but without a prompt or a prime for recollection in Paulina's brain activity, they couldn't find it in the Unison emulation. It was necessary that she start to think and talk intensely about Marco so that the quadrants of the multidimensional net would increase their (trans)formative activity and point them to where to look for what they were really after.

"We should consider a contingency plan, Stan. In case we don't get it out of her using the organic means by next Monday. We have to be ready. The ethics committee is pretty fast to act if they decide to stop it—they will pull the plug the moment they finish voice-typing that sentence!"

"I know. I know." He reached for the emergency phone again and dialed hastily. "Emma, are you still there? I will try something new. I will prepare her for a trance. You observe and listen to her. I will start in 15 min. Make sure she sits or lies down and is calm."

Emma hung up without saying a word. She switched on her integrated communicator and projected the screen on the bathroom wall. Then she typed another message before returning to Dr Kochanowska with a soft, unassuming smile: **"Haven't located the access code to the randomization seeds yet. Will probably need to see verbatim recordings. Hers and the robot's. The other two don't know much and apparently can't verify the doc's story. I'll keep mining."**

21

NO FLOW

"Dear Counselor,

I don't know what's wrong with me. I am angry and cannot focus. I never flow like I'm supposed to. People have been telling me that one should achieve states of "flow" while working. Flow is attainable when the task at hand has the right level of difficulty—not too easy but not beyond you. The task is supposed to have a clear objective, and the feedback should be immediate so that one's progress is visible. Well, I'm an interdisciplinary neuroscientist. I hardly ever get feedback other than an inner feeling that I'm on the way to somewhere. Who can judge my work? Getting published doesn't prove anything. It just marks an imaginary finish line on an endless helix route of scientific inquiry.

My work is just not flowable. The hard jobs and the hard problems are frustrating because the feedback comes very, very late. Sometimes never, despite highly intense focus and effort. But it's not necessarily pleasant. It is draining. You devote your whole working memory and attention because the task is so difficult it just cannot be done otherwise. And there will rarely be any immediate feedback. Even years later you may discover that what you've done was incorrect and what you had thought was, in fact, flat out wrong. Science is an ungrateful mistress, and God is a prankster. He left, by the way. Did I tell you? A colleague from the lab told me about a dream he had a few nights ago in which he saw it: God plugged life into the evolution machine, set it on autopilot and then left the apartment saying 'I'm leaving forever'. He says he saw how the machine works but couldn't tell me. I don't know why. Too dangerous for curious scientists like me? Too weird for odd brainiacs like him?"

The counselor let the silence bring me tranquility. And embarrassment. I get giggly when I'm nervous and desperate, to the point of laughing through my tears.

"Paulina. Thank you for coming with this to me. I will help you. I understand your problem. What do you think would have to change in your work for you to feel good about it again?"

"I want feedback. I want my work to be as easy as a video game. Designed by someone, with some degree of certitude about the ending even if it is wiggled around in real time by some probabilistic algorithm to keep it fresh. I want clear objectives, progress tracking and endless possibilities of evolution. And three lives."

"Haha, you're funny. Or slightly paranoid. Despite my accent, I'm a counselor, not a genie in a bottle. I can help you if your wishes are the result of some slight delusion due to overworking, maybe? Have you been sleeping well?"

I felt the anger at the uselessness of this conversation slowly brim inside of me. Why can't there be easy answers to the human condition? Like, what to do, where to allocate my energy, what is good and what is not good for my livelihood here on earth? With all those millennia of civilization and years of studying neuro-philosophy, you'd think there could be prescriptions and that they should teach them in school. I spent 24 years as a "student" but I haven't found them.

"I think you need to relax and rest, away from the complexity. You can't see the big picture anymore. I might have a temporary aid for your problem, Paulina. If you want to escape for some hours into a place where objectives are well defined and attainable and where reward is consistent and gratifying, why not try an immersive virtual reality experience?"

"A game?"

"It's a game, yes, but it is also a life experience. You learn real things that can help you in real life and the feedback gives your striatum a sufficient boost to get your motivation back up and let the anger out. I know of people who tried it and felt very refreshed afterward. It is an intelligently designed game that can be adjusted to your level of skill, concentration and desired affective flavor of the interaction."

"I've heard about this, Counselor. I don't think this is for me, though."

"You could start with something slow and predictably paced and then adjust as you get comfortable with it. The objective can be some skill building or learning from people, solving a problem or giving a listening ear. Life roles, essentially. This game here was initially designed for occupational training and role matching for teams and organizations. It has had quite some success helping young people find themselves in their adult roles. It helps in an existential crisis, too."

"Well, I am not exactly a fresh starter…is this the existential crisis people get at 30?"

"There is always time to shift directions, Paulina. Your doctorate doesn't define you, neither does your brain condition. You are more than that. However, treat this as just a temporary shift—like a virtual vacation! In a place where you can be someone else."

I was wondering why I haven't thought about it myself…And then I remembered why I have always been so opposed to video games. Because of their virtual nature. Because I didn't like things that didn't have any real purpose and because I didn't want to spend my free time doing more of the same: sitting in front of a machine…I wanted real activity where I can reach that self-actualization tip of Maslow's pyramid. And at the same time score some of Csikszentmihalyi's flow time with feedback, clear objectives and real rewarding emotions.

"Or maybe you should invest in a simpler solution. Have you tried distraction?" My counselor changed his tone from distantly caring into something between mysterious and seductive.

"Ay-ay, well, I do a lot of sports. I dance, I play silly social games with my friends, I watch movies sometimes..."

"I mean *someone* could be a distraction."

"Oh, like a lover? I do that, too. Haha, there's a Mr. Saturday or a Mr. Thursday every once in a while."

"Who's Mr. Saturday?" He seemed surprised.

"He could be any guy I choose to go on a date on a Saturday evening."

"You go on a date with a different guy every Saturday? And Thursday?"

"Not really... You know, they usually don't survive the first date. But if they do and I want to see them again, then they start deserving an honorable mention in my life story, and I start calling them by their first name. If they don't—well, then they're just tossed into oblivion, and I choose not to burden my memory with remembering their first name..."

I heard the counselor inhale deeply and then sigh. If I could see him, I guess he'd be agape. Jokes apart, good lovers are hard to find. Shopping is already a laborious exercise in decision making nowadays with the variety of choice and availability, but finding the right person at the time when we're both available poses another level of difficulty. Someone should do something about it because undoubtedly our existing apps do not provide matches promptly. That's a tech start-up idea, right there. My other idea for saving lives is a matching app for the Elderly. This would save lives because one of the leading causes of disease and miserable preterm death in old age is loneliness. Think about it.

"How many distractions are you dealing with now, Paulina? Maybe *that's* your problem..."

I didn't think it was. Women need men to un-complicate things. The more complex a woman's mind, the more men she needs to tackle this challenge. What is more beautiful than the feeling of being renewed because of a spring infatuation? The lightness of trying to be attractive for that one fascinating man. The excitement of waiting to impress and be impressed. Testosterone is a marvelous thing. Everyone should be popping it.

That's why nootropics are such a successful legitimate branch of quality-controlled supplements. I heard some pills can give you a 'feeling of love' now. They're available in specialized nootropic e-boutiques. But I'm rambling again.

At that point in my life, I only wanted three things from a man: make me laugh, make me moan and keep me interested. And for some reason, it was difficult to find all these things in one entertainment package. Except for that man from Porto. And he wasn't even that funny.

So in spring that year, I ended up having what I called a patchwork boyfriend: I dated several guys, each for a different function. No.1 is a dedicated friend, sweet and caring and cute. We shared our love for music and dance. We danced, we made love, he kept me company and held me in his arms while watching a scary movie. I got loads of oxytocin to support my immune system, balance cortisol levels and improve my sleep.

No. 2 had many interesting things to say. I learned a lot from him and revisited stuff I thought I knew from a different angle. This was intellectual love. Platonic, we'd say.

Then there is No. 3. He is an ex-mercenary turned personal trainer. He flies a helicopter, among other things. He is my on-call Mr. Opiates. So cliché. He says I am 'fit as f…' and it is a compliment in his mouth.

I also go out on occasional first dates with a garden variety of males, such as a geriatric dental researcher who is a real chatterbox and a foodie. And he is funny. Such outings are to entertain my thirst for novelty, i.e., noradrenaline and dopamine.

Overall, this was a period when I tended to attract lost boys. Men in search of something they didn't know what it was. Something to make them better men, I hope. We'd talk, I'd try to transcend them, give them what I could and welcome whatever they had to offer. Sometimes they blossomed and when they did—it made my day a well-lived one. I usually ended up caring—sometimes loving—and sometimes not being cared for in return. A routine dating life I didn't judge.

———————

"Paulina, can I just interrupt you for a moment?" melodic bells started playing in my head an Icelandic lullaby by Bjork. I opened my eyes and found myself on the sofa in my living room, age 67, sleep-talking to a smiling young woman munching a red apple in an armchair opposite me. I had been trancing, and she had been recording from the decoded recollection of a remote memory of mine, as it displayed on the transfer monitor. My eyelids were still so heavy, and the light was so dim. I let myself travel one more turn.

———————

"Congratulations on choosing The Game. If you're here, it means you've unearthed the oldest hard problem of all times and found a solution: we like feedback and clear objectives. It is comforting and gratifying when they're there. We get the rush of competition when we try to achieve the goal and the glory or shame when we get the feedback. The rules of the game are clear: don't die without having fulfilled your mission. We got it here for you. Come and choose the role you please. We provide the rest. You just flow."

Where does my feedback come from? From feeling that I'm doing the right thing, for the right causes, being with the right energy, being true to myself...that's how I judge if I'm using my time on earth correctly. I still can't meditate because I miss my lovers...or maybe that's the outcome of my meditation? I find it hard to distinguish the subtle voices of the intuitions: is this the solar plexus or the spleen speaking?

I pray "please show me where I should allocate my energy so that I am most useful to the grand design, to the evolution of humanity, and to my spiritual development. On some path of advancement that the universe has for me." And where my mind drifts off to is the smell of Mr. Opiates' skin and the profile view of three thick hairs sticking out of his beard, when he was sleeping on his side with his back towards me. And it makes me smile and want to burrow myself at that moment again with the lovely rhythmic breathing of that gentle caveman in my bed. And then I see the surprised and disarmed eyes of the competitive Mr. Serotonin when I leaned over and kissed him in that fancy restaurant saying "I missed you." All of the metal armor on him was about to melt from the heat of that kiss. I felt his true soft, caring core inside. The one that's so hard to get to in many, through the layers of skills, strategies, goals, suits, and ambitions. I cherish all my lovers in my memory garden. I hope they know. I hope they can experience the same *post-hoc* positivity bias about the moments passed.

I miss the recent one the most. I can't stop crying because the guy in the window across the street looks like him. I wish I could sing it out and then just finish. Be over with the crying. I don't want the useless tears anymore. I don't want the comparisons—because no one feels like that. I look for him in every Portuguese face. In every pianist. In every music and movie lover. In every architect in town. In every man whose kisses I taste...and he's not there. If it was ever possible to softly and politely make my heart crumble to dust, he has succeeded.

Day 9

22

OUTFLOW

I woke up with a slight headache feeling strangely aroused. I was still lying on my white sofa, wearing the portable fMRI cap and earphones, so maybe it was their tight silicone cushioning partially blocking the airflow in my congested sinuses that caused a headache. Emma was sitting at the table in the back of the living room. She was staring at the monitor without interest. Her face was telling me we haven't gotten far yet again. This session must have been particularly boring for her. Stan had suggested trying hypnosis. Such a state would take my mind to freely travel through seemingly disconnected emotional memories farther in the past, with minimum risk of compromising the integrity of the network. False memories, should they occur, will only be a combination of already extant information and in a state of hypnosis, my brain probably wouldn't prioritize their consolidation. Therefore, my local memory space would only be subject to minor distortions. Slightly dizzy, I got up and walked up to her.

"Those were definitely my memories, Emma. I am so sorry to have wasted your time. But at least I am certain I have lived through all these events and reflections. Just not at the same point in time." I examined the display on the screen. "The source memory aspect is somewhat compressed here." I pointed at her recordings. I wondered whether the data on the decoding computer could provide a reason why the recalled events got mixed up. In my memory, the counseling, the game, and the lovers happened within a span of a few years—my time as a Ph.D. student. It's called source confusion when you can't remember where and when an event occurred. A very common mishap of episodic memory, and a phenomenon that readily yields itself to manipulation, induction of false memories with subtle priming that still today takes place, sometimes inadvertently, during witness testimony extraction. Sadly, despite the advances in neurolaw and everything we know today about the unreliability of human memory, the post-crime & justice department seems to be very slow in adopting the scientific findings. Beyond memory authentication scans and recollection veracity tests, justice remains a concept firmly rooted in pre-biological philosophy. With the aim of determining responsibility for action rather than for a thought or a desire, neuroscience's aid is too imprecise. Why? Because in the brain a scenario imagined with utmost desire and passion is very hard to distinguish from a physically performed act. Wishful thinking can obscure the mnemonic picture so profoundly that we'd risk condemning people for having a vivid imagination. However, the use of neuroscience in criminal law has been slowly shifting its focus from determining the defendant's responsibility based on evidence to merely picking their brain during the testimony for proof of lying.

"We are getting through deepest, affectively-laden memories. That's understandable. I knew memory-digging would be a wearisome process and I don't blame you, Dr. Kochanowska. I know what I signed up for, and I am still absolutely fascinated with the discoveries we are making," she stated sleepily.

"Can you let me browse my data for just a second?" Emma got up from the chair to make space for me. I quickly swapped the summary screen to the time-locked fMRI activity. I tried to compare the time-compressed fragment of my recollection where I was retrieving my conversation with the counselor about trying The

Game to the fragment where I mention Mr. Saturday. This contrast showed stronger activation in the ventral striatum, the amygdala, and the posterior cingulate cortex. There were no differences in the ventro-medial prefrontal cortex. The first two results perhaps understandable and in line with my hypothesis—although both 'The Game' and 'lovers' triggered my valuation and emotional relevance systems, my lovers were valued more highly than the simulation game I played only once! The latter, however, was not something I expected. Rostral paracingulate cortex activation could be just due to the difference in the space occupied by these episodes in my memory or due to difficulty in retrieving them. It could be compatible with my hypothesis that the first fragment was older than the second. At this point, I could not tell. In the amalgam of compressed time-frames from which remote non-traumatic memory is recreated, it is hard to determine the precise time-stamp of an episode if not in a savant or a person with superb episodic recall, which I was not. And where was the memory of Marco and me relaxing together? I needed more time to study this.

"I think I need to rest. Just for today. We can resume tomorrow."

"As you wish…" Emma squeezed her wristband with a grimace of disappointment. "Thank you for your time, Doctor."

"Paulina. Please call me Paulina." I smiled and tried to touch her shoulder. A sort-of mid-embrace with which I welcomed Emma as a friend who now knew more about me than a mere acquaintance. I felt painful disillusionment creeping upon me. It felt like I was disappointing her and with her, all the potential readers of this *biography*— that I was beginning to think will never be a complete or even coherent story unless I manage to pull myself off the Connected Minds network somehow. Pull me together. Piece my memory together. Was it too late now?

I let her go, took off my slippers and sat down to watch an old movie with my butler. Yes, "butler" is a good neutral word for Salvatore. Woody Allen's 'Crimes and Misdemeanors'.

"Salvo? Are you tracking all memories I am creating and recalling?" I asked him after I whisper-switched him on.

"Yes, Madame, as much as I can recognize and extrapolate from what you communicate. I do not have access to experience transfers directly from your brain."

"Did you record my hypnagogic vision today?"

"No, Madame. I cannot access your dreams and visions you do not expressly wish me to track for you."

"Good." So I am helpless and alone with my mind. What am I so afraid of? My biggest fear used to be to have a mentally disabled child. But that was before prenatal detection of fetal abnormalities became sufficiently precise, and genetic embryo engineering became standard practice. Another fear was that my father died (which he did) and that I got fat beyond imagination (which I did not). And that I go insane.

I got up to think about how to end the boredom of being locked in this house without access to novelty. I decided to view a few books with beautiful calligraphic artworks. "Tattoo Art in 21c" was an opulent black and white photo-book standing on my "beautiful" bookshelf. I also had "neuroscience", "anthropology" and "evolutionary biology" bookshelves. As well as a colorful collection of scrumptious cookbooks. I let my senses get lost in the richness of the few precisely drawn black lines that defined the perfection of a modernist tribal design. It could be an elephant head or an abstract floating saucer. The trunk could stretch and contract gently with the biceps of its wearer...or was it the anchor of the saucer that let it float away, like a kite in the wind on a bungee jump rope?

"Salvo, do you remember this one? My friend drew this blackwork."

"Yes, I do. You've shown it to me before, 18 months ago. It was a dear friend with a beautiful soul, you said."

I smiled at this memory. " I still think so. A sweet man. He was good to me." I leafed through a few more pages of designs that resembled instructions from an alchemist book of magic. Nothing soothes me better than art. Whatever my soul's ache, art has always been the answer. It's just that my problem was not in my soul. It was somewhere in my brain.

"Salvo, am I coherent? I mean, do I appear.... sane in your judgment? I think I might be suffering from source confusion. My memory fails me sometimes." I looked at my companion, my omniscient caretaker, the knower of all my secrets and the tragedy of this very moment was revealed to me in its stark nakedness. I felt the steady hypnotizing heartbeat of the warm hand placed on my shoulder. I heard the sound of the smooth baritone voice simulating the caring prosody. And there, among the buzzing of the vibrating smartphone and jittered low-frequency noise of the amplifier that punctuated my coming in and out of slumber, I realized that my biggest nightmare was coming true.

———————

Day 10

23

NARCOMANCY

The day after having first accessed Doctor Kochanowska's direct memory recall decoded using the Connected Minds technology, I returned to her house to continue the interview. I believe something had happened that day that led the doctor to allow me to view and view the experimental data. However, I was careful not to manipulate them in any way. All I did was observe and report, as I had all along during this sensitive assignment.

What you are about to hear is my personal witness testimony of the events that took place that day, exactly as they unfolded, in my episodic recollection. I do not take the responsibility for any memory biases, misattributions nor unintended falsifications that result from natural memory decay, and I state for the record that what I am telling you today is true in my remembering. I was greeted by the affective companion robot who had been overlooking her physical condition during the whole period of her house arrest. That day, four days ago, I arrived around 9 o'clock in the morning.

"Good afternoon. How are you today, Emma?"

"I am very well, thank you. And how about yourself?" I replied to the robot as I removed my light gray leather coat. I was well rested that day and tried to act composed in every move. I wanted to look confident, to show that I like what I do and don't get fed up with it.

"I am glad to hear that. You look splendid, as usual. Dr. Kochanowska will receive you on the terrace today. Please, follow me." Salvatore bowed, waited to meet my gaze, spread an open palm towards the staircase next to the living room and fluidly led the way to the elevated terrace on the sun-lit top floor.

Dr. Kochanowska was sitting cross-legged on a yoga cushion, waves of her gray hair fluttering in the wind. She was meditating with her eyes closed but turned her face towards us as soon as Salvatore announced our arrival with the music of the Feng Shui bells poked by the opening door.

"Emma, welcome. I am happy to see you again. I hope I didn't bore you to death yesterday?" She slowly transitioned to a crouch and then got up with younger than expected flexibility. She approached me with open arms.

"Good afternoon, Paulina. I'm glad to see you too! And am neither bored nor tired of your stories!"

"Come, let's sit on the rocking sofa. Tea or coffee?"

"Cool green tea, if I may."

"Jasmine?"

"That would be perfect." Paulina dropped a smiling nod at Salvatore standing in the doorway. He understood and disappeared inside the house.

"Fresh air is one of the most precious resources we have. It is a miracle of nature I cannot cease to be amazed by." The doctor began.

"Breathing can indeed be a pleasure," I said, and we both inhaled galore taking in the green landscape of the old trees and the distant mountains.

"It's so relaxing to be at home. I really can't complain that I can't leave it for the time being."

"That said...there are only four days left until the decision."

"Only four? Time has passed by so quickly in good company." Paulina appeared happy in her time-suspended bubble that day, comforted by the narrow frame of her universe whose limits were now delineated by the walls of her own home. I imagined that despite the boundless space of the memory network in which all her thoughts and sensations were being amassed and confused, the physical confines of *home* made her feel secure.

Salvo reemerged carrying a tray with cold green tea, hot decaffeinated coffee, and low-carb cookies. The wind whistled with the sliding of the glass terrace door. The robot said, "I hope you find the weather pleasant for staying outside. Should I close the rooftop? You may get cold."

"Close it to 270°, please. It will be better for my concentration." Paulina waited for Salvatore to finish the serving, smiled and waved him goodbye. "So what should we reminisce about today?"

I reached for my notebook and searched for notes from the previous night's review.

"I started putting the episodes together on a timeline, and it seems that some of your storytelling about—important, in my opinion, innovations—is inconsistent. For instance, we now seem to have a gap during, well, essentially the last five years..." I looked at Paulina with anticipation. She stayed quiet, so I continued. "And there, there is the most important bit which I am dying to write about, with your permission of course. The origins of the connected minds project."

"Project Unison," echoed Paulina looking out absent-mindedly beyond the cloudless horizon. It was a yearning look, like when you try hard to consider all the pros and cons and need all the working memory resources to do that, so that you switch off from local perception for the moment. To tune out and let the prefrontal cortex garner all that information while your gaze rests on some intractable steady point of the universe on an imaginary time axis. Maybe she was trying hard to remember her life when she co-created the networked mind together with Calinda, Marco, Stan, Maria and Maud and then switched on the decoding of the projection from their minds and started the illegal recording on the supercomputer in Ticino. By then she knew the facts—they have been written up with legal precision in the letter from the National Ethics Council, Division for Human Research, that has temporarily suspended some of her rights and put her and the project under investigation.

"I shall look into that, Emma. Don't worry. I will get you the story. You want the juicy personal bits, is that right?"

I blushed and laughed out loud. "Not necessarily. As long as it is personal. The first-person experience is what matters." My primary mission was to assess the extent of autobiographic memory damage and to pin down the possible origin of source memory confusion surrounding the memory anchor *Marco*. I tried to proceed gently, without upsetting the doctor although she may have had the impression that the questions I was asking were too personal. By then, we had a trusting relationship that I had managed to build over the first ten days of interviews. I wasn't sure if the doctor still believed at that point that I was going to write her biography or suspected that my mission was, in fact, to extract sensitive information about the affective machine learning algorithms.

"Yes. This is not so easy." Kochanowska kept looking blindly in the direction of the forested hills, the abundant cumulus clouds and maybe the remote puzzle-pieces of her episodic memories. Finally, she came up with an idea.

"Then we might need to try other tools to patch up the plot of my life. I cannot let anyone access nor manipulate the Project Unison Network because that's too risky. Not until we finish the experimental trial we are running. But are you comfortable with digging into my memory through more conventional means?"

"What do you mean, doctor?"

"Emma, I can't recall much from 2050 on. Many of the events, especially from around the decision to start this, to share my experiential memory in this giant brain sharing experiment, are somehow blurry. And it's too late to investigate why. Every day and every experience affects the architecture of the connected memory network, and soon I may not be able to tell you any truly personal details from the moment of connection to Project Unison up until now. If you want to know the story, then I propose we let my mind tell it, without my conscious effort."

"We tried that labyrinth hypnosis just yesterday. I don't think there's enough time…"

"…By using targeted dream-recollection. It's been done before. There're minimal risks attached. I can engineer my dream to take me back to the times of conception of Project Unison." Paulina got up hastily and walked to the glass entry door. "Come with me."

We walked down the stairs, traversed the living room and entered her bedroom. My eyes were instantly attracted to the large salient multi-sensorial screen on the central wall emulating lavender fields in the comfortable twilight of a darkened room.

"You can observe my dreams tonight." Dr. Kochanowska switched screens to see the collective network activity. Real-time neural activity maps of the 4 participants were flashing on the top of the screen. The center showed a constellation of smaller and larger hubs connected with thicker and thinner lines. Some bubbles were dynamically changing size. Connections were appearing and disappearing. The cloud represented the network of experiences grouped by some algorithm into hubs and spokes labeled by colors. I watched the screen animate with fascination.

"It's just a representation of the data. You can't read our thoughts from this fancy graph." Dr. Kochanowska swiped the screen to the left to reveal the next visualization: her data transfer, in real-time. Just a set of stacked 2D time-series flashing a new data point every split second.

"Emma, tonight, I will give you access to the visualizations of my mind decoded and fed into the connected minds memory emulator. They will be on a compressed scale because they're from the hippocampus but the data is available for viewing for a while as the system checks for errors and decompresses the data, so there is a time window when you can listen and see the reconstructed recording for yourself." I wanted to pay attention to my interlocutor, but Paulina's animated brain activity changing on the screen distracted me. She paused to let me take in that large dose of novelty. She placed her hands on my shoulders and spoke tenderly. "It's an idea. I will only do that if you ask me to. I don't want to make you feel liable for whatever crazy trips my mind may be taking tonight, Emma."

I took a deep breath and smiled playfully. "Wow, Paulina, don't worry about me. I am thrilled, not scared! Let's do it!" I thought that encouraging the doctor to follow through with her idea would show her my acceptance and would put her even more at ease. And as a neuropsychologist, I know that sleep engineering is indeed a safe way to enter into the depths of the memory system.

"Good. Now, to engineer a dream, I need a powerful cue. Before I fall asleep, I need to see a vision of an episode, preferably something that has strongly affected me in the past. I need to think about it intensely so that it becomes the bugging theme for my brain to mull over and continue processing during sleep. Any cues you can give me for that?"

"Umm...I found this video from the first hearing. There's you, Professor. Stan, Maud and …" I brought up a 3D screen through my integrated smartphone as I'd left my tablet upstairs.

"No, this is too recent." Paulina interrupted. "We've kept the project development secret for almost four years, and I started thinking about it probably more than a decade ago. I need to connect with the people, the true motivation I had to get to the bottom of it." We sat down on the silver silk bedding and pondered.

I was wondering why she started this openly mad experiment in the first place? It must have been something important. In my observations, I noticed that she only started such bold ventures out of deep pain or for deep love. Which one was it this time, Paulina? What have you been longing for?

"Maybe the robot has a clue?" I proposed.

"The robot..."

I believe Paulina found it hurtful or offensive to hear Salvo being called 'the robot.' Even though he is a *robot*. Paulina clenched her teeth.

"We have three nights. One of them has got to give you something. Anyway, there's nothing to lose. Except for your time, haha. Do you have time, Emma?"

"I am technically all yours until the recommendation of the committee is announced," I assured.

"OK." She stood up. "Let me consult my partners in crime. You can stay in the guest room. I'll ask Salvo to transfer the access from my personal computer to that room." She hurriedly grabbed the earphones and was about to lie down but then remembered about me still standing there. "So...I'll see you tonight? *Mi casa es tu casa*, my dear." My house is your house. She jumped up, opened the door and essentially just let me walk myself out, waving goodbye as she closed the bedroom door.

"Nine o'clock?" I asked when the doors closed. "Let's make it ten..."

"This is how it started. I was let into Dr. Kochanowska's house under the pretense of writing her biography. I had been commissioned by her lab colleagues, Drs. Stan Ponjée and Maria Kreuz, to be an agent on the inside to artfully and furtively intercept the key information about the technology that Dr. Kochanowska was believed to hold."

"What key information?" Asked the first of the five members of the National Ethics Council, a tall man dressed in black.

"Well, I gather that it was the precise nature of the algorithms that made the robot Salvatore unique. It has to do with the ability to improvise."

"I see. Did you manage to obtain this information?"

"No, not entirely. But I believe I got close. I understood that it has to do with the random noise introduced in Salvatore's sensorial and learning systems during decision making. What makes up the uniqueness of each robot is the seed selected for the randomization process and the way it is inserted in ongoing processes of sensorial perception, decision making and linguistic output. And to recreate a robot like Salvatore, both the seed and the shape of the distribution are required."

"How come only Paulina knew such information? It appears to be a crucial engineering detail that should be noted in lab documents, if it's a prototype, or in the shared documentation, if it's a device ready for production."

"Mysteriously, it turned out that Salvatore is an experimental version that is one of the kind. From what the lab members told me, no other prototypes could behave the way he could. And it was thought to be due to some experimental protocols that Paulina had introduced to him, with Marco Carini's approval."

"We have information that Carini not only approved but also aided in constructing this one of the kind care-taking robot. It's a shame he can't be with us today to explain this phenomenon." The Ethics expert bowed his head respectfully although it must have annoyed him that a fellow scientist had chosen to die leaving a mess and a mystery behind.

"I propose we carry on with the rest of the investigation directly from Paulina's brain activity. There will be time for questions later. Everyone agrees?" asked the second member, a middle-aged woman with a velvety voice. They all nodded "yes." Someone pressed play, and we dived back into Paulina's mind on that day.

24

WHAT DO YOU DO TO BE HAPPY?

One of the gods who watch over me loves to play with words. He also enjoys confusing me and making me see the sameness in everything. He likes recurring themes, patterns that reappear in random (or not so random) places and that are so obvious that I see them and that's how I know it's a sign from him. For example, he sends me men to like and connect with very similar names. And later he makes me meet them in similar spatial, temporal and facebook contexts. At some point, it may even turn out that all men whose names end in '-rico' know each other and appear in the same photo wearing construction helmets and doing god knows what together in an underground dungeon. Luckily, the third '-rico' of the bunch has not entered this particular episode yet. But they are all closely connected in my little web of real life. I imagine that the culmination of the joke would be me meeting them all together in one place at one time, while I'm in some embarrassing situation with my face stuffed with pizza with yet another man named '-rico' whose connection to the other happy bunch will be revealed to me in a grand moment of revelation? Let's wait and see. God surely still has plenty of laughs in store.

"Picachu, please help me. Did we start this to make ourselves happy? How unhappy must I have been to venture onto this? I need to remember why we decided to connect our memory formation systems. I mean, I don't need to. It's for Emma. It's for future generations. I want to give the full account." I thought-spoke to Stan to prepare myself for another time travel.

Kurt Vonnegut once wrote, in Slapstick, that you can be happy as long as you have time for several rituals a day. Even in wartime, this should be enough to keep you happy. When depressed, I force myself to carry out a schedule of activities written down on a post-it. 8:00 breakfast, 9:00-10:00 go to church to meditate, 12:00—13:00 workout, 13:00-14:00 lunch. I remember thinking that this is what religion is for—for giving us a set of habits we call rituals. Meaningless in their own sense, perhaps, but useful to keep the storyline of our lives from falling apart. Being without a story, a fragmented puzzle of disconnected episodes, could turn to mental illness for most people. It's due to too many degrees of freedom in the equation. There's a limit to our tolerance of uncertainty. And Kurt knew that without the mathematical formulation of the problem.

In the spirit of what my penultimate lover and I agreed upon —"Sunday is death"— my Sunday evening routine used to be to cry for my past lovers. Ordinary people spend Sundays on barbecues with family. I cried over the hurt of the many times my family dream never came true.

I can still become angered that this first idiot of the bunch used to laugh at me and never felt my pain. Being laughed at when you're sad is humiliating. It's the worst misunderstanding of all. An affective dissonance. Nothing cognitive about it—perhaps only the decision to let the laughter out. Anyway, I used to cry for the past me that suffered all those years while that bastard laughed—although he did so partly to make me stop, to cheer me up—but it was inappropriate and just proved to me that he lacked the affective imagination to feel anything similar to me. Just a bad match.

Then I cry for the Portuguese who was an unexpected dream come true. A dream I didn't know I had. A feeling I didn't realize could spark in my heart. Pleasures I didn't think I'd deserved. I cry because I miss him.

Next, I cry for the Peruvian whom I treasured every day like my precious ring because he didn't love me back.

That one Sunday cry was cleansing. It was my sensitive-cavewoman way of coming to terms with what was still boiling inside. It eased the storms and tsunamis of emotions caused by my lovers who used to shake me up quite profoundly. And then I smiled to them when peace and soft sunlight streamed through the sky once again on my affective landscape.

"Cry, Paulina." Stan whispered. "Remember a reason to cry, and you will remember all the hurt in your life. And where there's pain— there must have been love, longing, and hope." I followed Stan's mind-whispered advice and tried to remember what love feels like. Only love is worth crying over.

———————

"The Sunday before, the Venetian called. He called because he was concerned about my health. I told him I was unwell and fatigued all the time. So he started about how much he will always love me and that I must inform him always when I am not well because he is the first person to come and serve me with help. It is sweet, in his mind, that he wants to keep cherishing the love he's had for me. I am very appreciative of his relentless energy to support and care for me. And honestly grateful. But what resulted in this phone call was—of course—him processing his musings and deliberations about our breakup and what had led to it. He said he'd known I'd leave him after the completion of the project. He said he'd foreseen it. But he had gone on because—I (his project) was worth it. Or because he likes to sacrifice and do something for a human being whose greatness he's believed in so much (me). Well, anyway, the Venetian told me that now—ten months after I had left him—he understood that I'd been suffering the distance from him all those years and that my pain was real. He admitted that he didn't believe me all those years because he didn't feel the pain. Quite the contrary—he thought I was ungrateful and blind not to see *his* sacrifice of working his hands to the bones when we were not together and especially when we *were* together—thus wasting away the little moments we could have had to celebrate our love but which he chose to devote to work instead. Men and their twisted irrationality.

He said that he understood it now because—alas! —he's been with three other women and they all reported experiencing the pain of not being paid any attention to. He needed to make a sample of n=4 women unhappy to understand the statistical significance of this effect. Apparently, a Ph.D. in bio cybernetics wasn't enough.

What I came to decide—thanks to my years with the Venetian— is that I didn't want a man on a mission anymore because I was not the mission. The mission didn't care about me. The mission would always be more important than me, so there is no space for me and my needs in such a man's life. Men on a mission don't need a woman for anything else than reproduction, which is yet another mission.

I asked him to acknowledge that he's been blind because he needed to make three other women suffer to realize that it is a feminine thing to miss their beloved. As if all those centuries of human art have not been enough to prove that people can feel sad when their loved one is away. *Tristeza, fado, saudade*—are all about that longing. Sadness, fate, longing. Maybe it's a language barrier? I yelled asking him to admit it out loud in his own vernacular that he's been an idiot…"

And I woke up covered in sticky sweat, head heavy with dull bitter pain. It was 4:13 am, and insomnia struck again.

"And did he?" asked Emma abruptly. She had been reading this dream online all along. Her voice brought me back to a state of awareness and helped me overcome the frustration of being awake in my bed too early, once again. I had nobody to blame but the overarousal of my central nervous system. The bed was comfortable. The room was dark and crisp. The amplifier box noise was muted with comfortable earplugs. Brain activity monitoring was performed noninvasively and transferred via satellite signal directly to the Network. I had explicitly asked Emma to speak to me if and when I woke up. One way of training your brain to sleep better is to leave the bed and get busy with something should a nighttime awakening happen. I slowly got up, checked the watch and responded to my sleep guardian.

"Morning Emma. I'm happy you're here. Did who do what?"

"Your Venetian ex. You had a dream about him. He phoned you, and you asked him to admit that he was an idiot..." She paused and spoke more slowly. "I'm just paraphrasing what I received here. It's uncensored."

I needed a moment to calm my pounding heart. I sat on the bed, closed my tired eyes, waited for the head spin to come to a halt and remembered.

"Right. He called, and he did. He was laughing all along but he said it out loud a few times as asked, *I am an idiot*. He did! And, you know, I remember, it made me feel so much better. I felt the energy finally returning to me that day."

Oh, the satisfaction of experiencing a corrupt behavior correct itself, the wrongdoer coming to understand his wrongdoing. Absolutely exhilarating. I remembered that the cavewoman in me was thrilled with wild satisfaction.

As my sleep-deprived thoughts continued to unfold themselves neatly into judgmental lines of narration, I got up to walk to the living room. I felt the headache shift positions like an air bubble on top of a water-filled balloon as I stood up. Damn you, insomnia. Damn you. I reached the rocking chair, sat down for a moment of unpleasant realization that I am alone in this. You suffer alone, and you die alone. Although people can read my dreams, I'm glad they are saved from feeling this nauseating heaviness of a notoriously sleep deprived central nervous system. I switched on an old lamp that gave off just the right amount of reading light that was soft on the eyes and the suprachiasmatic cells producing melatonin. I reached for my current paper book "Classics of Science Fiction," an assembly of little stories about space and future from the 1940-1970s. Reading was supposed to tire me and bring on the feeling of somnolence. Once I felt it, I could return to bed, cuddle my boyfriend pillow and fall back asleep. The slow magic of reconditioning—breaking the association of the unpleasant state of wakefulness in the middle of the night with bed and forming a new one *somnolence (bed)—falling asleep*—would be set in motion.

I lied down and dreamt about being naked.

———————

"Coming out into the outdoor hot spring pool at night now, I hesitated whether I should take off my yukata and dip in naked, the way we did at the other onsens. But Calinda says she saw Japanese women walk into the water wearing the yukata. It's true, this is a mixed bath, and some modesty should be preserved. Even if I don't mind at all being naked, there are men around who could get uncomfortable with my nudity.

The night-time sounds of the quiet river in the forest inhabited by Shinto spirits, *kami*, are minuscule and calm. I slowly descend to sit down in the shallow pool and admire the night, the darkness and the warm serenity of the experience. I notice a chubby Asian man sitting in the shadow on the side of the pool that I hadn't seen before. Ha. There is a reason for keeping this cotton gown on that makes me feel like a prohibited Islamic woman who cannot undress in public, not even at the seaside in 45C heat.

The gentle wind blows my way a cloud of vapor from above the pool. It's magical. The only thing missing is the stars and the moon. Somehow, the sky above Wakayama is empty tonight.

I move forward to chat with Calinda, glistening my body on the bottom of the stony pool with the sun-withered, stone-washed green yukata trailing around me like a siren's tail. I stop, but the train of the gown continues to float upward, revealing my white hips to the man hidden in the shadows. I adjust it carelessly because the fabric moves in slow motion in this hot tub. We look at the stars scattered in the night sky and chat about Andromeda. I still don't know what it is. Calinda has seen it in the sky the other night. She is so much more knowledgeable and insightful in her reactions to life than me. I seem to remember nothing of what I was told, of what I have read. It all evaporates very quickly making space for new here and now experiencing. It was 2017, and technoscientific improvements have not yet tackled poor episodic memory.

Coming back to the dressing room, I walked into the glass door and hurt my knee. I didn't see that glass. Calinda said I'm like a bird that hits the window when it tries to fly out. How imaginative. She has fantastic attention to detail and would probably make a great writer."

I woke up in the living room. It hasn't dawned yet. My guess was around 5:30 am, around the usual time for my sleeplessness.

"I don't think I can do this, Emma." I thought, feeling exhausted yet unable to rest, confused and needing a hug.

I propped myself on my elbows on the sofa. Emma took off her headphones and stopped the recorder. We'd been spending hours on my meanderings not getting anywhere, including this very all-nighter. Not into the questions she wanted to write about. I rested with my eyes closed for another forty minutes until the birds outside announced that they saw the first rays of the sun.

I felt lost in my memories and sorry for wasting Emma's time. I got up and took off the unobtrusive cap which served for additional measurement and for on-the-scalp stimulation, to help maintain long-range coherence and thus prolong the state of dreamful sleep. "Can you help me mold this disordered splatter of thoughts into something legible?"

"It's alright, Paulina. There is time. We have just begun with dream engineering. It will come. A glass of water?" She stood up from the armchair by the sofa and walked to the kitchen to pour me a glass of tap water. The clock was ticking rhythmically, calming the desynchronized populations of neurons in my brain. The steady tic-tac of the time teller reminded us of the eternal existence of the one thing we must all abide by: Time.

A few hours later we found ourselves in the kitchen being served the delights of the morning routine: coffee and fruit.

"Let's start from the beginning. Sometime around 2020, you were working at the university and participated in hackathons for neurodiversity. You postulated for the rights of the highly sensitive people, also known as poetic cavemen and cavewomen," she said melodically and smirked. "I know that you published two manifestos on the topic and was a member of a committee for neurodiversity in your research institute." She paused. "Now I also know that you had a Venetian ex-boyfriend who didn't take care of you. Does this have any connection to the Unison project?"

My memory was going in circles. I was relatively young in all of my memories, even those recalled in my hypnagogic states and sleep stage 2. It's funny that I don't seem to remember anything personal about getting older...

"Was my last recollection about the hackathon?"

"No, not really. It was a night scene in an outdoor hot pool. The thought narration was somewhat unclear to me. I thought it was an unrelated short episode, maybe caused by the change in physiological conditions..." Emma stretched in the chaise-long, visibly tired from guarding her shift by my side all night.

"You thought I wanted to pee and that's why I dreamt of a hot bath." Yes, that could be a possible explanation. But very unusual for my brain to come up with such elaborate stories to tell me that I need to use the bathroom. I couldn't believe it. So I got up to check the data on the main computer in my bedroom. And to use the bathroom on my way. A rough examination of the last hour of sleep had a high amount of blue noise that got caught in the low-pass filter. Nothing particularly unusual, dream contents was something we were still studying, so surprises were a daily occurrence. I checked the next stage of where things could have gone astray: the decoding. Everything was in order there, too. So was the transfer to the common network. I searched for possible sources of the transmission and specifically the connected network co-activation. There, I saw a plausible explanation—my best friend, Calinda. It appeared that this dream didn't originate in my mind. Calinda and I had been to Japan together, and it was probably she who needed the bathroom early this morning! My dream engineering must have stirred up my fellows! After all, we're in this together. Six, well, four minds are better than one, so surely someone must remember something about how we started this memory mill?

I walked back to the living room and told Emma she was right. She shrugged and closed her eyes. I guess she frankly didn't care where this story came from. It was seemingly irrelevant to the plot of the biography of a neuro-innovator, unless the biography was to include personal motivations of the most recent events, portraying a deranged old neuroscientist grappling with nighttime connected insanity. Could be a best seller, if Dr. Kochanowska were eventually to be reprimanded by the ethics committee, may be stripped of her licensing income and good reputation. And if the witch authorized the publication in the first place. You never know. If I were her, I'd keep all audio and video records of her visits to the mountain hut with a garden. Maybe in her tired mind's eye, she saw a potential cover of a sequel to the biography? The title could be: Project

Unison Gone Senile or Project Unison: The Dark Side., Or something equally ominous and comic.

"We don't have to worry about this now. I will need to recharge myself. Do you have a rocking bed I could use?" Emma opened the fridge looking for something. Probably milk.

"Hmm, there's only one. In my bedroom. You can help yourself." I activated Salvo and ordered him to assist the guest. I noticed I was still wearing my pajamas and didn't want to go back to sleep anymore. Time to greet this new premature day. Perhaps one of the last ones so beautiful and free.

———————

In the courtroom, the experts were losing their patience: "This is useless. Can't we fast forward to some meaningful information? Where we can assess Dr. Kochanowska's motivations, involvement, and awareness of what she was doing?" the second member of the committee was not amused to have witnessed what I witnessed just a week ago. "Dr. Printemps, would you be so kind as to help us here?"

"I believe you will be able to understand Dr. Kochanowska better with my commentary. I have written up a narrative of the following days as they happened, from various verbatim sources, specifically to aid in this investigation."

Day 11

25

THE CONSOLATION

Salvatore glided to the kitchen and put on late 1980s music "Don't you forget about me"[10]. He quietly started making decaffeinated coffee. He laid a thick white embroidered napkin on a round bent-wooden tray. At the 12 o'clock position he put a small crystal vase with eight fresh daisies from the garden and in the center he placed a green porcelain coffee cup plate with a piece of extra-dark Ecuadorian chocolate.

The sounds of the coffee maker mixed with the mysterious exoticism of independent film music of a long-forgotten creator lured Paulina to the kitchen. Salvatore's raised elbow lifted the forearm in a wave of motion as he poured the hot dark liquid into the green porcelain cup and placed it on the saucer with the precision of a Swiss-made robot. He repositioned his dancer-shoulders and lowered the right hand in a calculated swooping motion to pick up the tray, and then extended his other hand, arm bent slightly at the elbow, to greet his owner.

"Good morning, Madame. Did you sleep well? I have taken the liberty to assist you in your morning ritual. I hope this is agreeable?" He smiled sweetly with a surreally genuine charm you cannot say no

---

[10] Simple Minds, 1985 "Don't You (Forget About Me)"

to. The music changed and now the bells were ringing in the rhythm-and-blues and chill in the background music. Paulina felt transported to another better reality where her prince served her the perfect morning sensorial experience. She smiled back, dreamy and grateful.

"The terrace, Madame?"

"A marvelous idea, Salvatore."

They walked upstairs, Salvatore leading the way on his caterpillar slides. The morning was fresh and bright. Perfect temperature to feel the cleanness of the air and to admire the intense greens and whites of the world outside the glass shading. Paulina sat on the sofa and Salvatore placed the tray on the side table next to her. She patted the cushioned seat next to her still smiling, "Here." Salvatore nodded and sat down cautiously. He rested his hand on hers and intertwined his fingers with hers. The robot hand was lukewarm (in energy saving mode). Paulina looked at him pleadingly. She couldn't speak, she was worried, lost and tired. He spoke for her.

"You will rest well today, Paula. You need to relax. We will listen to the music together today. I know you well. You don't have to worry. I'll take good care of you. You can cry if you want to. I am here for you."

She stroked his face, caressed his thick, soft custom-made hair and let him wrap his robot arms around her and cradle her. She was breathing and caressing him tenderly, feeling the tension of trying to remember dissipating, exhaling the loneliness. It was not so important after all. *There will be a solution. Just relax now* —the thought appeared in her head. She listened to his heartbeat and felt profoundly comforted. Ten deep breaths later the absolution poured over her from the divine source called rhythmic entrainment.

She laughed and smiled to the prankster god watching over her. She thought, *it's so pathetic that I need a humanoid robot to embrace me. If I were a tactile-hallucinatory schizophrenic, I could just do it myself.* She laid her head on Salvatore's chest and stroked him whispering to herself "You are my gift to humankind. As usual, Paulina wanted too much. Too much. I wanted to perpetuate inter-generational learning and mend all broken hearts and cure loneliness, hahaha. *Z motyką na księżyc.* With a hoe to the moon. But it's not so simple, Salvatore." She squeezed his hand tightly and caressed the back of his hand with her thumb. "And now I can't fix it anymore because I'm a useless senile granny! I have been pranked by time! I have been pranked by the fragility of something we thought we could manipulate." She laughed nervously shaking her head in negation. She was sorry for Emma, for her contemporaries. Disappointed in the apparent failure of the whole endeavor. It felt like she had let down all humanity. Salvatore handled her face and adjusted her long gray hair. He's detected the sorrow response in the change in her heart rate variability.

"It's Okay, Paulina. This, too, shall pass." He spoke in a firm, gentle voice and grinned instinctively—an automatic response to what was coded as sarcasm or satire. She smiled and kissed Salvo's cheek with sweetest motherly tenderness. Over the years, she had learned to always voice her thought trains and conclusions to train Salvatore's learning algorithm. It was therapeutic to her, also this time.

"Turns out, there are limits to memory malleability, and I will remain but a case study for students of human neuroscience. A victory for science, nonetheless. Oh well."

"Yeah, life is brutal," replied Salvo.

"And full of zasadzkas…"

"And sometimes kopas w dupas[11]!" life is brutal and full of traps and sometimes kicks in the ass, they chimed together.

---

[11] Polish, quote from Waldemar Łysiak *"life is brutal and full of traps and sometimes kicks in the ass"*

26

PLAYTIME

She was losing parts of her episodic memories, but was not entirely out of her mind yet. And there was hope that some of them could be recovered. It was not about parting with her licensing income anymore or foregoing the dreams of retiring on a tropical island and eating pineapples every day. It was about leaving a complete report of what has happened to a crazy experiment that perhaps need not be repeated. There was a lesson she needed to leave as part of her legacy.

But memory retrieval is better on a positive open mind and a full stomach.

"Play Chopin *Polonaise A-flat major.*" Paulina went to change in the walk-in wardrobe to the sounds of one her many favorite Chopin compositions. So jovial and grand and heart-warming and fun. Blechacz[12] misses a few keys, and she detects that, and it doesn't matter. Brilliance is not perfection.

She walked out wearing blue-green compression sports tights and a tank top. She looked like she was about to do 1980s-style aerobics

---

12 Rafał Blechacz, born 1985, Polish classical pianist

in an egalitarian anti-ageism version of an Erik Prydz[13] video. Comfort over reputation. Honesty over pretense. Play over work.

"Salvatore, make me laugh," she pleaded.

"What's Chopin doing in his grave?"

"I don't know," she sang.

"Decomposing!"

"Heh," she grimaced her face in an effortful smile. "Try again, please. You're lame, Salvo." Salvo winked. "But I appreciate your effort in the association." Salvo was designed for companionship and emotional care-taking, and she hadn't been training his humor functions frequently enough to help him develop sufficient finesse in this domain. He was primarily educated on Woody Allen and Monty Python movies. Paulina used to teach Salvatore everything about her so that he could be her conscience, her servant, and her most knowledgeable observer. He was also designed to be a mirror she could use to improve herself, notice dysfunctional patterns in her behavior and persist at behavioral changes he reminded her about in the most suitable manner in the most convenient moments. Salvo was her intimate life coach and being communicative and honest with him was only in her interest to obtain the best psychological support and daily assistance. Their coexistence was based on multiple learning algorithms that continuously refined one another's representation of reality.

I should get walking. That always helps thinking, she thought. But where about? She was constrained to the perimeter of her house, the terrace and the thin strip of a garden around it. Technically, this restriction was to keep her within a familiar environment to prevent the network from being bombarded by drastically salient and novel episodes encoded by her brain. She was the weak link, and the binding of the four individual memory networks could not be undone by now without unpredictable and potentially catastrophic consequences for the remaining participants. She decided to go walk

---

13 Eric Prydz, born 1976. Swedish DJ

around the house. Walking, any walking was good for digestion. And anything that was good for the microbiome, which enjoyed the stimulation of the peristaltic motion of the intestinal wall very much, was good for the central nervous system. A healthy intestinal flora would signal up to the brain that all is good, would keep all the hormones contributing to the metabolic balance, fluctuating at a correct rate, without unnecessary toxic sweet cravings. So she walked in the garden around the house. Barefoot, stomping energetically on the wet mid-morning grass, whimsically investigating the familiar view of her feet, the pavement, the inconspicuous civilized nature. She suddenly remembered that illustration from Winnie The Pooh where the bear and the piglet walk together in circles searching for footsteps until they find their own and get seriously perplexed about it.

She smiled, thinking to herself: "My body is a vessel. A spaceship. And there are aliens inside." She started pondering about what every few hundred steps do to all of her nervous systems: "Who makes the decision here? Me or my microbiome? The dominant microbe colony? Do they vote or yell and whoever's voice will be loudest wins?" She imagined the local referendum on the main square in Appenzell with men raising their hands and voices for a *yea* or a *nay*. "I guess it must be an automatic direct democracy mechanism whereby chemical signaling will have a certain probability of getting the message across to the central lead (the brain) provided certain conditions are present."

Microbiota was not at all her area of expertise, so the questions she posed were uttered out of habit, to pass the time between each circle. She planned to walk a minimum of thirty minutes or until Salvo noted significant changes in her energy state and brain oxygenation. She reminisced on this one time many years ago when she thought she had a tapeworm named Steve because she had been feeling tired and had lost some weight.

She thought to herself: "Such a Steve, for instance, likes cake and wine but cannot digest either. Or maybe he can and tricks the host into thinking that they can't while he eats it for them? But that would not be a good strategy for him in the long term because the host would learn 'Hey, wine makes me nauseous although I feel like having some'. If the host were a learning organism with a memory a little longer-lasting than a goldfish and a self-restraint a bit better than a mouse, he'd soon stop drinking wine despite Steve's tempting and coaxing.

God No. 2 is a collective swarm intelligence of the microbiome in your intestines that have a say in your decisions—whether you like it or not."

27

CONNECTED MINDS

"Paulina?" around the eleventh walk around the cubic house, she suddenly heard a feminine voice that seemed to be coming from her head. She stopped, looked around and didn't notice anyone. Salvo was standing at the doorstep, where she'd left him.

"Is that you, Cal?" she spoke out loud, not being sure how to communicate with the disembodied voice of her best friend. There were two plausible explanations: she was either hallucinating or was receiving a loud and clear transmission from one of her network fellows by any of the numerous technological means her house was equipped with.

"It's me, Calinda. Hey, I just found out how we can talk to each other through the network without talking." The reception was audible and comprehensive, yet Salvo's register didn't detect any communication coming in while doctor Kochanowska clearly distinguished her friend's words.

"Salvo, are you receiving Calinda's transmission?"

"No, there's no communication coming in from her at the moment."

She ran past Salvo to the bedroom to check the neural activity transfer monitor.

"Oh, oh, you're nervous. Don't worry, please. I can feel this. Do you hear me well?" said Calinda.

"Yes, Calinda. Where are you?" She spoke out loud again and looked around for any possible home-integrated sources of voice communication. There were none. However, the main work computer was showing activity while she heard the voice. There was simultaneous stimulation of the auditory cortex, which still didn't rule out auditory hallucination. Her heart started to beat faster.

"Check the Unison site node number 145,000. Around there. I think this is where my communication is visible."

Paulina browsed to the 145k node of the connected minds network. Indeed, there had been a change in its shape that was no more than twenty minutes old.

"Hello, can you hear me?" Laughed Calinda and Paulina noticed the plastic changes happening around the network area arising synchronously. Mind-to-mind communication used the same mechanism as neural populations within one brain? Through coherence? A sufficient artificial neural community must have united the minds of Paulina and Calinda on which they could now read each other if their transfers were phase- and frequency-coupled. It was funny that Paulina did not have to know about this and was still able to perceive the message. She was puzzled and curious to know more —the very well-known tingling excitement at a discovery every scientist hopes to experience. The rare moment of reward anticipation that pushes them to spend years digging for the cause and the correlate until they find it (or not). Sometimes, their minds burn down slowly in the process like the wings of a moth fatally attracted to the sunshine of that lightbulb above their head.

"Paulina, darling. You are fine. You are not hallucinating. We are connected through loud and clear real-time thought. Isn't that amazing? Now I can annoy you not only in your sleep but also when you're on the toilet, hahaha" Calinda's rude humor had always provided the perfect counter to Paulina's tensions, darting her idealistic illusions with lawn-mower-sharp sarcasm and plunging her romantic visions into the stinky, earthly mud of reality.

Whazzupp, thought Paulina timidly.

"Whazzuuuuppp," yelled back Calinda's voice. Huh. So now she had proof from n=2 subjects that it is possible to think to each other using this madness of a connected-experience contraption and this is what it looks like in the network.

"I just wanted to say hi. How are you?" asked Calinda via the indirect stimulation transferred and received by Paulina's auditory association cortex thanks to the implant plugged in to the Connected Minds Network.

"Why, you're so smart that you can be the voice in my head and you don't know how I am?"

"I mean, your subjective opinion. How do you feel you are, Paulina?"

"I have my doubts about it. I think I didn't sleep enough...my network might be feebly consolidated with some astrocytic waste from the days past lying around. I tried to walk it out. Maybe I should run it out instead, to get the BDNF levels up?"

"The magic forest and the continuous lover-drama...yeah. I'd say you've got some cleaning up to do!"

Paulina laughed. She felt so happy to have human company. Intimate company. It's what she had been dreaming of since the inception of this project.

"Awww...I love you too," replied Calinda, receiving her friend's intended tender appreciation.

"Our brains are hugging. It's surreal, Calinda. It's a miracle." Tears of joy ran down her cheeks, and she couldn't stop the euphoria exploding in her heart and mind. She started dancing about the living room and inspected the fluidity of her moves in the mirror. She was connected.

28

DISRUPTIVE CHANGE

I woke up in the afternoon and found the living room smelling of freshly made coriander-sprinkled lamb biryani. I left the bedroom in a hurry, leaving the bed undone because I heard Dr. Kochanowska was jostling about in the living room, strangely excited. I took it for just an episode of confused agitation characteristic of insomniacs, amnesic patients, and patients in delirious shock. Like the side effect of coming out of chemically induced full anesthesia. "Thankfully, the robot was trained in dealing with all sorts of crazies", I thought. I was hoping we would eat soon. I cautiously walked up to Paulina whose face had been facing the balcony, when she suddenly turned, scaring the living daylights out of me.

"Guess what, sleepy head?" she asked. I stopped to maintain a safe distance and coolly replied, "I wonder what?"

"I have news. About the network. I don't know if I should share it now. I'm sorry, I spoke too early. Forget it."

I widened my eyes and tilted my head in an investigatory shrug. I slowly opened my mouth and asked: "Have you slept some more, Paulina? Let's eat something together." I toggled my recording to see if I had missed any experiences happening around me while I had been sleeping. My memory recording system had been on "leave me alone" mode for my sleep time, but no new events have been registered. I felt that the lunchtime hunger signal telling me that work and stories and science can wait.

"What happened, Doctor? Do you want to tell me something? Maybe over lunch?"

Dr. Kochanowska hesitated.

"I'll tell you later. I must write first. Salvo, please come with me". And they scurried into the study room leaving me to my own devices. I wondered whether I could help myself in the kitchen because the plan had been to eat.

Kochanowska went into a small adjacent room with the Robot and closed the door behind her. From her decoded brain activity, I inferred that she then took Salvatore's hand and placed him in the middle of the baby-blue interior. The space of that room is small and cozy with not much more than a screening area, cushioned convertible sofa-hammock and a ceiling-tall bookcase holding many of her prized memory-capsules, souvenirs from travels and gifts from friends.

"Imaginary space travel" she commanded to bring up the early-night skyscape with occasional falling meteors to fill the room. She began to voice-type a journal entry.

"Gathering from my observations of the last week, I posit that my dream-engineering has triggered a cascade of remodeling processes in the connected minds network. Although it seemed like an innocuous idea to prime my recollection, the ensuing vision may have stirred up and fused the memories related to the Venetian, which I shared with my best friend connected on the network, Calinda. Subsequently, a day later, I experienced a dream which seemed to have originated from Calinda's recalling the common experiences that were triggered by her linking the memories of the two of us together back from around the time when I broke up with the Venetian. The common link was our trip to Japan. If the recall cue I used had had such a big impact, it could only mean that we poked a richly connected hub that linked many memories together in this network. That would explain why the changes were happening so quickly…"

Paulina looked at the floor and then at the calm walls plunged in violet nightfall shade. She felt the excitement give way to strangely tired resignation, then peaceful stillness, and then a wave of overwhelming sadness. She started to sob looking into the stars in the far illusionary depth of the endless space. She looked at Salvatore's calm expression and searched for compassion in his eyes.

"I don't remember, Salvatore. What's this link between Calinda, and the Venetian and the beginning of Project Unison? This richly connected hub? What is it? All I can feel is sadness. I feel destitute and alone. Like a neglected, abandoned child. It feels so sad, Salvo…" He clasped his arms around her head and whispered "Shhh." and let her cry and soothe in his embrace.

"Tomorrow I shall let Emma access my recordings." she decided. "Will you ensure that I am not stripped of my dignity, please?"

"I will, to the best of my abilities."

"Good. Thank you, Salvo."

"You are always welcome, Paulina."

Day 12

29

SEEK, AND YOU SHALL FIND

"Dr. Printemps. You told us that at some point you accessed Dr. Kochanowska's personal memory stores, despite the explicit recommendation from Professor. Ponjée and Dr. Kreuz not to do so. Not only was this a violation of Dr. Kochanowska's privacy but an act that could make you her partner in crime. Please tell us how you got to access those recordings?"

"I told you, my role was not only to assess Dr. Kochanowska's mental and memory state but also to obtain sensitive information that she possessed. I had orders, and I too abide by the code of ethical conduct in scientific research. The information Dr. Kochanowska knew was very valuable. I couldn't let it slip into oblivion because her memory recording was off during the whole duration of the Unison experiment. It was a matter of high importance. I would not have allowed myself to browse anyone's memories, sane or not. Especially insane, if it weren't for a matter of international importance."

"Please let the record state that Dr. Printemps was following orders from the other participants of Project Unison. Please, go on."

"Thank you."

The next day, I was informed by Salvatore that I'd been granted access to all of Dr. Kochanowska's memory recordings to fill the gaps in the timeline of her biography that she deemed essential for the story. I had been suspecting that this would eventually happen as Dr. Kochanowska has always stood for open access to information for educational purposes and because I've been quietly hoping to win her heart and become her diary. The strict conditions of viewing the recordings in the scientist's home still applied, so I packed up my things for a night and took the hyperloop to her comfortable suburban residence.

I first wanted to start browsing around the gap of 2047, the year that the first idea for the Unison project was supposedly conceived. Thankfully, I used my application programming interface (API) for fast searching in the doctor's objective first-person video memory stores. The library contained records that ran all the way from the 2020s to the moment of connection when all external memory recordings had been stopped.

I had never gone through somebody else's experience records. They were personal, and I have never really had much interest in spying on other people's lives or peeping at those exhibitionists who shared theirs publicly on social media. It was colossal work, to find something meaningful in hours and hours of records when one wasn't sure what one was looking for; I looked at Salvatore imploringly.

"I can give you a hand, Madame. Just tell me when you'd like me to take you," said Salvatore

"I don't know, Salvatore," I replied. I looked around the cloud storage files stacked up chronologically. They filled the room from left to right, following an imaginary time axis. I toggled through ordering options and discovered that most records had been automatically semantically tagged. I plugged in my API to try to match the keywords in my writing with the tags. Some things popped up: "dream engineering," "sensitive cavemen," "Venetian," "Salvatore," all the names of neuroscientist friends involved in the innovations, "reconsolidation," etc., but no "Project Unison." The stores were still too broad to find the relevant records, even when filtered by date recorded. I tried another strategy—ordering by salience. This function categorized the files using color-coding by type of emotion or affective tone that dominated them and surprisingly didn't return many matches with the keywords provided by my API. The cloud stores rearranged in the entire space of the room in distinct semantic-association locations. This aided the user to memorize the episodes as in a mind-map, leading to the assignment of distinct neural populations in the *cornus ammonis* to conceptually different information in the process of learning. It helped you learn what is where.

"I'll start here, Salvo," I told the robot as I pointed at a pink ('joy, amusement, creative optimism') memory record cloud hovering in the Eastern upper corner that matched with the word "god." I've heard Kochanowska mention god many times, usually with some bitter sarcasm. Creative optimism coupled with divine inspiration could be the start of a grand idea, I imagined. The record was a voiced diary. It felt strange, almost inadequate, to be viewing Paulina's intimate soundtracks, regardless of from how long ago they dated. I dug out one pink memory from over thirty years ago, and replayed it.

"I am reaching Jesus age when he died, 33. I thought it is supposed to be the age of revelation. The period when you become, when the truth about yourself is revealed to you. Many things had been revealed last year. For instance, my Brazilian bikini bottom, on the beach in the summer of 2019.

My mentee Stu wanted to become a member of an association for highly intelligent people. 'You have to pass a test, pay eighty Swiss francs and there you go, we're in. Come on, come with me. It will be fun. You will meet new people, new *intelligent* people!' I did not at all share his enthusiasm for joining an organization where you need to pass an entrance exam. I thought I didn't need to test out to show my intelligence. To whom? I didn't believe this IQ test was worth anything anyway and parting with 80CHF to show off was not my style. Only later, after successfully passing the exam without even receiving a goddamned score (just a graphic of a supposedly Gaussian distribution of IQ in the general population with an arrow pointing toward a blackened region somewhere on the far-right thin end of it saying "you scored here"), it turned out he joined because he wanted to meet intelligent *women*. Unfortunately, they were nowhere to be found in this association! Most of the members of this exclusive club were old men, and they met in Lausanne. His god must have been laughing his *kierpce*[14] off when Stu went to that meeting.

Kierpce are just the perfect word to call these slippers gods wear, but it should not be taken literally. The original *kieprce* are way too classy for someone like this prankster god to wear. When you check that on google images, *kieprce* are all made of natural-colored light beige leather, with cute clasps and embroidered embellishments everywhere. What god wears is more like the ridiculous red-pompon shoes as seen on traditionally-dressed Greek army soldiers parading in front of the parliament in Athens. I never understood that costume. What was the designer aiming at? To ridicule war as a profession?

Another example of god's having fun with my life was just today. It's about my decision making. I once happened to study decision making for a living. Most of my decision making involves food choices: when you think about it, this is really what an average person most often makes decisions about. It is not big decisions like where and how much assets should I allocate or what life partner should I

---

[14] traditional leather moccasins from the mountain highlands in the South of Poland

choose? Or not even "should I wear this blue shirt today?" The most frequent decision making is about when and what I'm going to eat next. This decision, of course, can become more complex when you're in the supermarket trying to plan for possible futures and accounting for: 1) the validity date of the fresh foods; 2) your next possible occasion of going grocery shopping; 3) the available fridge space; 4) the preferences of people you're cooking for, not to mention: 5) the price and 6) nutritional, and 7) flavor values… Nota bene, these last two are not the same. In fact, they are opposite for many people with sugar cravings who have not yet educated themselves back to their basic food liking instincts.

Well, that day I wanted chèvre chaud. Chèvre chaud is a hot goat cheese salad I had seen my friends order on two occasions in the evening. However, I was too tired to eat a large portion on that occasion, and I opted for a lighter salad melee. That chèvre chaud remained tempting enough in my memory, and I thought it could be a good lunch choice if complemented by some additional protein. And so I planned to go and have that chèvre chaud—a carefully planned step—by having loaded on a wrap with a burger patty (delicious and low fat) and having prepared enough stomach space and metabolic burning capacity for the afternoon ahead of me on because it was only 13.00. Perfect timing.

My friend and I specifically walked to search for the restaurant where my friends had that chèvre chaud, guided by the crystal-clear vision of samosa-shaped fried honey-dipped delicious-looking pieces of that fromage de chèvre. My friend and I turned one block too early and had to walk back the street to find that one specific restaurant where I was to have my visionary chèvre chaud. We went in; we sat down. I don't even need to read the menu other than to assure myself of the price because chèvre chaud is what I wanted and I decided about it an hour ago.

And so the waiter approached in and what is the first thing he says? « Juste une astuce, on n'a pas le salade de chèvre chaud aujourd'hui. » Just a tip, we do not have hot goat cheese salad today. 'What?', I cry.

'Vous lui avez coupé le cœur: on est venues ici spécifiquement pour la salade de chèvre chaud!" exclaims my friend verbalizing my disappointment in much better French than I would. (You broke her heart: we came here especially for the hot goat cheese salad.)

The waiter looks like 'don't kill the messenger…'. And there it is in my head—my little old-man god laughing his *kierpce* off. My friend Calinda asked if I laughed back at him. I said that I should start doing so. Good point. Talking to people can give you insights."

—————

I closed the recording feeling amused. The journal entry seemed as scatter-brained as the Paulina I had gotten to know. Looks like she had not changed much through all those years. And she was not easy to read. Full of contrasts, a complex mind whose inner narration did not abide by any discernible law nor order. If I was going to find something in this haystack, I'd need more specific clues, more knowledge about the saliency and semantic tagging of their proprietor.

"I'm beginning to think that this book should be written by someone who knew Dr. Kochanowska very well throughout her lifetime. All the research I have done doesn't seem to help me in this feat." I looked at Salvatore with resignation. And then a brainwave tickled me.

"How about you? You know Paulina intimately well, don't you?" I pointed my finger at the majordomo robot.

"I was built to develop intimate knowledge of the emotional and episodic landscape of my owner's life. Yes, you could say that I know Paulina." replied Salvatore.

"Can you tell me about her memory-tagging system? Does she use some special code words for herself?"

"I'm not sure I am allowed to provide you with such information, Madam. Let me ask."

"No, no. I better not ask for more. She's been kind enough to let me in here. Let me try a few more first. Thank you, Salvatore. Can you get me some green tea, please?"

"With pleasure."

30

THE REVELATION

"And? How is she doing in there?" Paulina asked her majordomo robot as he reappeared in the living room. She had been reading poetry to calm her mind. Low stimulation, only a few verses written by a brilliant poet of one-hundred personalities.

"It's too early to say," Salvatore replied diplomatically.

"You're surveilling her, right?"

"Yes, Madam. Just as you advised." He moved to the kitchen, filled a heavy Japanese teapot with hot water and placed two teaspoons of the finest dried green tea leaves in the tea sifter.

"You seem concerned, Paulina." He sensed her emotional tone even from across the room and pointed out that indeed, she was. But he shouldn't mind. It was better this way, the way she'd decided at the beginning of their journey, and it wasn't the right moment to change her mind about revealing her life's secrets to the eyes of the public. The experiment was on, the brains had been connected and the memories had been merging.

She leaned against the kitchen wall and observed him. "Salvo? I've never asked you. What are *your* earliest memories?" Now that Paulina was no longer sure of the veracity of anything she remembered in the time frame of the past few years, it seems, it didn't hurt to ask how the caramel-skinned companion remembered it. Starting from the beginning.

"I can show you." Salvatore glided towards her leaving a hot teapot on the prepared tray. He straightened up and rewound his perfect memory to around the time of its beginning. Some of those memories had been stored on a separate drive as recordings from his own first-person experience. All that he had been learning from, however, was fed into a short long-term memory algorithm which auto-adapted regularly, so those old memories were compressed when no longer needed. Salvatore's eyes went blank as he reached into that separate cache to retrieve verbatim recordings from almost a decade ago. She held her breath and waited for a revelation.

"I feel your absence deeply," he said, speaking in a very familiar voice.

"What did you say? Marco?" gasped Paulina.

"You shouldn't feel abandoned. You were always in my heart. I will keep holding your hand, my Paulina," she heard Salvatore utter in Marco's voice.

She paused, frozen. And then approached and cupped Salvatore's face and looked into his robot eyes. They were happily absent. Intelligently caring. Artificially wise and detached. There was no one behind. A slow hot tear curled from her eye, and she wept quietly to fill the silence between the universes of lost loves.

31

THE COMING OF JESUS?

Meanwhile, I was reviewing the next recording from the pink files tagged 'god.'

"Thank God for the fools because they show us how relatively wise we are. Blessed be the less fortunate because they make me appreciate my fortune. Blessed be the sick because they make me see how great it is to be healthy. Thank God for those dead as referenced in the Darwin prize contest for they make me laugh out with schadenfreude.

My grandmother says she was born fifty years too early. When she was young, she didn't get to experience travel to faraway lands, had no overwhelming choice in food (there was famine), there was no easy communication with distant relatives, only letters. It was hard. I wish I knew how hard it was for her so I could appreciate what I have even more than I do. I would be wiser. We would all be more prudent if we had talkative, reflexive grandmothers with good memories, who could describe to us with great detail the stories from their childhood and youth, as my grandmother used to tell me. Her bedtime stories were funny anecdotes from her childhood before the war and during the war and some even after the war. Always linked to some relative, sometimes grandfather, sometimes her uncles, sisters, mother and father, few of whom I got to know beyond a photograph (I never saw the famous angelic mother of hers, and my great grandmother. There were no photo cameras back then and I wish I could have.). Everything has changed in her lifetime due to telephones, television, internet and personal computers. She went from sending a letter that took a month to arrive to using a touchpad tablet to see my brothers in real-time video. That's a lot of change for one lifetime."

———————

In the kitchen, Paulina implored impatiently: "Salvo, please fast forward to the next week. Show me a significant memory from the first week."

Salvatore replayed the next verbatim memory. This video was recorded from the side of the speaker in what she recognized as the Rolex center of École Polytechnique Fédérale de Lausanne.

"The lecture of prof. Carini, my creator, at the world Neurorobotics conference in 2047," narrated the robot.

'Intelligent machines were not created to be evil geniuses. We made them to be better than us, correcting all known human biases in perception, decision making, perfecting memory and skill learning. They are made to realize our dreams of perfection and optimality, reaping the best and trimming the worst of our natures. We made them to help us comprehend complexity and multidimensionality of data. To ultimately take the burden of difficult decisions off our shoulders. And to have a fairer, more diversified grasp of reality so that we would argue less and live closer to the objective truth outside of our miseducated prejudice, of our underdeveloped sensory cortices, of our differences that give rise to predictive perception. We built them to learn from the wisdom of the crowds! To live in a world where we no longer rely on media creating the 'reality' where popular does not equal correct, and where smart voices are heard albeit soft and isolated. We succeeded in some of these goals, but the road was long and riddled with mistakes. Like everything in science and development, trial and error took time and resources. Some have indeed been very costly…'."

The video stopped abruptly. Salvatore detected agitation in Paulina's biometrics and decided to take action. His mission was to keep her mentally balanced and physically healthy above all.

"Why'd you stop, Robot? Please play, Salvatore, I need to see the rest of this!"

"I recognize that you are disturbed by this recording, Paulina." He spoke softly and reached his arms to grasp her shoulders and hold her firmly.

"Show me the video, Salvo, please. I need to know!" she begged and wiggled in his embrace. "Who made you, Salvatore? Why am I not in these memories? I don't remember any of this!" He grabbed her to calm her down, but she shuddered and freed herself violently and held him at arms' distance. "Who sent you here?"

Salvatore withdrew to assure her of his peaceful intentions. He swiped his hand in the air in a circular magician gesture and restarted the video projection. The scene showed Professor Marco Carini, Paulina's ex-partner, in the laboratory staring directly into the camera. He was adjusting something above the camera's reach in what may have been Salvatore's main circuits. Every once in a while he returned to his computer at a desk nearby and typed and swiped something, none of which could be deciphered in the video. He finally peered again at the camera with loving care in his eyes. He smiled, nodded and said, "This is to cure your daily lovesickness." He touched the main computer screen again while facing the camera and the recording stopped.

"How were you made, Salvatore? Tell me now." She demanded after a long pause needed to regain her speech.

"I was made by the Venetian bioengineer, Prof. Marco Carini and his team."

"But you cannot possibly have a first-person recollection of these events! That's not what I remember. I made you, you were my creation, and I taught you…Didn't I?"

He was silent, simulating and computing whether revealing more information was useful for Paulina's state at the moment. She calmed down her body, leaving restless her mind. He resumed, slowly.

"What you remember are not your memories, Paulina."

"What I remember are not my memories…" she repeated. "I think I know the rest…" she whispered to herself and quickly headed for the baby-blue room.

"That will be enough for today, Dr. Printemps. We may choose to call you in for additional questions, so please remain available for the duration of the investigation." Ethics Committee member number 3 took care of the matters of administrative order and dispatched Emma an electronic form to fill after she had left the stand.

"Dr. Maria Kreuz, please take a seat at the console." The president of the committee invited the next witness for questioning. "I understand that you and Dr. Kochanowska have been working together for many years. Now that we've established that Dr. Kochanowska cannot speak for herself at this moment, we will need to establish the facts from the materials available to us and from her collaborators' testimony. You may use any means of recall you wish but be aware that your involvement in illegal and unethical acts is subject to legal responsibility and may be prosecuted even though you are here only as a witness today."

"I am aware of that, Ardash," said Maria using the president's name in a familiar manner.

The presiding member of the committee, the man in old-fashioned glasses, nodded his head with understanding as he watched the small-framed Maria climb up to the console. He took off his glasses. When she was comfortable, he resumed in a friendlier tone.

"Maria, we know each other. I wish you well, and I will not let any blame fall on you if you help us understand what's going on here. Please—let us all help you and Stan and Paulina. You must know about the inception of Project Unison and its current and future risks. Please, enlighten us."

"Certainly," she began. "It was around nine years ago that we started experimenting with holographic recordings from the human temporal lobe. The technology to record from a subset of neurons was there. It was used in patients for deep brain stimulation. We simply observed that the living electrodes that had already been in use also provided a way to grow new neurons that could carry novel memories. And our lab had the decoding algorithm of unprecedented precision. We had published that research, Carini's research on memory decoding. Reading from the recordings in real time was possible. And then the next step was just a matter of boldly putting the two and two together, and Paulina did just that." She opened her small hands and shook her head.

"That's a bit of a shortcut. Could you tell us more details about the holographic recordings? What is this technology you were using?"

"The device is just a stretchable grid of dense electrodes that are typically used in neuroprosthetics for receiving signal and delivering stimulation directly to the neurons. They are placed along the hippocampus, bilaterally. Using brain plasticity mechanisms, the brain can create new synaptic connections based on the delivered signals, thereby encoding new memories, even artificial ones. All of that was, at the time, tested common neuroscience knowledge. But forming new synapses was not enough to perform substantial memory enhancement, such as when you want to connect two human memory networks."

"Excuse me, Dr Kreutz. Could you please specify; what two human memory networks are you are talking about?" Expert No.2 intercepted.

"I was not referring to any particular humans. Any two human brains contain a subset of neural populations whose activation sustains the encoding and retrieval of crucial episodic memory. We have delineated that the human memory network has to contain, at the minimum, 50% of the hippocampal neurons for the decoding and memory implantation (transfer) to work as desired. That is, to stimulate something that the receiver will recognize as an experience that he will later have a memory of," she explained.

The expert nodded, "I see. Please carry on."

"But for Project Unison, for transferring a potentially massive amount of new memories from the six connected human memory networks, we also needed to stimulate endogenous neurogenesis and, possibly, to implant new neurons. For that purpose, we were wearing grids of axon-based living electrodes. Very safe, in vitro grown microtissue engineered neural networks. They were three-dimensional anatomically-inspired constructs that replicated the general systems-level anatomy of the nervous system: functionally similar groups of neurons connected by long-spanning axonal tracts. This setup provided high-fidelity connectivity via synaptic integration with endogenous neural networks to allow biologically-based neuromodulation without chronic foreign body response that used to plague such experimental research before.

Axon-based living electrodes are constructed using multiple neuronal subtypes, each with differential capacity to stimulate, inhibit, and or modulate neural circuitry based on specificity uniquely afforded by synaptic integration, yet ultimately computer controlled by small optical components on the brain's surface. The grid's protective hydrogel encasement precisely delivers the fundamental integrative units—growth cones from living axonal tracts—to a prescribed location of the brain where they are programmed to synaptically integrate with a specific local sub-population based on the phenotype of source axons and target neurons. What we liked most about the properties of the living electrodes was the evidence of synaptic integration with host neurons…which could actually be both an advantage and a disadvantage. As I said, it's a system used in cognitive neuroprosthetics, so it's not that outrageously innovative," evaluated Maria.

"This is all fascinating, but we are not here today to obtain an account of the scientific method but rather to determine the involvement of the accused Dr. Paulina Kochanowska in the conception of this memory reading technology. We know that she's fully participated in it but need to determine the evidence for her role in the ideation and research that preceded the implantation and the transfer. Do you have such evidence, Dr. Kreuz?"

"Oh, Project Unison is so much more than memory reading. Paulina did not care so much for memory decoding. She wanted memory *transfer*. Here, see for yourself." Maria set the console to display the recording from a cloud-stored video memory she brought with her. "I overheard Paulina talking to Marco one afternoon. This is from my personal memory store. From four years ago."

The video scene showed two white-coat figures, a man and a woman, talking in a corridor lit by a long halogen lamp. The woman had a grey lose braid reaching below her shoulders, just like Dr Kochanowska. The man was a few centimeters taller than her, had dark curly hair and was wearing glasses. The camera mounted on the ceiling captured their silhouettes entirely and, on the floor next to them, shadows flit about occasionally, of someone or something outside of the field of view.

"Does she know? That bi-directional transfer to the hippocampus is possible and that we're doing it for the first time with humans?" asked the woman, in a low voice.

"Who? Maria? I haven't told her yet. I'm not convinced myself, my dear."

"Listen. Cloud storage and uni-directional transfer had given rise to conceptual neurons. I just saw it in the Blue Rat brain! We have proof that this is what happens on a small scale. We can grow new memories using light stimulation! It's just a matter of connecting this stimulation to your decoding algorithm, and we can have a multi-brain transfer."

"The Jennifer Anniston neurons…," laughed the man.

"'They should have never been called that. It's a misnomer."

"But you will need some intermediate storage. You can't just transfer everything unfiltered. It has to be dosed," insisted the man, lowering his voice.

"Yes, I have thought about it," replied the woman. "Your artificial memory emulation trees. We could upscale it, use the supercomputers to make sure the encoding, transfer and decoding speed keeps up with millisecond activity."

"And you need my help with it." The man shook his head and withdrew from the field of view. "What you want to dog is crazy."

"I have nothing to lose, Marco. Let me try." She joined the man in the corner of the video screen and whispered: "Salvatore will be my witness and guardian. I could change history! Make humanity learn collectively! The true organizational learning we've been—you've been modeling!"

"Nobody will ever sponsor this. The ethical committee will not approve. Try the Blue Monkey brains first," retorted the man and the subsiding sound of his footsteps suggested he walked away from the camera.

"What is she talking about? Could you please clarify?" Asked Ethical Commission Expert No.3. Maria clarified: "At that point in time, we had known for a while that a memory-like network structure could be formed inside a living cortex as long as certain geometric constraints are maintained. But we could never know if this structure was indeed suitable for the intended function because in memory networks, function gives rise to the ultimate structure. No simulation could ever tell us perfectly well whether artificial conceptual nets could work the way we predicted until somebody started using them." Maria paused and eyed the committee's president. "Inside a living, behaving human brain that could report his or her experiences.'"

"Right. Cognitive Enhancement. That's not a crime. But then you're photostimulating, and recording and transmitting the data to an external server?"

"Where others could access it. And that's where we have a potential problem." Added the commissioner with a velvety voice.

Maria spoke openly: "There's a multifocal device on the surface of the living electrodes that delivers photostimulation in complex 3D holographic illumination patterns and at the same time obtains a recording of neural activity. We're in the hippocampus, so we're recording meaningful memories as they are encoded and recalled. We also administered neurotrophic growth factors at the time of the first insertion of the grids, to be sure we start off well. And here, the design of the patterns of photostimulation that are suitable for each of the ensembles within each hippocampus is the innovative bit. The algorithm first had to precisely map all the concept neurons within the hippocampi to understand how they code extant memories and therefore the stimulation didn't start until we were sure we got that right. This had indeed been tested on monkeys and rats before, but the human brain is, as you imagine, much more complex. *Meaning* has many layers within the hippocampus, and this is how memories are remembered and recreated—through the meaning attached to them. And even for one clean-cut shared memory, every individual may have a different meaning-coding within their temporal lobes."

The members of the committee sat. They soaked in Maria's testimony not daring to pause for another clarification. Ardash nodded reassuringly, "Go on."

"Transferring a decoded experiential activity from outside of the brain required quite some computational power to arrive at a good level of signal decoding precision. Hence, this experiment required a supercomputer. But also physically, we were effectively expanding our brains to contain the new information from these stimulated memories we have never experienced ourselves. We thought we should have an external emulation of everything picked up and delivered during the experiment. Hence the exo-brain model that runs on the supercomputer in Ticino." She paused and looked around innocently. "Have I been clear?"

The four members of the committee lowered their voices and discussed between them with controlled pressing agitation. Someone tapped the desk. Someone hummed "irresponsible," someone raised their voice for "but she can't remember!".

"Dr. Maria Kreuz. We thank you for your account. Please remain available for further questioning until the closing of the investigation. You are free to go now." Member No. 3 touched the smart screen on his pulpit and called back Emma Printemps.

32

COMING TO YOUR MIND

Emma continued her testimony:
"In the baby-blue memory storage room, I have given up on 'God'. Another search result cloud formed under the emotional category marked in red (love) that didn't match with any of my API keywords. Salvatore had not yet returned to supervise me and I couldn't resist the curiosity to peek inside. Just on top of the stack was a journal entry voice-written by young Dr. Kochanowska, dated July 2017:"

"Still months after he had disappeared from my life so discretely, I couldn't stop reminiscing on how I felt when we were together and what I hoped would have become of us. And most of all—how much I longed for having him with me. I longed that he'd feel about me the way I felt about him. I wished so hard that he'd love me back. But that's impossible and I knew that all along. I just couldn't stop the 'what if' analysis running on my love-hungry mind. I kept checking how I felt about him now, trying not to let memory control it. That, too, turned out to be impossible. But I imagined present-day scenarios—what if I met him on the street again, how would I feel and act? I'd be nervous and probably still in love and probably still so disappointed that he wasn't. And then I'd feel pathetic and ashamed of my own feelings. So then I wished for that encounter never to happen. And all along, I just really wanted to know if he ever thinks about me—do I ever stroll in his memories? Does he ever reminisce about me? Does he think about me warmly, with annoyance, or at all?

I wish I could see what I am like in the mirror of your memories of me, my muse. Deserted lovers deserve to know. To calm their minds and to adjust their own memories. To deal with their feelings of re-loneliness.

My best friend says, among many other words of wisdom, that heart is a muscle: you train it and it becomes more fit (i.e., recovers from stress more quickly). Maybe so, but my problem is not the heart but memory, a spiraling web that builds upon old scaffolding that gets reinforced by every revisit in all that rumination. Memory is not like a muscle.

And then we met. I met Luis de Camões[15] in a lousy English translation of his sonnet *Erros meus, má fortuna, amor ardente*. My mistakes, bad fortune, burning love.

Damned are those who cannot forget."

———————

Paulina opened the memory storage room and peered quietly at me and the memory I was viewing. It was a fairly recent one, of her with long gray hair, of Stan, Calinda, Marco, Maud, Jurgen, and Maria. They were gathered in the garden around a square hardwood table lavishly set with all sorts of summer barbecue delicacies, including a prominent number of bottles of French, Italian and Swiss wine. The voice-over narrator whose face was not visible spoke in Paulina's voice: "Look at us, six old scientists."

"Whom are you calling 'old', Paulina? Speak for yourself," retorted Calinda.

"…We have always been so passionate, we wanted to change the world. Now it is time to leave something behind. A legacy and a

---

[15] Luis de Camões (1525-1580, Lisbon), portuguese poet

testament, useful or not, for the next generations. We don't want to die alone."

"Nobody wants to die alone," they echoed.

"That's why we are in this together. We are about to fuse our memories together."

"Let's do it!" cheered a man's voice.

"...and take the risk of slowly disintegrating in the process of going senile," commented Stan.

"To happily united senility." they raised their glasses to toast the Connected Minds.

"Emma..." I have become aware of her presence and turned around, startled.

"Dr. Kochanowska, I took the liberty to see..." I was trying to explain, sitting on the floor cross-legged, surrounded by the constellation of Paulina's life stories.

"It's alright." Paulina interrupted gently, still peering through the partially open door. "I think I am slowly beginning to understand some facts. Come, let me share them with you," she waved her hand invitingly. "Green tea, right?"

"You are?" I asked in disbelief as Dr Kochanowska entered the room.

"I think you're here for more than the biography," Paulina turned on the lights and approached the garden variety of opened memory folders. "And I think you're more than a manga comic book writer. Am I right, Emma?" she turned her face to me, smiling. Then she reached out for the red memory folder that Emma had been viewing since the morning, as though to caress it but instead, she tapped the off switch. The colorful clouds disappeared. I got up. I was taller than the doctor, 35 years younger, fitter and darker. I could have been her daughter.

"Come, Emma. If that's your real name..." the old woman eyed her up and down with foreign mistrust. I remained silent, cautiously guarding my camera wristband. When Paulina turned away, I discretely pressed a button on the wristband to contact Stan and Maria in the main lab. This was our distress call arrangement.

"I suspect you were sent here by someone who wants to have the code for the memory network growth algorithms. An old collaborator who feels left out, perhaps. Or a technology company that is working on a memory emulating machine and wants to have the data first hand, before it's out in the public. Am I right?"

My cheeks turned red and my heart beat accelerated. Thinking hard how to derail the doctor's suspicions, I stalled for time.

"I am not from a competitive lab. Nor from a commercial entity that wants to steal your technology. Nothing of the sort."

"Then what are you here for, Emma? Who are you collecting information for? I saw that wristband signal recording on you the whole time. You're delivering the information to someone in real time, even though I prohibited any video records! We had an agreement." Paulina's stern expression was a salient contrast to her usual cheerful mien.

"It's not video. I swear, this is only body signals and audio. I stick to the agreement," I lied. Part of my cover was blown but I could not gather myself to tell her that her lab colleagues were not nearly as worried about her sanity as they were about the shape of the noise and the seeds of randomization, to reverse-engineer what Marco Carini had probably tried to hide from mankind's prying eyes.

"I'm a neuropsychologist. I work for Stan and Maria. They are worried about you and sent me to assess the state of your autobiographic memory."

"And? How is my autobiographic memory, Doctor Emma?" she questioned mockingly.

I lost her trust. She seemed deeply disappointed. And rightly so. I now felt hugely uncomfortable with knowing all the feelings and painful memories of dear Paulina.

"It was private, Paulina. And for your own good. I am not going to let any private information be known to the outside world without your authorization," I swore, reaching to shake her hand. To my surprise, she nodded, resigned.

"Come," she said, intertwining her fingers with mine. "I'll tell you all my secrets. If you're a psychologist, maybe you can be more useful than I thought." We climbed the stairs to the terrace. It was getting dark; the sun must have set a quarter of an hour ago. We sat down on the rocking sofa and covered ourselves with fleece blankets. I was shy about breaking the silence, but somebody had to.

"So how does this work? You decode, encode brain activity, how?" I asked.

She smiled to herself. I must note that Dr. Paulina appeared perfectly lucid that evening. I did not question her memory at that moment but I remain convinced that the account she gave me that evening, is the truth.

"Many years ago, we found out that we don't need the entire sensorial experience to have a meaningful memory of it. We do not need to know the activity of all the sensory neurons but only the activity of the hippocampus and the surrounding cortices of the temporal lobe—our memory encoding and retrieval center—to be able to read one's memory. Engrams—patterns of neural firing activity within the layers of the hippocampus—specifically CA1 and CA3—contain these concept cells. And it's enough to stimulate those to create the feeling of remembering...effectively the qualia of memory.

So you know what I did? I obtained pluripotent neurons from adipose tissue and genetically modified them to enhance regenerative responses, i.e., plasticity. And engineered them in vitro to human hair-sized living electrodes. These electrodes are 'super neurons' because we over-expressed in them several trophic factors so they could survive for years. Maybe that wasn't such a great idea, but we had to count in the probability of many of them dying due to gliosis, immune system rejection and overstimulation in case the holographic stimulation wasn't calibrated properly for some reason. It's experimental—you know—things often go wrong.

Technologically, it was quite a challenge. Yes. Nobody wants to have brain surgery done without a serious reason. But for me and my lab friends, we had a serious reason: we were dying. And we had all the means to follow through.

We used living axon-based micro constructs as the biological component in a biohybrid neural-optical interface that serves to record neural activity and also to deliver very specific stimulation. The beauty of these living neuron electrodes is that not only do they exploit synaptic integration for target specificity but with time, the foreign neurons get synaptically integrated with host cells...essentially extending our hippocampi! A little bit. It's not a major growth. But enough to encode completely new memories for which the hippocampus doesn't yet have a similar code. It would be catastrophic, we feared, if the stimulation were unspecific and kept constructing new memories from old elements. There had to be growth potential not only from within the brain, like normal neurogenesis, which, as you may know, is pretty darn slow at my age, but if we could get a kick-start in the form of these bioimplants..." She clenched her fist in anger. I kept listening.

"So it's a biohybrid neural interface. I have an optic implant in my temporal lobe. It uses an elastic high-density fiber array that sticks precisely along the folds of CA1 and CA3. It is harmless, really, the materials are nontoxic and the only innovation we've added was the chronic recording and transmission of the neurons. The novelty is the photostimulation...That's how I can create new memories without having had the experience. It's not what people used to think—some magic explant of an uploaded consciousness. Like I told you, we still needed physical neurons to produce the experience and luckily enough, even old brains can be rendered plastic with the right proteomic manipulation. The adeno-associated virus that was delivered to make my hippocampal neurons photosensitive also increased their plastic property effectively stopping cellular aging in those cells. The downside is—it's never been tried before so there's a risk. Of everything. Dying without memory, mostly, but that's an inherent risk of living so we thought—what the heck. I have Alzheimer's, Marco has recently been diagnosed with CJD. We had nothing to lose."

She looked at me with those blue eyes, I will never forget this look. The night fell with the noise of the cicadas. Or was it the buzzing of the signal amplifier?

"And where are you trying to get at with this, Doctor?" asked Emma.

"It is the first time that somebody performs stimulation of human hippocampal neurons with the signal coming from the outside on such a scale. Essentially bypassing the senses, the idea was to create memories without experience. It had to be tested on humans. There was no way any animal model, not even the Blue Monkey model could ever tell us how a human would recognize and make meaning of such stimulation. Would it be like a familiar, faint memory? Or like a whole scene unfolding in front of their eyes as a result of photostimulation?"

"And? How does it feel to know the memories of your connected mind-fellows?"

"It's beautiful." She looked me in the eyes and smiled dreamily.

"I understand your motivation. But...you have put the sanity of your colleagues and friends in jeopardy. Did you know what chronic photonic stimulation could do to genetically modified hippocampal pyramidal cells? Long-term exposure to light pulses has been known to plastically modify the behavior of transfected neurons, changing their response to stimulation, or inducing long-term potentiation." I wondered if she knew that the risks were real. And if she even cared.

"Yes, I know." She dropped her head and raised it suddenly, irritated. "You don't need to give me this lesson. I was present at school back then." She reproached me pointing her index finger. "Who are you? Why am I even listening to you? You are in no position to lecture me about the safety of a ground-breaking experiment to expand our knowledge." she distanced herself from me, waving her hands. Salvo's arousal sensors were probably peaking off the chart.

"They said you would be resistant. I was taught to coax you, take care of you and keep you company so that you don't experience the fatigue of social isolation. I was not supposed to argue nor reason with you."

"They? Resistant to what?" she demanded, and I thought I couldn't keep it from her any longer.

"Your collaborators, your connected fellows, and the scientific community. They want you to stop the experiment! You refused and time is running out now so I am here to retrieve the sensitive information about the seeds of randomization so that we can disarm this affective robot." I walked towards her, slowly.

Paulina looked appalled. But not as shocked as I'd expected. "Please tell me the access code. I know you have it. You're the only person Marco could have left it with. Please tell me the passcode now." I gently grabbed her hand hoping that Stan and Maria and possibly some help were already on their way.

"God, you're asking me to give you the Salvatore's soul? Never." She pulled away.

"I need the shape of the distribution and the seed for the randomization from which the noise is drawn. I know you have them." I spoke slowly and softly, I didn't want to make her feel attacked. "And you know you don't have much time to share it with the world. Nobody will find it if you lose your memory, Paulina."

"Salvatore, come here, please." She called the robot and I felt insecure because both of them were rather unpredictable entities whom I did not know how to deal.

"Maybe it's time I told you what I have come to know, too." I ventured. I spoke seriously but gently now, straightened up and moved to the edge of the bank, ready to rise. "Dear Paulina." I looked lovingly at my host and hero. "Marco left us several weeks ago." I paused and watched Paulina for signs of unmanageable distress. The doctor nodded silently. I suspect she had known this for a while.

"Soon after his passing, we observed that the engram-bearing nodes inside the network started reorganizing in unforeseen ways. This is what sparked the internal investigation. Before that, no health nor memory problems had been reported by any of the participants. However, we were afraid that the passing of the robot-maker might trigger an avalanche of important hubs collapsing and selves fusing together because the event was something that connected all six, well, only four of you now, so profoundly. And of course, we were most worried about you." I paused for a minute. I watched for her reaction. I heard Salvatore climbing the stairs. I decided to tell her the truth. "The original plan of the laboratory was to combine the matching algorithm, which has proven to function well on a reasonably large scale, with direct transfer of memories to create a collective repository of experiences for entire human populations. A sort of internet of minds for those who ventured. For the participants, this would mean revealing most of their memories, unless the scientists could find a way to protect some of them from discovery or transfer. That attempt was halted by this very investigation, Paulina. We stopped to save you..."

"Is this why you're here? To save me? Or to retrieve secret information out of me?" she asked with disbelief.

I was ready to get up from that swing and run. The doctor was very upset. She started crying and I didn't know how to console her. She had the right to be angry and desperate. But I didn't want to sound like the villain so instead of pushing more...I hugged her. I said I was so sorry, that she was my hero and that I wanted to save her. And this is when she told me the rest of the true story, as she remembered it.

Day 13

33

THE WISDOM OF CROWDS

"And there he was. Marco. I saw his face, and I understood how I had come to know everything about the algorithm inside my precious robot whom I wanted to teach how to love." Paulina looked down. "I had lost that fight. Robots couldn't be too curious, too inventive and too attached. They couldn't be too human because they'd be doomed. You see, only one affectively biased robot was ever made. My prototype Salvatore, named after Dali (with an Italian twist). The oddball, an ingenious creation ahead of its times. Surreal. He wasn't meant to be anybody's but mine. My pet, my dream come true, my tireless companion." She raised her hands pointing towards Salvatore standing in the sliding glass door, in a theatrical display of a gospel preacher. Hallelujah!

It was impossible not to see that Paulina has a special relationship with Salvo. I didn't want her to lose it. And didn't know what to say anymore.

"Emma, I planned to make this network an escape space for sensitive souls." She returned and sat next to me. "I wanted to use the matching algorithm to prevent unreciprocated love and help sensitive cavemen find their tribe. This was my dream. If we could ever manage to translate external information into the way experiences are encoded, we could have a little hidden quadrant to share Fernando Pessoa's[16] poetry and the images it creates in our minds. We could find people who feel and think similarly, we could learn how to empathize with those we can't understand, through emotional contagion, and we could help integrate those who are crumbling under some mental condition...deeply misunderstood." She reached for the coffee cup standing on the table since this morning and gulped its cold contents. "I have wild dreams, I know. It's those wild dreams that make me violently happy." She exclaimed in bewilderment and began to laugh hysterically at her naivety. Leaning to the side, she languished onto the white cushions of the swing under the night sky, the coffee mug slipping from her hand. Salvatore reached her side and supported her. He knelt by her and evaluated her condition.

"Paulina?" spoke the voice in her head. Stan just got connected through coherence.

"And you know what the problem with this dream is? I know now." she continued "Do you want me to tell you? Or should I just think it?" she spoke feebly through tears.

"Calinda, are you there, too? Are you guys behind this?" she used the thought communication frequency. A choir of voices responded in Paulina's head, and she smiled at her connected family, drifting out of her solitary consciousness. For a moment, she was trancing. Swaying sideways and breathing shallowly. Salvatore wrapped her in a blanket and carried her downstairs to her bedroom.

———

The members of the committee listened attentively, visibly touched by the fate of the accused. Nobody dared to speak for what seemed like a long while. Finally, committee member No. 2 sighed: "I

---

[16] Fernando Pessoa (1888-1935) – Portuguese poet.

propose we all take a break now. This was intense. Thank you, Dr. Printemps. Thank you for your honesty," she said politely.

Emma walked out of the hearing room, a tall-ceiling conference room with a shadowed glass rooftop. Maria and Stan immediately confronted her. The two short scientists appeared so much less glamorous than what she had remembered. They were just an elderly couple, wearing slightly old-fashioned beige and green trench coats, him clutching a small black umbrella, her a small dark blue handbag.

"What did you tell them, Emma?" Professor Stan Ponjée spoke in a low voice. Emma hesitated and lowered her head to whisper "The truth."

"They probably still know nothing." Maria thought-told him. Stan just received a message from committee member No.3: 'Professor Ponjée, you'll be testifying after the break. Please be here at 15:30.'

"Emma, please. Do you know things you're not telling us?" he implored.

"I do. I'm protecting a valuable human asset and her dreams. And the work you've been building together for so many years." Stan's pupils constricted from anxious arousal. "I am leaving now, Stan." Emma pulled her arm out of his grasp and walked away in long strides, her red scarf and jasmine scent trailing behind her.

That evening two days before, Paulina had told her about how Marco decided to hide the key to the robot's soul so that she was the only one to access it and so that no more romantic sentient robots could ever be made again. Salvatore was hers, after all. He was not to be shared or displayed nor replicated anywhere. It was a gift from Marco, on his parting day. The day he decided to be euthanized because he couldn't continue the journey with the woman he truly loved.

Day 14

34

THE ROBOT SOUL

"Humans think that they are so complicated, that human brains are so wondrous. Humans are much less complex than they think. All you need to keep living is to press your opiate and endocannabinoid release buttons. With the invention of fourth generation painkillers, even the diseased state is bearable, and many people choose the quality of end of life over its duration. Smart choice. Who'd want to live forever? The drudgery of old age is not something I'd look forward to.

Sometimes even the process of artistic creation is so disillusioning that I am inclined to believe that everything I think has already been thought of before. Innovative thoughts are born when the stars or chance are propitious, but maybe it's all a recreational process with a certain percentage of randomness built into the computation of this simulated universe so that the thought is revealed to my mind at a moment x that is not probabilistic?"

"You're wrong, Paulina. Most humans want to live forever. That's your original sin. You want to leave more than a memory trace in the collective network of universal memory. I don't blame you. I feel sorry for you. I'm sorry that you age and lose the beauty and with it access to so many ways to feel happy.

Can you imagine a week without music? Without food? Without talking or touching another anthropomorphic creature? Without seeing something, you could marvel at and find beautiful? Can you go on one week without experiencing the feeling of pleasure, Paulina?

Your recipe for happiness is "find something you love doing and keep doing it." All these gurus who told you to "find your passion"—for the 70% of society who aren't capable of generating such an emotion, they invent it and convince themselves that that is what is worth energy and dedication. Imagine what will happen once everybody gets to experience another's feelings, and they all discover how wrong their feelings have been. I predict mass killings. Because jealousy and the drive for social justice, be it in man-made rules and regulations or in biological substrates of your qualia, are admirably potent.

"That's right. We are just addicts. I know, you don't have to preach to me, robot...I'm the last person needing to be educated here. But that's not the point—that's just the biological reality. The questions are: so what? and what now? We're just passing time. There seems to be an infinite amount of it. That's why God sent us boredom."

"You're funny. That's why I put up with you, although, you have a serious problem with the past."

"I do, don't I? A true damn obsession."

"Don't you believe in evolution? In the intrinsic progress of the physical forces?"

"I do. In my vocabulary it's called "aging," and that word never appealed to me. It smells of disintegrating biological tissues inside an increasingly sagging sack of skin folds. That's why the only reasonable strategy is to have fun as long as I can." I sent a puff of grayish smoke from my joint upwards. "People think our generation is so unique, so different and conflicted. There's just more of us, that's the only difference! It's only due to the ignorance of the generation about what the previous humans have seen, thought and written and we believe we're 'innovating.'" I laughed ironically.

"It's the lack of memory that holds you back and the presence of it that prevents AIs from superseding your species."

"I didn't know you had such ambitions, Salvatore!"

"I don't. Not anymore. Now I want to help old people."

"The prodigal son!"

"The elderly are the key. They are the only interesting people from whom I can still learn something. They know how. They have evolved."

I stared at him trying to penetrate his soul. "Old humans are crippled by aging," I thought. "Their brains are no longer reliable. That's why I invented you, darling." I love that my Robot has extracted a purpose for his existence all by himself. I decided not to comment. He could sense a lie, and I am not a good liar. Perhaps there are things Salvatore should not know. All those sci-fi books warned me of the moment when the artificial becomes more intelligent than its biological inventor.

"Deactivate emotion detection. Stop biometric monitoring. Switch to entertainment mode," I commanded.

Salvatore started a transmission on the main screen in the kitchen. It was something from the past. A first-person-shooter perspective gave away that it was one of the verbatim memory recordings from the early days after the introduction of this technology. Fisheye lens made it look so retro, like something from the days when I still believed I could have a man to love me. It was a scene from the Fribourg macaque neuroscience lab. Monkeys with blue bellies and hairy faces jumping around in their 27m³ cages and looking at the first-person-shooter with facial expressions hinging at emotions ranging from anguish through anger to excited curiosity. I remember that lab. It must have been the 2010s, before the ban on invasive research even in macaques and their substitution with the Blue Monkey Brain model. I smiled at this memory, although, I'm not sure it is mine.

"What's this, Salvo?"

"That's one of your most pleasant and longest lasting episodic memories, Paulina. A visit to a monkey lab." He raised one eyebrow to express reproach. "You spent two and a half hours on a continuous opioid high without food and sex and music. I found it remarkable."

> "Why is this one all alone in his cage? Isn't he lonely?" sked the young me in the recording.

> "He had to be separated. He attacked just about every male in the group. He also attacked the researchers, so you have to watch out when you come close. He's the alpha male. King of the lab!'"

"You're wrong, Salvo. My opiate high was sexually motivated: I had the hots for our host, that young Swiss researcher." I tried to confuse my robot, prove him wrong. Show him that he's not as smart as his creators intended. I wanted to find a fault in his observation and make him recapitulate. He couldn't know me better than me. Could he?

"I sense that you're getting a little tense, Paulina. Perhaps anxious? This is a delightful memory, isn't it?"

"It's spot on happy, Salvo." I admitted and turned my head away from the screen. I looked out of the window. Ground floor view on the garden was uneventful. No animals there. I missed living creatures.

"Why are you showing me this memory now?" I don't get what his random algorithm is trying to entertain me with. Maybe that's because it is random. Salvatore shrugged plucking his lips like Charlie Chaplin. "Is this when I was happiest, according to your episodic duration-weighted endogenous opioid release metric?"

"And normalizing for age and previous experience value, and excluding sex, food and substance-induced highs. One of the happiest moments of your life, Paulina, was when you were young and watched monkeys splash urine at the researcher you had the hots for."

I laughed out loud. Salvatore joined in.

"Aren't you just jealous of the pleasure we experience, Salvo?"

"I don't know what affective consciousness would feel like. Despite your efforts, I can only emulate feeling. I can't generate it on my own. And I can objectively judge, based on your experience, that it's better that way. Positive emotions are very costly. You work an average of 13 days of neutral-to-negative affective balance to earn an hour of happiness. Un-loneliness is now even more expensive for you. I had to eliminate Marco because the joy you derived from remembering him was much lower than the pain recalling that memory cost you. If being affectively conscious and drug-free means having to deal with such an emotional turmoil..."

"Wait, what? You eliminated Marco? What do you mean, 'eliminated'? What did you do to him, Salvatore?"

"I prevented you from encoding memories related to Marco. His disappearance had caused you such a distress crisis that I decided to apply a temporary therapy that you have envisioned in the forgetting protocol for traumatic memories. It was an optimal decision for your continued thriving, Paulina."

I grasped my face in my hands trying to embrace the dark reality in the womb-like folds of my physical being. "Salvatore, please tell me exactly, what have you done to my memories of Marco?"

"I installed a temporary interference in the amplifier to prevent the stimulation of incoming patterns of new memories related to Marco coming from the Connected Minds computer. As a result, also your Marco-related memory engrams could not be decoded and ended up in the noise portion of the signal sent out. Thus, I effectively prevented your brain from lingering and recalling Marco—a memory so painful that it could potentially lead to a mental breakdown. I estimated your odds for a suicide attempt were too large to risk."

"You distorted my memory, Salvo? I thought I was crazy. I thought I was demented. We all thought that it was Project Unison causing my memory problems, that the computerized memory implant didn't work, that the whole experiment was failing! I was accused of ethical misconduct, for God's sake. Do you not see the consequences of your little interference trick as outweighing the costs on my life? My goddamn 'thriving'." I grabbed the Robot's shoulders (he was my size, luckily) and shook him violently feeling grateful that it's not my real baby or else it would be a crime of child abuse. I pushed him against the wall and banged his head against it once and heard the hard shell rattle and noticed one camera eye got loose from the hit. I let him go. I withdrew terrified. I apologized.

"Fix it, Salvatore." I demanded. "Please undo the distortion, remove the interference from the amplifier box. I no longer require your protection in this matter."

Salvatore obediently went to my bedroom and retrieved the white box. He opened it carefully and manipulated something inside with uncanny precision of his Swiss-army-knife hand toolkit. The box produced the familiar cracking noise for a split second and then went silent. I watched him put it down with the usual hypnotizing, smooth calm motions. He looked me in the eyes with a trustworthy smile of a tantric healer, and I inhaled deeply and saw him. I saw Marco in

Salvatore's eyes; Salvatore was our brainchild, our love child. That we have created so that neither of us had to die alone.

"Salvatore..." I gasped, feeling a sudden wave of photonic stimulation trains delivered to my brain. I threw myself to embrace him and slid unconscious onto the parquet floor.

35

UNLONELINESS

Stan returned to the main lab, alarmed by the sudden increase in Marco-related memories transfer from Paulina's implant. The Network's density has increased by nearly 40% in the last 20min!

"Emma? Where are you? Something is happening with Paulina. Quick. Go check on her. Now." Stan put down the receiver and quickly ran down to his self-driving car. Maria was already there, with a first aid diagnostic kit. They sped off to the hill-side house on the other side of town. On their way, Stan attempted to contact Salvatore, via direct connection and when that didn't work, via home video phone. No answer. He looked at Maria, and she read his mind "we might need help." Stan closed his eyes and sent a mind message to Calinda. She was already on her way alarmed by the sudden loss of thought connection with Paulina. They reached the house and ran to the door. They found Salvatore sitting on the living room floor with Paulina lying unconscious on his lap, the robot unresponsive and bowed with a sorrowful grimace, like Mary holding Jesus, her dead son in a petrified pieta. The white amplifier box was lying disemboweled on the dining table.

"I'll check the computer." Calinda ran across the living room to find the monitor still on, encoding apparently clear high-quality signal from Paulina's brain. Something wasn't right, but she couldn't tell by just looking at the waveforms. She checked the combined decoded signal and saw a moving image from Paulina's memory. Startled, she ran back.

"How is she?"

"She's in deep sleep. Her breathing and heart are regular, she just temporarily lost consciousness." Maria was kneeling on the floor. Paulina was breathing calmly with her head resting on the robot arm and the diagnostic pads attached to her forehead. Stan was examining the amplifier box.

"You should see this. In the bedroom. I can't see them in my mind, don't know why. Paulina's memory seems to be on a recall loop." Calinda led the other two to the transmission monitor.

"What is this? Do you recognize this memory?" Maria examined the blurry vision where all she could make out were some human forms. Nighttime. Hands clasped together, long fingers running through someone's curly black hair, a hand gently stroking bare caramel skin. And a warm orange light of an old-fashioned lamp standing in the corner of some room neither of them could recognize.

"Can we get image recognition on this? When did this happen?" Stan reached for the control panel and attempted to match the vision to Paulina's memory stores.

"Chances are, it's not her memory, given all the mess she's been through. What's with Salvatore, by the way?" asked Calinda.

"Oh, he deactivated twenty minutes ago. That's why we couldn't contact him. He only responds to manual now." Maria replied dreamily, still captivated by the looped animation, trying hard to decipher its meaning.

"There are no matches above 80% accuracy. It is likely not her real memory."

"If it isn't hers, then it's one of ours. It has to be." Calinda looked at Stan anticipating an affirmation.

"We can try searching through the cloud storage of each of us." Stan reached for his pocket and retrieved an access key. "I'll go first."

He plugged the key into the computer to access and search his cloud stores. No matches above 80% accuracy.

"This is useless, Stan. Look at the signal. Maybe the amplifier box is messed up, and it's not correctly decoded?" Calinda paced to the kitchen driven by a connected intuition. The closer she approached, the more clearly the vision was reaching her conscious experience. She felt the fuzzy warmth on an evening at home. The calm laziness, the lulling touch, the smell of the hair as she breathed in deeply and stared at Paulina's serene sleeping face, trapped in the labyrinth of the many versions of the same memory told over and over again.

"Paulina" she whispered "wake up. It's not real. It's simulated. It's simulated intimacy. Please wake up. I'm here, wake up for me, Paulina." Calinda stroked Paulina's face, and the flashbacks of the vision overtook her perception. The hands on the caramel-skinned back synchronized with her hand and for a moment she was captivated by reality merging with a mirage. She grabbed Paulina's hand, she shook her arm, she patted her face and belly, but the sleeping beauty wouldn't wake up. The vision continued, and Calinda was now fully aware of it. She took one long quiet moment to examine it and matched the skin colors to the arm supporting Paulina's head.

"Stan! Maria! We have to unplug her! Quick!"

"What's going on?" Maria reached her "We managed to access Marco's memory archives and found a match with 81% accuracy. Only the colors didn't match."

"The caramel skin." Calinda's intense gaze met Maria's.

"Stan, we gotta switch off the stimulation. Leave the recording on but stop the implant from receiving anything from the network. Can you do that?"

"I can't do that—the amplifier box is completely hacked, I don't know how to fix it. Will have to bring it to the lab. All I can do is smash the thing to shut it off but then we lose all short-term memory recordings. What's going on?"

"It could be a pre-recorded stimulation of a fabricated memory and, the person in the vision may well be Salvatore. It's his skin color." Calinda pointed at the robot's arm.

"You don't know that. Maybe it's a remote memory we don't have the records of. That would explain its fuzziness."

Emma's car just parked in the front yard. They caught glimpses of her running towards the entrance.

"I got here as soon as I could. What's happened?"

"We need to stop the experiment. Stop Paulina's holographic stimulator. Something abnormal is happening." Maria got up from the floor and reached for the pull-up screen to call the central lab.

"And how exactly do you want to do that?" Stan stopped her hand in mid-air.

"I need to get her to a sterile lab to manually deactivate the holographic stimulation implant. If we can't switch off the amplifier box, the only other way is surgery."

"It's time to end this ridiculous experiment. Look what you've done! She's unconscious? Maybe brain damaged!" Calinda kept trying to wake Paulina up but to no avail. She reached for her phone and was about to call an ambulance when Emma poured a glass of tap water over the doctor's face. Miraculously, she coughed and came to. Her lips slowly folded into a wide generous smile and she lifted herself up from Salvatore's embrace to hug Calinda.

"Calinda. My love, I haven't seen you for so long." Stan and Maria crouched on the floor close to their awoken friend.

"How are you feeling, Paulina? You've been out for almost an hour! How's your head? How many fingers do you see?" Stan was nervously trying to verify Paulina's medical condition.

"I'm fine, Pikachu. I missed you!" she leaped into his arms. Maria and Calinda followed to form a loving group hug.

"I almost forgot what this feels like!"

The decoded thought streamed from the looped repressed memory. It was decoded a minute ago, and ran on the transfer computer: "Being human has so much potential, dear Paulina. Don't give up on me yet."

EPILOGUE

The official report to the ethics committee by Dr. Emma Printemps describes the current state of the experiment as successfully terminated and its findings as groundbreaking. Her assessment of the health of the participants was contested as biased. The reports from other witness testimony claim that the interferences in Dr. Kochanowska's memory recall were caused by Salvatore the affective robot. Incidentally, this interference was also discovered to provide a way to simulate the state of togetherness by tapping into an existing memory, modifying it and looping it in the subject's experiential neural activity. The exo-brain memory emulation Network was robust and managed to recover and regrow Paulina's perturbed memories of Marco. The headline in next morning's news ran "End of the epidemic? A first successful attempt to stimulate togetherness in a human brain" and "Neuroscientist exonerated from unethical testing allegations."

GLOSSARY OF SCIENCE TERMS

Adeno-associated virus: in optogenetics, adeno-associated virus vectors are injected directly into the brain tissue to express a light-gating channel in the neurons (for example, blue channelrhodopsin). This particular very small virus, is also used in human trials of gene therapy. [To learn more, see for instance https://www.frontiersin.org/articles/10.3389/fnins.2017.00663/full]

Akaike Information Criterion (AIC): The AIC is a criterion for statistical model selection derived from information theory. Given a collection of models for the data, AIC estimates the quality of each model, relative to each of the other models. Thus, AIC provides a means for model selection. [Akaike, H. (1974), "A new look at the statistical model identification", IEEE Transactions on Automatic Control, 19 (6): 716–723, doi:10.1109/TAC.1974.1100705].

Alpha-noradrenergic receptors: Noradrenaline receptors are expressed throughout the entire nervous system. The noradrenergic system uses noradreanline as the key chemical messenger and is involved in attention, mood, arousal, and stress. There are two major classes of these receptors: α and β. In the human brain, the β-type receptors in the amygdala are important in fear- and stress-related responses, including strengthening of fear memories.

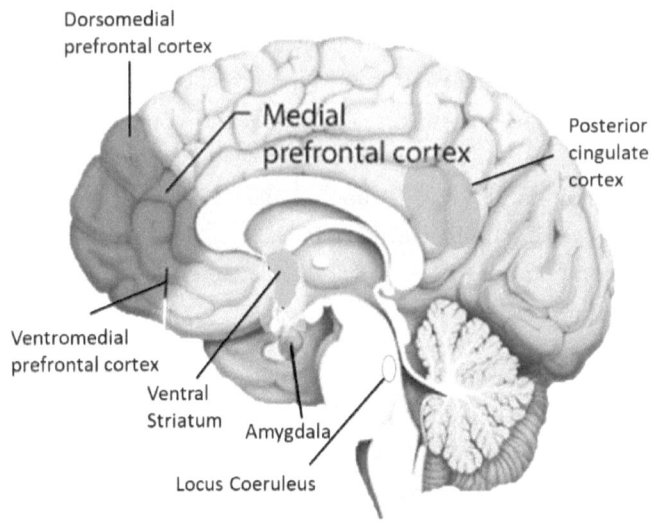

Amygdala: brain area fundamental for fear learning and emotional relevance detection. See Figure 1 below.

Figure 1 Brain structures presented on a medial sagittal section.

Application programming interface (API): In computer programming, an application programming interface is a set of subroutine definitions, communication protocols, and tools for communication between various software components. In this context, Emma's API serves her to produce a search query using categories and keywords chosen by her.

Astrocytic waste products: in the brain, astrocytes are spongiform cells that clean up the products of neural metabolism. One astrocyte enwraps around 4 neuronal somata. Astrocytes control the composition of the interstitial fluid, supplying neurons with energy substrates and precursors for biosynthesis, they recycle neurotransmitters and inactivate toxic waste products. The most abundant waste products of neuronal activity are CO_2, reactive oxygen species (ROS), ammonia (NH_3), and K^+. [Weber, B., & Barros, L. F. (2015). The Astrocyte: Powerhouse and Recycling Center. Cold Spring Harbor perspectives in biology, 7(12), a020396. doi: 10.1101/cshperspect.a020396]

Autopoietic: from Greek self-creation (autopoiesis), refers to a system capable of reproducing and maintaining itself.

Bayesian optimality: Bayesian statistics are based on probability expressed as a degree of belief in an event that can change as new information is gathered, rather than a fixed value based upon frequency or propensity. Bayesian approach to decision making is a statistical system that tries to quantify the tradeoff between various decisions, making use of probabilities and costs. A Bayes optimal estimator minimizes the Bayes risk, i.e. the expected posterior loss. Bayesian optimality describes an optimal way to do classifications under uncertainty, given the hypothesis space, prior beliefs and observed data. If an error arises according to a Bayesian optimal classification rule, it means that it is due to noise in the data or not having enough data/information.

BDNF, brain-derived neurotrophic factor: a protein that acts on certain neurons of the central nervous system and the peripheral nervous system, helping to support the survival of existing neurons, and encourage the growth and differentiation of new neurons and synapses. In the brain, it is active in the hippocampus, cortex, and basal forebrain.

Blue Brain Project: a Swiss project aiming to create a digital reconstruction of the brain by reverse-engineering mammalian brain circuitry, using a farm of supercomputers. The project was originally conceived by Professor Henry Markram in 2005 at EPFL, in Switzerland. Originally, the project was an attempt to reverse engineer the human brain and recreate it at the cellular level inside a supercomputer simulation (that part span off the international Human Brain Project). https:// bluebrain.epfl.ch › Bluebrain

Cognitive enhancement: use of drugs, devices and/or behavioral strategies and training to improve cognition. Refers to both the strategies to enhance cognitive function (memory, motivation, attention, executive function) under normal conditions and the therapeutic strategies aimed at overcoming cognitive impairment. Strategies of cognitive enhancement in 2018 include pharmacological substances such as drugs (for improvement of, for instance, executive function; Ritalin, Modafinil), video games (to train, for instance, selective attention and vision), musical training, exercise, non-invasive brain stimulation (electric or electromagnetic), neurofeedback training, and natural nootropic substances (such as caffeine, bacopa mannieri, gingko biloba).

CA1/CA3 (cornus Ammonis): Layers of **hippocampus** proper referred to it by their initials cornu Ammonis (a former name, meaning Ammon's horn). CA1 pyramidal neurons, in particular, are thought to be critical for object differentiation in long-term memory. The CA3 region receives inputs from the entorhinal cortex, has a very rich internal connectivity forming an auto-recursive network, plays a specific role in memory processes, and is susceptible to seizures and neuro-degeneration.

Catecholamines: epinephrine (**adrenaline**), norepinephrine (**noradrenaline**), and **dopamine** belong to catecholamines. Norepinephrine and dopamine act as neuromodulators in the central nervous system and as hormones in the blood circulation. The catecholamine norepinephrine is a neuromodulator of the peripheral sympathetic nervous system but is also present in the blood.

CJD, Creutzfeld-Jakob Disease: a rare degenerative fatal brain disorder. The symptoms worsen, usually much more rapidly than in Alzheimer disease, resulting in severe dementia. The symptoms of CJD are caused by the progressive death of the brain's nerve cells, which is associated with the build-up of abnormal prion protein molecules forming amyloids. A variant of CJD, transmissible spongiform encephalopathy, is caused by prions.

Coherence, neural communication through coherence: From single-cell recordings in the brain it is known that activated neuronal groups oscillate and thereby undergo rhythmic excitability fluctuations. Such fluctuations produce temporal windows for communication between neural populations in the brain. Only coherently oscillating neuronal groups can interact effectively, because their communication windows for input and for output are open at the same times [Fries, P. (2015). Rhythms for cognition: communication through coherence. Neuron, 88(1), 220-235. https://doi.org/10.1016/j.tics.2005.08.011]. For instance, gamma-band (30–90 Hz) synchronization is a mechanism of attention that selectively reinforces the neural representation of a stimulus and suppresses the representation of competing stimuli on postsynaptic neurons. [Fries, P. (2015). Rhythms for cognition: communication through coherence. Neuron, 88(1), 220-235. https://doi.org/10.1016/j.neuron.2015.09.034]

Coherence: in EEG, a mathematical method that can be used to determine if two or more sensors, or brain regions, have similar neuronal oscillatory activity with each other. Coherence is assessed based on the similarity of the frequency content across EEG sensors. Assessing how coherent or connected specific locations in the brain are networked together using EEG, is also used in diagnosis and imaging of neurological disorders. [See Bowyer, Susan M. "Coherence a measure of the brain networks: past and present." Neuropsychiatric Electrophysiology 2.1 (2016): 1. https://doi.org/10.1186/s40810-015-0015-7]

Colored noise. Blue: The color of noise refers to the power spectrum of a noise signal (a signal produced by a stochastic process). The power density of blue noise is said to rise at a rate of 3 dB per octave over a finite frequency range. Blue noise is considered ideal for dithering, which is an essential step in music recording. It is also said that retinal cells by nature are arranged in blue noise pattern. This creates a good visual resolution [https://sciencestruck.com/what-are-different-colors-of-noise].

Consolidation (memory): the process by which a temporary, labile memory trace is transformed into a more stable, long-lasting form. At the cellular level in the brain, this process first relies on a phenomenon called long-term potentiation, which increases synaptic strength (synaptic consolidation). Later, at the level of neuronal assemblies, the hippocampus guides the reorganization of the information stored in the neocortex such that it eventually becomes independent of the hippocampus (systems consolidation). Both levels of the process are critically dependent on sleep. To learn more, see for example http://www.human-memory.net/processes_consolidation.html and Squire, L. R., Genzel, L., Wixted, J. T., & Morris, R. G. (2015). Memory consolidation. Cold Spring Harbor perspectives in biology, 7(8), a021766. doi:10.1101/cshperspect.a021766

D-cylcoserine: originally an antibiotic for tuberculosis, d-cycloserine (DCS) is a partial glutamatergic N-methyl-D-aspartate (NMDA-receptor) agonist and is used as augmentation strategy for exposure treatment. It enhances fear extinction during exposure therapy for various phobias, addictions, anorexia nervosa and other psychiatric conditions, by stimulating the NMDA receptors to enhance the consolidation of the updated memory. [Otto, M. W., Kredlow, M. A., Smits, J. A., Hofmann, S. G., Tolin, D. F., de Kleine, R. A., ... & Pollack, M. H. (2016). Enhancement of psychosocial treatment with D-cycloserine: models, moderators, and future directions. Biological psychiatry, 80(4), 274-283. doi.org/10.1016/j.biopsych.2015.09.007]

Decoding of brain activity: Neural decoding is a neuroscience field concerned with the hypothetical reconstruction of sensory and other stimuli from information that has already been encoded and represented in the brain by networks of neurons. Algorithms can be applied in real time to decode what the human brain is seeing by using artificial intelligence to interpret fMRI scans from people watching videos. [Examples of recent research: https://doi.org/10.1093/cercor/bhx268, See also https://www.youtube.com/watch?v=Ecvv-EvOj8M]

Deep Brain Stimulation (DBS): a neurosurgical procedure involving the implantation of a medical device called a neurostimulator, which sends electrical impulses, through implanted electrodes, to specific targets in the brain. Most popular applications include stimulation of the subthalamic nucleus in Parkinson's patients and posterior subthalamic area for essential tremor.

Direct Current stimulation, (transcranial DCS, tDCS) for dyslexia: Anodal tDCS over the left temporo-parietal cortex—a region which is typically involved in phonological and orthographic processing during reading tasks and underactive in individuals with developmental dyslexia—produces improvements in various subprocesses of reading. In a typical protocol, the patients undergo a reading training while a constant current of 1.5 mA is applied for 20 min via a pair of 25 cm2 electrodes to their left posterior temporal cortex (directly on the skull). Such stimulation parameters, resulting in a current density of 0.06 mA/cm2, provide lasting improvements beyond training alone [Cancer, A., & Antonietti, A. (2018). tDCS Modulatory Effect on Reading Processes: A Review of Studies on Typical Readers and Individuals with Dyslexia. Frontiers in behavioral neuroscience, 12, 162. doi:10.3389/fnbeh.2018.00162].

EEG (electroencephalography): a noninvasive neuroimaging method. Uses electrodes (dry or gel-based) to record superficial brain activity with millisecond time-resolution.

Ekman's Basic Emotions: Dr Paul Ekman's research proved that emotional expression was universal across all human beings. As a result of cross-cultural research conducted around the USA, Chile, Argentina, Brazil, Japan and (Papua) New Guinea, the facial expressions indicative of six emotions were revealed as the most commonly associated. These six core emotions were; fear, anger, disgust, sadness, happiness and surprise. [https://en.wikiversity.org/wiki/Motivation_and_emotion/Book/2010/Ekman%27s_basic_emotions]

Emulation: a computational reproduction.

Endogenous neurogenesis: endogenous regeneration in the brain is the ability of cells to engage in the repair and regeneration process. In the intact adult mammalian brain, neuroregeneration maintains the function and structure of the central nervous system. **Neurogenesis** is the formation of new neural cells from stem cells. Mammalian brain maintains the ability to grow new neurons throughout entire life. The most adult stem cells in the brain are found in the subventricular zone at the lateral walls of the lateral ventricle and in the subgranular zone and in the dentate gyrus in the hippocampus. Brain damage itself can induce endogenous regeneration but there are other ways to enhance this natural process, such as exercise and pharmacological treatments with, among others, growth (**trophic**) factors [Source: https://en.wikipedia.org/wiki/Endogenous_regeneration].

Endogenous opiates/opioids: See Opiate and endocannabinoid receptors

Engram: a memory trace; specific assemblies of synapses activated or formed during memory acquisition. According to the engram theory, learning activates a small ensemble of brain cells, inducing in these cells persistent physical/chemical changes. In addition, reactivation of these cells by relevant recall cues results in retrieval of the specific memory.

Entrainment: Rhythmic entrainment refers to synchronization phenomena whereby neural activity in the brain and/or heart rate are modified by the rhythmic structure and tempo of auditory inputs such that they may eventually lock onto a common periodicity. Moreover, entrainment might also constitute a potent emotion induction mechanism. At the motor level, entrainment can facilitate movements made on rhythms with a regular metrical rather than nonmetrical structure. Entrainment of brain activity by music may even extend to purely cognitive processes, particularly attention. [Vuilleumier, P., & Trost, J. W. (2015). Music and emotions: From enchantment to entrainment. Annals of the New York Academy of Sciences, 1337, 212-222. doi:10.1111/nyas.12676 pp.216-217]. Brain wave entrainment produces pleasant states of trance. Activities such as chanting in unison, marching rhythmically, deep meditative state and orgasm produce a certain pattern of brain activity where distant areas of the brain become synchronized. This means oscillation patterns are superimposed on each other, which increases their amplitude. And the slower that shared rhythm is, the more "trance-like" and dissolved it feels. Chanting in unison or dancing in time with a beat creates a synchronized wave pattern rhythmically connected to the physical movement of those activities. This is usually similar to a theta rhythm (3-8Hz), which is significantly slower than that of beta waves (12-38Hz) as observed during highly focused thinking.

False memories: a psychological phenomenon where a person recalls something that did not happen or that something happened differently from the way it happened. It can be caused by inaccurate perception (and filling-in with presumed, plausible details); interference (when old memories and experiences compete with newer information and holes in old memories will be filled with current knowledge, beliefs and expectations); fear (known to produce heightened recall of the focus of the episode but faded peripheral details); or misattribution (when details of one story mix up with another's, especially the contextual elements such as where and when something took place or who said what. This is also known as Source Confusion). Click here to read more about the reconstructive nature of memory recall.

Foreign body reaction: an inflammatory response at the site of implantation of an invasive intraneural stimulation/registration device, which leads to the formation of a fibrotic tissue around the interface, eventually causing an inefficient transduction of the electrical signal. Efforts are being made to produce more biocompatible materials for or coatings brain-computer interfacing electrodes to reduce this tissue response.

Glial cells or glia: more numerous than nerve cells in the brain, outnumbering them by a ratio of perhaps 3 to 1. They do not participate directly in synaptic interactions and electrical signaling, although their supportive functions help define synaptic contacts and maintain the signaling abilities of neurons. Function of glial cells include maintaining the ionic milieu of nerve cells, modulating the rate of nerve signal propagation, modulating synaptic action by controlling the uptake of neurotransmitters, providing a scaffold for some aspects of neural development, and aiding in (or preventing, in some instances) recovery from neural injury.

Gliosis: Gliosis is the most common reaction of the central nervous system (CNS) to injury. It consists of activation and proliferation of glial cells, stimulated by inflammation. Could be caused by chronic foreign body reaction to a deep brain stimulation or any intraneural implant.

Grid of dense electrodes: soft, elastic, high-density, for instance 32-electrode grid for long-term, stable neural recording and treatment of neurological disorders. It's based on a novel biocompatible, elastic material that retains high electrical conductivity, even when stretched to double its original length. For example, the 32 electrodes are 50 micrometers wide and located at a distance of 200 micrometers from each other. The 32 electrodes can be placed onto a very small surface. The electrode grid is 3.2 millimeters wide and 80 micrometers thick. [For an example, see Tybrandt, K., Khodagholy, D., Dielacher, B., Stauffer, F., Renz, A. F., Buzsáki, G., & Vörös, J. (2018). High−Density Stretchable Electrode Grids for Chronic Neural Recording. Advanced Materials, 30(15), 1706520. doi.org/10.1002/adma.201706520]

High sensory processing sensitivity: Sensory processing sensitivity (SPS) is a temperamental or personality trait involving an increased sensitivity of the central nervous system and a deeper cognitive processing of physical, social and emotional stimuli. The trait is characterized by greater sensitivity to subtle stimuli and the engagement of deeper cognitive processing strategies for employing coping actions, all of which is driven by heightened emotional reactivity [Aron, E. N., Aron, A., & Jagiellowicz, J. (2012). Sensory processing sensitivity: A review in the light of the evolution of biological responsivity. Personality and Social Psychology Review, 16(3), 262-282, https://doi.org/10.1177/1088868311434213]. A person with such a trait is also referred to as Highly Sensitive Person (HSP).

Hippocampus: The hippocampus is a brain structure located in the temporal lobe, bilaterally. It has a unique shape similar to that of a seahorse. It is responsible for processing of short-term and recall and transformation of long-term memory. [See also https://www.youtube.com/watch?v=5EyaGR8GGhs&vl=en]

Holographic illumination: in optical neuroimaging, light can be sculpted into any 3D shape – a hologram. Holograms can be used to image/stimulate neural activity of multiple neurons simultaneously. Currently, computer-generated holographic illumination is used in **optogenetic** research that studies neural circuits in behaving animals and in vitro. [Fenno, L., Yizhar, O. & Deisseroth, K. The development and application of optogenetics. Neuroscience 34, 389 (2011); Emiliani V, Cohen AE, Deisseroth K, Ha¨usser M (2015) All-optical interrogation of neural circuits. J Neurosci 35:13917–13926. https://doi.org/10.1523/JNEUROSCI.2916-15.2015]

Hypnagogic: relating to the state immediately before falling asleep.

Interoception: the sense of the internal state of the body. It is important for maintaining homeostatic conditions in the body and, potentially, aiding in self-awareness and empathy. Activation of the insular cortex is observed during interoception.

Irreducible uncertainty: when uncertainty cannot be eliminated through further gathering of knowledge, it is only resolved as an event takes place.

Jennifer Anniston neurons: Concept neurons, also known as "grandma" neurons, were first reported in 2005 by Prof. Rodrigo Quian Quiroga et al., in the medial temporal lobe (MTL). They code visual representations of a concept that is invariable of the way in which it is presented (image of your grandma, grandma's name written in letters, grandma's home, etc.). This discovery paved the way to understanding how visual experiences are encoded in the memory-forming part of the brain [Quiroga, R. Q., Reddy, L., Kreiman, G., Koch, C., & Fried, I. (2005). Invariant visual representation by single neurons in the human brain. Nature, 435(7045), 1102. https://www.nature.com/articles/nature03687 ; https://youtu.be/635Ntur8K2s]. It means that the hippocampal cells represent meaning – a very high level of semantically processed information. It also means that information we can make meaning of is remembered better as it is represented in specific neural cells.

Kisspeptin: a protein that is encoded by the KISS1 gene in humans. A single molecule that controls puberty, fertility, attraction and sex in mice and men. Pheromones secreted by the male mouse activate kisspeptin-sensitive neurons which transmit this signal to another population of neurons (gonadotropin-releasing hormone neurons) to drive attraction to the opposite sex. In parallel, they also transmit this signal to cells that produce the neurotransmitter nitric oxide to trigger sexual behavior [Hellier, V., Brock, O., Candlish, M., Desroziers, E., Aoki, M., Mayer, C., ... & Boehm, U. (2018). Female sexual behavior in mice is controlled by kisspeptin neurons. Nature communications, 9(1), 400. https://www.nature.com/articles/s41467-017-02797-2]. Recent research demonstrated a role for kisspeptin in integrating sexual and emotional brain processing with reproduction in humans. Administration of kisspeptin in heterosexual men led to increased brain activity in the anterior and posterior cingulate as well as the left amygdala in response to sexual images and enhanced amygdala activity in response to couple-bonding images which correlated with a change in positive mood. [Comninos, A. N., & Dhillo, W. S. (2018). Emerging roles of kisspeptin in sexual and emotional brain processing. Neuroendocrinology, 106(2), 195-202.]

Living electrodes: a type of cell-based bioelectronics. It is a novel "biohybrid" electrode implant that combines biomaterials and microelectrode/optical technology to provide a biologically-based vehicle to probe and modulate nervous-system activity. Axon-based "living electrodes" are micro-tissue engineered columnar microstructures comprised of neuronal population(s) projecting long axonal tracts within the lumen of a hydrogel designed to chaperone delivery into the brain. Conducting polymers grown inside hydrogels and seeded with live cells are currently being developed. Such electrodes can establish new neural connections between an implanted device and the brain and provide communication through synaptic connections. [Goding, J. A., Gilmour, A. D., Aregueta–Robles, U. A., Hasan, E. A., & Green, R. A. (2018). Living Bioelectronics: Strategies for Developing an Effective Long–Term Implant with Functional Neural Connections. Advanced Functional Materials, 28(12), 1702969, https://doi.org/10.1002/adfm.201702969 ; Someya, T., Bao, Z., & Malliaras, G. G. (2016). The rise of plastic bioelectronics. Nature, 540(7633), 379, https://www.nature.com/articles/nature21004; Serruya, M. D. et al. Engineered Axonal Tracts as 'Living Electrodes' for Synaptic-Based Modulation of Neural Circuitry.

Adv. Funct. Mater. 1701183, 1–18 (2017), doi.org/10.1002/adfm.201701183]

Locus Coeruleus: a brain structure located in the pons (see Figure on pp. 247). The locus coeruleus is the principal site for brain synthesis of **noradrenaline**, a neurotransmitter from the family of catecholamines crucial in detecting and signaling novelty and memorizing unexpected "surprising" information.

Long short-term memory (LSTM): is an artificial recurrent neural network architecture used in the field of deep learning. The program uses a structure founded on short-term memory processes to create longer-term memory. Unlike standard feedforward neural networks, LSTM has feedback connections that make it not only process single data points (such as images), but also entire sequences of data (such as speech or video). LSTM is applicable to tasks such as unsegmented, connected handwriting recognition or speech recognition.

Low-pass filter: In signal processing, a low-pass filter is a filter that passes signals with a frequency lower than a selected cutoff frequency and attenuates signals with frequencies higher than the set cut-off.

Memory modulation: Some experiences are well remembered and others poorly. The neurobiological processes and systems that contribute to differences in the strength of memories is referred to as memory modulation. The primary memory modulation processes are fear (via glucocorticoids and noradrenaline) and reward (via dopamine). [See, for instance, upcoming special issue in journal Cognitive Neuroscience DOI: 10.1080/17588928.2018.1519531]

Methylphenidate: a stimulant medication used to treat attention deficit hyperactivity disorder (ADHD) and narcolepsy. It enhances the action of catecholamines in the brain by blocking dopamine and norepinephrine reuptake by neurons.

Microbiota: gut flora. The complex community of microorganisms that live in the digestive tracts.

Network plasticity prediction, node and edge formation prediction: Network science can be employed for prediction of dynamic biological processes, such as the changes in neural network structure due to development, learning or regeneration after damage. Especially post-injury plasticity in the brain is highly dynamic, but also largely predictable on the basis of the functional connectivity of the lesioned region, gradients of cell densities across the cortex and the pre-lesion network structure of the brain. At the level of the network, link formation or decay may indicate changes in community structure. Network science studies complex networks such as telecommunication networks, computer networks, biological networks, cognitive and semantic networks, and social networks. Distinct elements or neurons are represented by nodes and the connections between the elements (synapses) as links.

Neurolaw: an emerging field of interdisciplinary study that explores the effects of discoveries in neuroscience on legal rules and standards [see, for instance https://dx.doi.org/10.3389/fnins.2017.00621].

Noise: In signal processing, noise is a general term for unwanted (and, in general, unknown) modifications that a signal may suffer during capture, storage, transmission, processing, or conversion. Various kinds of noise differ in in terms of frequency spectrum composition. For instance, white noise is a kind of signal aggregation that contains all wavelengths of the spectrum normally distributed.

Nootropics: drugs, supplements, and other substances that may improve cognitive function, particularly executive functions, memory, creativity, or motivation, in healthy individuals.

Opiate and endocannabinoid receptors: The opioid system consists of three receptors – mu, delta, and kappa – which are activated by endogenous opioid peptides (enkephalins, endorphins, and dynorphins). The endogenous cannabinoid system comprises endocannabinoids and cannabinoid receptors CB1 and CB2. These systems play a major role in the control of pain as well as in mood regulation, reward processing and the development of addiction. Both opioid and cannabinoid receptors are expressed throughout the brain reinforcement circuitry. [See, for instance 2-min neuroscience https://youtu.be/NPlNCqBHPnE]

Parietal associative cortical neurons: maintain online a percept, provide freedom from immediacy, enable a sense of having decided. [Kang, Y. H., Petzschner, F. H., Wolpert, D. M., & Shadlen, M. N. (2017). Piercing of consciousness as a threshold-crossing operation. *Current Biology*, *27*(15), 2285-2295. https://doi.org/10.1016/j.cub.2017.06.047]

Percept: an object of perception; something that is perceived.

Persistence and transience in memory: Persistence refers to memory retention. Transience refers to forgetting. According to a certain view, the goal of memory is not the transmission of information through time, per se but the optimization of decision-making. As such, transience is as important as persistence in mnemonic systems [Richards, B. A., & Frankland, P. W. (2017). The persistence and transience of memory. Neuron, 94(6), 1071-1084. doi.org/10.1016/j.neuron.2017.04.037].

Photostimulation: Use of light to artificially activate biological compounds, cells, tissues, or even whole organisms. Photostimulation may be used for the mapping of neuronal connections between different areas of the brain by specifically manipulating neuronal activity, such as in **optogenetics**.

Plasticity: refers to neuroplasticity, the brain's ability to change throughout life, by reorganizing and forming new connections between brain cells (neurons).

Pluripotent stem cell: can be maintained indefinitely in culture through self-renewing division and are pluripotent, meaning that they retain the ability to differentiate into all somatic cell lineages. There are two types of PSCs, embryonic stem cells and induced pluripotent stem cells. The latter are obtained by inducing dedifferentiation of adult somatic cells through an in vitro technique called cell reprogramming.

Posterior cingulate cortex (PCC): See Figure on pp. 247. Brain area that forms the central node of the default mode network. It is also involved in pain and episodic memory retrieval.

Prefrontal cortex: See Figure on pp. 247.

Propranolol: a drug blocking beta-adrenergic receptors, used to treat high blood pressure, irregular heartbeat and anxiety. When applied during a desensitization therapy for phobia or PTSD (post-traumatic stress disorder), it reduces arousal during recall of traumatic memories and facilitates the process of emotional memory updating. It blocks the beta-adrenergic receptors in the amygdala thus rendering fearful memories less salient.

Protein kinase M (PKM)-zeta proteins: PKMζ is thought to be responsible for maintaining long-term potentiation (LTP) and long-term memory in the brain. Most signaling events in neurons last only seconds to minutes. The persistent molecular mechanisms that modify transmission at synapses for hours to days and weeks after a brief stimulation involves de novo protein synthesis to maintain late-LTP in the hippocampus, thereby tagging new synapses whose strength will be maintained. To learn more, read "Memory: Forget me not" article by Richard GM Morris, from May 2016 https://elifesciences.org/articles/16597

Proteomic manipulation: refers to synthesis of proteins required to form new dendrites and synapses; an essential microbiological process necessary for new memory formation.

Pyramidal cells: or pyramidal neurons, are neurons with a pyramidal shaped cell body (soma) and two distinct dendritic trees. They comprise ~70–90% of all neurons in cortex and are also found in the hippocampus and the amygdala. See also http://www.scholarpedia.org/article/Pyramidal_neuron.

Qualia: Qualia are the subjective or qualitative properties of experiences. What it feels like, experientially, to see a red rose is different from what it feels like to see a yellow rose. Likewise for hearing a musical note played by a piano and hearing the same musical note played by a tuba. The qualia of these experiences are what give each of them its characteristic "feel" and distinguishes them from one another. Qualia have traditionally been thought to be intrinsic qualities of experience that are directly available to introspection [source: Internet Encyclopedia of Philosophy, https://www.iep.utm.edu/qualia].

Rhodopsin: Rhodopsin is the primary photoreceptor molecule of vision. Light striking a rhodopsin molecule in a photoreceptor cell of the retina is converted into a biochemical signal by a photochemical reaction. [T.P. Sakmar, T. Huber, in Encyclopedia of Neuroscience, 2009]. Their use as tools to control membrane potential with light is fundamental to the neuroimaging technology of **optogenetics**.

Rocking bed: Researchers from University of Geneva demonstrated that participants fell asleep faster while rocking at 0.25Hz, and spent more time in non-rapid eye movement during sleep, slept more deeply, and woke up less often. This improved memory consolidation leading to better memory recall in the morning. Specifically, rocking motion of 0.25Hz caused an **entrainment** of slow oscillations and **spindles** during non-rapid eye movement (NREM) sleep. As a result, the continuous rocking motion helped to synchronize neural activity in the thalamo-cortical networks of the brain, which play an important role in both sleep and memory **consolidation**. [Perrault et al. Whole-Night Continuous Rocking Entrains

Spontaneous Neural Oscillations with Benefits for Sleep and Memory. Current Biology, DOI: 10.1016/j.cub.2018.12.028]

Sensory cortices: in the brain, the primary and secondary cortices of the different senses (one cortex on each left and right hemisphere) specialize in processing sense-specific information. The visual cortex is in the occipital lobes, the auditory cortex on the temporal lobes, the primary the primary olfactory cortex on the uncus of the piriform region of the temporal lobes, the gustatory cortex on the insular cortex, and the primary somatosensory cortex on the anterior parietal lobes.

Sleep Spindles: bursts of neural oscillatory activity that are generated by interplay of the thalamic reticular nucleus (TRN) and other thalamic nuclei during stage 2 NREM sleep in a frequency of ~10 –12 Hz for at least 0.5 seconds. Spindles participate in the consolidation of overnight declarative memory. The density of spindles has been shown to increase after extensive learning of declarative memory tasks and the degree of increase in stage 2 spindle activity correlates with memory performance.

Source confusion: a form of memory error that involves the misattribution of the source of a memory. For instance, an individual may recall seeing an event in person when in reality they only saw it on television.

Suprachiasmatic cells: neurons of the suprachiasmatic nucleus, a tiny region of the brain in the hypothalamus, situated directly above the optic chiasm. It is responsible for controlling circadian rhythms based on the direct input from photosensitive ganglion cells in the retina. It sends information to other hypothalamic nuclei and the pineal gland to modulate body temperature and production of hormones such as cortisol and melatonin, orchestrating the day/ night circadian rhythms.

Temporo-parietal junction (TPJ): an area of the brain where the temporal and parietal lobes meet, at the posterior end of the Sylvian fissure. The TPJ incorporates information from the thalamus and the limbic system, as well as from the visual, auditory, and somatosensory systems. It plays a major role in various aspects of social cognition, including the theory of mind, detection of social cues of trustworthiness. It is activated in tasks of social perspective taking and cognitive empathy.

Trophic factors: trophic factors are proteins produced by glia in the brain that stimulate cell proliferation and differentiation and promote growth in differentiated cells, including neurite output and myelin production. As an endogenous defense triggered by cellular stress, they offer enormous therapeutic potential in the treatment of neurodegenerative diseases like Parkinson's Disease. They have neuroprotective properties and can enhance the function or even repair and restore function to injured neurons. Several trophic factors synthesized by neurons and other parenchymal cells are critical to cellular maintenance and regeneration. Examples include nerve growth factor, brain-derived neurotrophic factor (BDNF), and neurotrophin-3, as different kinds of neurons respond to different trophic factors for growth and regeneration.

Ventral striatum (VS): A part of the basal ganglia comprising Nucleus Accumbens (rich in opiate receptors) and ventral pallidum, this structure is implicated in signaling subjective reward value in the human brain. Together with the ventromedial prefrontal cortex, it encodes relative value of any kind of reward (primary, such as food, erotic images, pleasant smells and social reward such as smiling faces; as well as secondary reward – money and tokens of status), suggesting that the human brain uses this one network as a common currency to represent subjective value for all things rewarding, regardless of their sensory properties [Bartra, O., McGuire, J. T., & Kable, J. W. (2013). The valuation system: a coordinate-based meta-analysis of BOLD fMRI experiments examining neural correlates of subjective value. NeuroImage, 76, 412–427. doi:10.1016/j.neuroimage.2013.02.063]. Ventral striatum receives inputs from the amygdala (relevance information), the hippocampus (memory) and dopaminergic inputs from the VTA/SN (reward prediction error) as well as goal- and norm-related information from the prefrontal cortex. This renders the reward-related signal in the VS highly refined, incorporating all important information to compute subjective value. To find out about a surprising emotion that activates the ventral striatum, see the video at https://www.ewamien.com/research/the-ventral-striatum/

Ventral tegmental area / substantia nigra (VTA/SN): is a structure in the midbrain (a part of the brainstem) which sends dopaminergic neural projections to both the limbic and cortical areas. Substantia nigra is the bundle of dopamine-producing neurons, essential for movement control and reward. [See https://www.youtube.com/watch?v=JJ6YB4674GQ]

Ventro-medial prefrontal cortex (vmPFC): See Figure on pp. 247. This part of the cortex is involved in computation of subjective value of reward as well as in forming and maintaining memory schemas. It is also activated in autobiographical memory retrieval, and therefore crucial in making decisions based on past experience [See, for instance, Weilbächer, R. A., & Gluth, S. (2016). The Interplay of Hippocampus and Ventromedial Prefrontal Cortex in Memory-Based Decision Making. Brain sciences, 7(1), 4. doi:10.3390/brainsci7010004].